As ever, for Suzanne & the Two Terrors ...

The Girl in Black

CJ Loughty

The first to ten goals would be the winner. They'd flipped a coin for who would go first and Archie had guessed correctly. Oliver, his brother, had positioned himself in the centre of the goal, his knees bent and feet planted firmly apart. Splaying his hands in front of him, he squinted in the sunlight and then gestured that he was ready.

Archie took his run up and blasted the ball as hard as he could. It fizzed through the air in a blur and smashed into the crossbar hard enough to make the frame shudder.

'*Wow!* You got a lot of force into that ... for a twelve-year-old!' Oliver said, pushing thick tumbles of curly brown hair away from his fringe. 'Just a shame your accuracy isn't very good. I don't think you're going to be the next Ronaldo.'

'Oh, and you're going to be the next Ronaldo, are you?'

'I'd like to think of myself as being more like Messi, to be honest.'

Archie scoffed, retrieved the ball, then lined himself up for another shot. This time he went for accuracy rather than power – and then fired the ball straight over the crossbar, over the fence, into next door's garden.

'You can go around and get that,' Oliver said.

Archie did not like the idea of going next door on his own. The house was spooky and the boys had convinced themselves that it must be haunted. It stood tall and lonely in the middle of Salt Road in the sleepy town of Waddington. It was the only detached property on a street full of semi-detached Victorian houses. Tiles were missing from its grey slate roof. The place was a mess. Both gardens, front and back, were overgrown. Paint on the windows was peeling away. The gutter pipes were rusted. The place was badly in need of renovation. It'd been empty for two years, since the previous owner, Mr Ticklesworth, had passed away at the ripe age of one hundred and two.

'Will you come with me?' Archie asked his brother.

'No. I went round on my own last time, so I'm sure you can manage it, bruv.'

'Please go with me.'

Oliver shook his head. 'Nope,' he said. 'You hit it over. You get it.'

'Pleazzzzze go with me!' Archie begged.

'Go where?' a familiar voice said.

Both boys turned to see their mother coming down the steps.

'Archie hit the ball over next door and he won't go and get it,' Oliver said.

'Yes I will,' Archie said. 'If you come with me.'

Oliver was about to say something, but Mrs Wiggins silenced him with a raised finger. 'Neither of you are going next door,' she said, 'so your ball's staying where it is for now, I'm afraid.'

'Why?' Archie said.

'The new people are moving in,' Mrs Wiggins informed him. 'A removal van and a black Mercedes have just pulled up outside. Things are going to be chaotic for them today and the last thing they need is you pair pestering them every five minutes for your ball.'

'We won't be pestering them every five minutes,' Oliver protested. 'If we can get it back, we'll make sure it doesn't go over again.'

'You leave that ball where it is,' Mrs Wiggins said, giving him a no-nonsense scowl. 'And don't go getting any ideas about jumping over the fence to retrieve it. I'd like to start on good terms with the new neighbours. If they see you pair trespassing in the undergrowth I'm sure it'd give them quite a shock.'

'Great,' Archie said. 'That's just ... great.'

'It's your fault that it's over there,' Oliver said.

Archie scoffed. 'Oh – and like you've never hit the ball over before, yeah?'

'Not as much as you have.'

'Please stop arguing,' Mrs Wiggins said. 'What have I just told you about making a good impression?' She focused her attention on Oliver. 'You're the older boy here, so please start acting like it.'

'I'm only a year older than him,' he muttered.

'What was that?' Mrs Wiggins asked him. 'What did you just say?'

'I said that we'll find something else to do,' Oliver responded. 'We'll play on my XBOX.'

Mrs Wiggins said. 'You've already had two hours on it. Wouldn't you be better off going to the park, or something?'

'That would be interesting if we had the ball,' Archie muttered.

'Don't you start talking under your breath as well,' Mrs Wiggins said, beginning to get quite flustered. She gave them one last warning: 'I don't care what you do, just do *not* attempt to get that ball back today. Do we have an understanding?'

'Yes,' Archie and Oliver said in low voices.

Mrs Wiggins put her hand to her ear and said, 'Sorry, I didn't hear you - what did you say?'

'*YES!*' the boys said in unison.

'Ah, that's much better,' Mrs Wiggins said. She gave them a nod and a smile, then disappeared back inside the house.

'So what are we going to do now?' Oliver said, throwing his arms up in frustration.

'We could play on your XBOX, like you suggested.'

'As if I'd actually want to play with you on my XBOX. I just said that to cover myself when Mum was quizzing me.'

'Oh,' Archie said. He made a suggestion: 'We could check out the new neighbours. See who's moving in next door at number 25. I hope it's not another pensioner. Especially one like old man Ticklesworth, who used to moan about *everything*.'

'You can do whatever you like. I'm off out.'

'Where are you going?'

As Oliver made his way up the steps, he tapped the side of his nose and told Archie to mind his own business.

'Can I come with you?' Archie said.

Oliver didn't reply. He disappeared through the back door, leaving Archie on his own, twiddling his thumbs.

Great, he thought, *what am I going to do now?*

Curiosity was stirring inside him. He wanted to take a gander at the new neighbours, but he didn't want to do it in an obvious way, which would risk the wrath of his mother. Bounding up the steps and into the house, he went to his bedroom and shut the door. Then he peeked through the closed curtains.

Farther along the street he could see the black Mercedes was parked by the roadside and that the van had been reversed onto the driveway. The rear shutter was up and the inside was crammed from top to bottom with kooky old stuff. Archie scanned the contents, hoping to see evidence of a kid: some toys, a bike, anything that would give him hope. Having a boy (or even a girl) of a similar age next door would surely be a good thing.

Two people appeared: a man and a woman. They began unloading the van. The woman was tall and slim with shoulder-length, straight brown hair. She was wearing a blue dress and high heels, which made clip-clopping sounds as she scurried back and forth. The man was short and portly, dressed in black trousers and a white shirt. His head was bald and shiny with sweat, as if he'd done a vigorous workout. Archie watched them for a few minutes – until his parents called up to him, telling him that they were off out somewhere. Hurrying down the stairs, Archie went to see where they were going.

'Nowhere interesting,' Mrs Wiggins informed him. 'We're just doing some food shopping and running some errands. We won't be long.'

'Are you going out now so you can talk to the new neighbours?' Archie asked her.

'No, we're going out now because this is when we planned on going out,' Mr Wiggins said as he appeared from the kitchen. 'You're welcome to come if you want, but I can't imagine it'll be particularly interesting for you, kiddo.'

'I'll pass,' Archie said.

After his parents had gone, he crashed out on the settee and played with his mobile phone. When he grew tired of doing that, he set it aside and wondered what he could do next to entertain himself. Bored, bored, bored. He figured he could play on Oliver's XBOX and switch it off if he heard anyone return. But the only game he liked playing at the moment was Fortnite and he wasn't keen on the idea of having to abandon a match midway through (plus, if his brother caught him, he'd go ballistic and snitch on him – he just wouldn't be able to resist).

Archie's best – and only – friend, Ryan Jackson, was out of town for the day, so that wasn't an option.

'Bored,' Archie said to the empty room. 'Bored, bored ... *bored!*'

The only thing he really wanted to do was practise his football skills, which he couldn't do, of course, because his ball was in next door's garden. He imagined himself jumping over the fence, retrieving the ball like a ninja, and then jumping back over without being seen by anyone. The new neighbours were busy unloading stuff from the van, so they wouldn't notice him – would they? Archie didn't think so. And if his parents asked him how he'd got his ball back, he would just tell them that someone had thrown it over.

Springing up off the settee with a grin on his face, Archie bounded out through the back door and down the steps. He went to the place where the ball had gone over and stood on a big rock so he could peer over the wooden fence. He couldn't see the house next door from this vantage point because of the bushes, trees and overgrown foliage obstructing his view. But this was a good thing. If he couldn't see the house, then that meant no one could see him.

He had jumped over the fence before, many times. But that'd been with Oliver helping him out. Without his brother around to give him a leg up, Archie couldn't see how he was going to get over on his own.

He checked in the shed and found a folded-up chair. Deciding that this would have to do, he took it back to the other side of the garden and unfolded it. He positioned it as close to the fence as possible. The chair wobbled about on the unsteady ground as he stood on it. Then, with a jump and a lurch, he hoisted himself up and over in one quick, fluid movement.

He landed squarely on his feet and immediately set about looking for the ball. Careful to make sure he was out of view all the time, he searched here and there – but he couldn't find it. After a few more minutes of searching, he began to get frustrated. He crashed through the undergrowth, twigs snapping under his feet, and then came to a dead halt when he remembered where he was.

Sure that he'd heard a voice, he cocked his head to one side, listening. He stayed still and continued to listen. Then, just as he was beginning to convince himself that it'd been his imagination, he heard the voice again. A girl. Somewhere in the garden. Somewhere close by.

Oh poop! Archie thought. He turned around and began making his way back towards the fence. But then he reconsidered and stopped. Curiosity was eating away at him. He wanted to know who the girl was and what she was doing. He decided that he would just take a peek and then be on his way (the ball would have to stay wherever it was – for now). If he was quiet enough she wouldn't hear him. But being quiet was proving to be a problem, though. Every few steps Archie would put his foot down on a twig and cringe at the noise. The girl's voice became louder and clearer as he edged his way toward her. Emerging from the undergrowth, Archie went past some trees, pushing branches out of the way. And that was when he caught sight of her: sitting on the lawn, amongst the high blades of grass, with a book in one hand and a stick in the other. Dressed all in black, she had pale skin, long dark hair and the biggest, brownest eyes that Archie had ever seen.

She squinted at the book, then pointed the stick at something and said some strange words: 'Motus Moblata!'

Archie watched in amazement as a large rock rose into view and came to a stop a few feet above the ground, hovering. The girl appeared to be doing some sort of magic trick – some sort of illusion. She kept the rock suspended for a while – until Archie shifted his weight and a twig snapped beneath his foot.

His breath caught in his throat as he as froze on the spot, wondering if the girl had heard him. Apparently, she hadn't – because she continued to make the rock hover, without so much as a bat of her eyelids. Archie was just about to let out a breath of relief when the girl said something:

'There's no point hiding. I know you're there.'

Oh poop! Archie thought again. He didn't know whether to run or introduce himself. He was sure that an explanation was in order, so he decided on the latter.

'Hi,' he said, stepping out in the open and blubbering his

words, 'I wasn't spying on you. Well, actually, I guess I was. But ... erm, that's not why I'm in your garden. I hit my ball over and I've just come round to retrieve it. Except that I haven't come round as such. I jumped over your fence. And d'you know what, I'm not even sure I'd have got back over without my brother to help, so it's not the smartest thing I've ever done. And I haven't even found the ball. Your garden is so overgrown; it's like a jungle! If you come across my ball, can you thr – '

The girl held up a finger, silencing him. Then she lowered the rock back to the ground and regarded Archie with a curious expression.

'That's a cool trick,' he said. 'How did you do it?'

The girl didn't reply. She just sat there in the grass with the curious expression still on her face.

'I should film you doing that and post it on Youtube,' Archie said. 'It'd get loads of views, I'm sure.'

'Please don't film me doing anything,' the girl said angrily. 'My parents would *not* be happy about that! And I wouldn't be either.'

'Okay, no filming – I promise. But how *did* you make that rock hover? I've seen plenty of illusionists on Youtube doing cool magic tricks, but I've never seen anyone doing anything like that right in front of me.'

'A magician never gives away his or her secrets.'

'Is that a rock real?' Archie clicked his fingers because he thought he'd worked it out. 'Magnetism?' he said smugly. 'That's it, isn't it? That rock is fake. It's got metal inside of it and there's a big magnet underneath it that made it hover. All of that stick waving was just for show, yeah?'

The girl fixed him with an icy stare. 'It's not a stick; it's a wand.'

'Whatever,' Archie said as he made his way through the long grass, towards her. He was determined to prove that his theory was correct. But when he picked up the rock it was very heavy and very much real. And there was no magnet beneath it. This left him scratching his head. 'Okay – now I'm flummoxed. How *did* you make that rock hover? Do it again, please.'

The girl looked up at him. 'I'm not sitting out here to put a show on for you,' she said. 'I've come in the garden to get away from my parents.'

'Shouldn't you be helping them to unload that van?'

'They don't need my help. And, to quote my mum: "I'd only be getting in the way"'. The girl pointed farther down the garden, to the right. 'I think your ball is in a bush over there. Feel free to go and get it.'

Archie looked down the garden, shielding his eyes against the sun with his hand. 'How d'you know where it is? You couldn't have seen it land from where you are, down there.'

The girl shrugged. 'I heard it land. And let's just say that I have a talent for finding things that are lost.'

'And a talent for illusions as well.'

The girl said nothing. There was a smile playing at the corners of her rose red lips, though, which made Archie even more curious than he had been before.

'My name's Archie,' he said, introducing himself. 'Archie Wiggins.'

'And I'm Isabelle,' the girl replied. 'Isabelle Lockhart. I'm pleased to meet you and all that, but I think you better get your ball and go back to your garden, don't you? My father isn't the most approachable person. If he catches sight of you, he's going to wonder how you got here. He'll start quizzing you and it won't be a pleasant experience, just so you know. You don't want to get off to a bad start with your new neighbours, now, do you?'

Archie looked nervously towards the house. A glimpse of movement behind one of the downstairs windows got him moving.

'Yeah, right ... right,' he said as he began backing away. But then he remembered that he wouldn't be able to climb over the fence without help. 'Erm, you couldn't give me a leg up, could you? I could try and scramble over on my own, but I might damage a panel. After what you've just told me about your father, I don't want to go annoying him by destroying the fence. And I don't want to annoy my mum, either, 'cause she can be a bit of a dragon, if the truth be told.'

Archie was sure that he caught another glimpse of movement in the house, which made him retreat a few more steps.

'Okay, I'll help you,' Isabelle said, standing up.

Archie led the way.

'Aren't you forgetting something?' Isabelle asked him. 'Your football?'

'Oh,' he said, staring off in the direction that it'd apparently landed, 'I'll worry about that another day. If you come across it, can you throw it back, please?'

Isabelle assured him that she would. 'Come on,' she said, gesturing for him to get moving again. 'Let's get you back in your own garden – and then I can carry on practising my "illusions".

As they made their way through the undergrowth, Archie said, 'So ... are you going to tell me how you made that rock levitate, or what? I'm still puzzled as to how you did it – and I'm genuinely curious.'

'As I said, a magician never gives away his or her secrets. That's a big no-no.'

'I guess you won't be showing me how to do it then,' Archie said. He held some tree branches back so Isabelle could pass by unobstructed.

She thanked him and then said, 'I'm afraid not. I'm quite angry with myself for allowing you to see me do it. Can you promise me that won't tell anyone?'

'Why would you be bothered about me telling anyone? If I could do a cool trick like that, I'd be showing *everyone*.'

'Well, I'm not you. Let's just I like my privacy. So can I get a promise from you, or not?'

Archie pretended to think long and hard about this and

then said, 'Yeah, I think I can just about manage that. As long as I get my ball back.'

'You'll get your ball back. Don't worry about that.'

Isabelle moved to the fence and laced her hands together, ready to give Archie a boost up.

'Can't you just levitate me over there with your sti ... sorry, I mean, wand?' he said, smiling.

'Maybe I can. And maybe I can't. But we'll try the non-wand method, if that's all right?'

Archie shrugged. 'Okey-doke. If you're sure you're up to it.'

'I'm up to it – don't worry; I'm stronger than I look.'

Isabelle bent her knees, ready to take his weight.

And Archie was pleasantly surprised when he put his foot on her hands and she boosted him up onto the panel. He sat on top of it, one leg on either side, looking down at her.

'Wow – you really are stronger than you look,' he said.

Isabelle just looked up at him and smiled.

'Oh well, thanks for the boost up. And remember that your secret is safe with me – as long as I get my ball back.'

'As I told you before, you'll get it back. You might want to get off that fence panel now, 'cause it's bowing under your weight, in case you hadn't noticed.'

Archie hadn't noticed. 'Oops!' he said as he gave a quick wave of his hand and then dropped back into his garden.

Landing in the flower beds, he narrowly avoided his mother's prized marigolds. Then he stepped onto the lawn and looked back at the panel he'd just jumped over, to see if he'd damaged it. Satisfied that he hadn't, he lingered there, wondering if Isabelle would get his ball now or later.

And that's when a large, white splodge landed on his shoulder.

'*Ughh!*' he said, making a disgusted expression. He looked up and saw a pigeon flapping about overhead. 'Thanks for that – you flying rat!'

Something bounced off the side of Archie's head, hitting

him hard enough to knock him sideways a few steps. He let out a yelp, more in surprise than pain, then watched as his ball went bouncing across the lawn.

'And thanks for that!' he said. He waited for a reply, but one did not come. He put the chair back in the shed. Racing back into the house, he took off his t-shirt and tossed it in the washing basket. Bounding upstairs, he got himself a clean one from his drawer and slipped it on.

Then he peaked through the curtains to see what was happening next door. To his surprise, the removal van had gone and there were no signs of activity. *That van was filled from top to bottom with stuff*, he thought, *so no way have they unloaded it already*. He was becoming more and more intrigued by the new family and he was intent on keeping a close eye on them.

Archie's parents returned thirty minutes later and he helped them carry the shopping into the house. In the kitchen, as they were emptying the bags and putting stuff away, he asked them what they thought about the new neighbours.

'They were eager to talk to us and were very pleasant,' Mr Wiggins said. 'As first impressions go, they get a nod of approval from me and your mother.'

'Did you notice anything strange about them?' Archie asked.

'Strange?' Mrs Wiggins said. 'What do you mean by "strange"?'

Archie shrugged. 'I dunno. I mean, they look a bit odd ... don't they?'

'I'm disappointed in you, Archie Wiggins,' Mrs Wiggins said. 'We've raised you to judge people by the content of their character, *not* by how they look. Don't be so superficial, young man!'

'Did you ask them where they moved from?' Archie inquired. 'And why they've moved here?'

'We've only just met them,' Mr Wiggins said, brushing past

him to put a box of cereal away in a cupboard, 'so we didn't ask too many prying questions.'

Archie nearly laughed out loud. He thought: *my mother, the nosiest person ever, didn't ask too many prying questions?* He didn't believe that for one second.

'How many of them are there?' Archie asked. 'Is it just the three of them, or does the girl have any brothers or sisters?'

Mrs Wiggins said, 'How do you know that they've got a daughter? And what's with all these questions? Why are you so interested in the new neighbours?'

Archie gave another shrug. 'While you were gone, I ... saw a girl helping the adults to unload the van. I figured that she must be their daughter.' He chose not to answer the second question. 'Did they give any indication as to why they've moved here of all places?'

'Colin and Kelly told us that Waddington is a lovely place,' Mrs Wiggins said. 'And apparently they're renting the house at a very reasonable rate (which has probably got something to do with the state of the place, I'd imagine). The Lockharts plan on making it as lovely as it can be, though. Colin is a salesman of some sort, just like your father. And Kelly is a hairdresser, which could be handy for me.' She gave her blonde bob an enthusiastic pat with the palm of her hand. 'Very handy indeed.'

'Where have they moved from?' Archie inquired.

'Somewhere down south,' Mr Wiggins said. 'I forget the name of the place.'

'Well, I must admit, I never thought you'd take this much interest in new neighbours,' Mrs Wiggins said to Archie. 'Is it the girl that's caught your eye? Is she pretty?'

Archie did not reply. He could feel his cheeks flushing with colour. A strong desire to get out of the room came over him. He decided that he wasn't going to get any more useful nuggets of information from his parents and went to watch some cartoons on the TV in the living room.

Later in the afternoon, when Oliver arrived back home, Archie cornered him in his bedroom and told him about his expedition into next door's garden to look for the ball. And he also told him about Isabelle and her magic trick, despite the promise he'd given her.

'The rock will be fake,' Oliver suggested. 'It's probably got a magnet inside of it or something.' He was relaxing on his bed with his hands laced behind his head.

'That was my first thought. But nope. I picked it up; it's a real rock.'

'She was using strings then.'

'Nope. There were no strings.'

Oliver gave it some thought and then shrugged his shoulders. 'I have no explanation. She's obviously a world-class illusionist, whoever she is. Or maybe she's actually a real witch and really *was* levitating the rock. Did you ask her how she did it?'

'Yes, but she wouldn't tell me.'

Oliver gave another shrug of his shoulders. 'I guess it'll just have to be one of life's unsolved mysteries, then, won't it?'

No, it won't, Archie thought. 'I'm going to find out how she did it.'

'Whatever,' Oliver responded, losing interest. 'Did you get the ball back? That's all I want to know.'

'Yes. But that's another strange thing. She knew exactly where the ball was, even though it landed nowhere near her.'

'Maybe she saw it come over the fence and followed the line of trajectory.'

'She couldn't possibly have seen it from where she was sitting. There was too much of that overgrown garden in the way for her to have seen where it landed.'

'Like I said, maybe she's a real witch ...'

'Magic isn't real. Witches don't exist.'

Oliver said nothing. He just smiled and shook his head.

'Those aren't the only weird things that have happened,

though,' Archie said. He explained about the removal van and how it'd been emptied so quickly.

'So the girl's parents are hard-working and just get on with a job when it needs doing. You could take a leaf out of their book the next time you have chores to do, bruv.'

'Says you, who's an expert at dragging his heels.'

Oliver's bedroom was at the rear of the house. But even from here, they heard the trundle of a van pulling up on the street and the sound of doors being banged shut.

Archie went to investigate. In his bedroom, he looked out of his window and saw that the van had returned next door and had once again been reversed onto the driveway. The short, bald man, Mr Lockhart, appeared from around the side and opened the rear doors. The van was once again crammed with stuff from top to bottom. This got Archie moving.

He raced back to his brother's bedroom to tell him about this. 'The van is back!' he said, getting excited. 'And they're about to unload it.'

'So?'

'I'm going to watch them do it. Are you going to watch, too?'

'Why would I want to watch someone unloading a van?'

'They emptied the first lot of stuff ridiculously quick. I want to see if that happens again – and I want to see how they do it. And our new neighbours told Mum and Dad that they're from down south. Aren't you the least bit curious as to how they've managed to reload the van and make that journey so quickly?'

'Not really. I think I'll just chill here for a bit, thanks. I'll leave the boring stuff to you.'

Archie tutted at his brother and then raced back to his bedroom. Peeking through his curtains, he saw that the van was still crammed with stuff. Good, that meant he hadn't missed anything. He waited ... and he waited ... and he waited. And then he began to get bored and frustrated. They had been eager to unload the first vanload, so why was it taking them so long to even get started with the second?

Mrs Wiggins called up the stairs to him: 'Archie, can you come down here, please! I need a word with you!'

What! No! he thought. *Not now!*

'I'll be down in a bit!' he replied loudly.

'No, I need you down here now!' Mrs Wiggins said. 'It'll only take a minute!'

Archie let out a grunt of frustration and then went to see what his mother wanted. In the kitchen, she quizzed him about a school trip which was taking place on Wednesday. She wanted to know which clothes he would be wearing, what he'd want in his packed lunch, and what time he'd return (even though it was four days away). After he'd given her all of this information, he raced back to his bedroom and once again peeked through the curtains.

To his amazement, the van had gone.

'No flippin' way can they have unloaded it *that* quickly!' he said. 'No *FLIPPIN' way!'*

His mother called up to him again: 'What's all the noise? Are you and your brother arguing again?'

Archie went onto the landing to find his brother standing there, giving him a curious look.

'No, we're not fighting,' Oliver said to her as she peered up the stairs at them. 'Archie just knocked over a Lego tower he was building. That's all.'

'Oh, right,' Mrs Wiggins said. 'Can you not yell out like that again, please? I'm on the phone to someone and they don't want to hear you ranting in the background.'

'I'll be quiet,' Archie promised her.

When she'd gone, Oliver gave him a searching look.

Archie explained the reason for his outburst. 'I was gone no more than a few minutes at the most,' he said. 'So how do you explain that? How could anyone unload a van full of stuff that quickly?'

Oliver shrugged. 'I dunno. Perhaps the stuff had all shifted to the back during their journey, so it just looked like the van was full. As with the floating rock, I'm sure there's a reasonable explanation.'

'You couldn't come up with a "reasonable explanation" for that and you're clutching at straws with one for this. The stuff in the back of that van was crammed in from the bottom to the top. If it'd all shifted about during the journey it would have been spread out more evenly, wouldn't it? That seems like a more logical explanation to me.'

Oliver gave another shrug. 'Look, I did suggest that the girl could be a witch,' he said with more than a hint of sarcasm in his voice, 'so maybe she's not the only one. Maybe a family of wizards and witches has moved in next door. I'm sure you'll see one of them flying around on a broomstick soon enough, if that's the case.'

He disappeared into his bedroom and shut the door before Archie could reply.

'Idiot,' Archie said in a low voice.

He stood there for a few seconds, wondering what he should do next. Staying in his bedroom to see if a third van-load turned up was an option (a very *boring* option!). He decided that he couldn't bring himself to do that, even though he was committed to proving that something strange was going on with the new neighbours.

In the back garden, he did some kick-ups with his football. From his vantage point, in the centre of the lawn, he could see the upstairs windows of the nearest side of the house next door. There was no movement behind the glass, no signs of life. *Keeping an eye on these people would be a lot easier if I lived in a house across the street*, he thought.

As if out of nowhere, Mrs Wiggins appeared on the steps and said, 'How did you get that football back? Please tell me you didn't ...'

'Someone threw it over,' Archie replied, cutting her off.

Mrs Wiggins' eyes narrowed suspiciously. 'Are you sure that's how you got it back? You know how angry I would be if you disobeyed me and jumped over the fence to get it, don't you? You know how angry I'd be if I found out you'd been trespassing, yes?'

Archie explained how the ball had sailed back over the fence and hit him on the head. And, as a diversion tactic, he told her about the bird that'd pooped on his shoulder.

'Oh dear,' Mrs Wiggins said, unable to suppress a smile. 'That is *most* unfortunate. What have you done with the top? It'll need washing on its own, that will.'

'I put it in the washing basket.'

'Ah, right, okay – I best go and sort that out then, before it dries and becomes a real pain to get off. Are you coming in soon? Me and your father are thinking of having a movie night. I can nip to the shop and get some goodies, if you're interested? Popcorn and some other nibbles?'

Archie liked the sound of that, so he gave his mother a thumbs up and followed her back into the house.

The movie selection turned out to be the usual debacle. No one could agree on what to watch. Mr and Mrs Wiggins wanted an adventurous film such as Jumanji, whereas Oliver was leaning towards something more Marvel-like. Archie, on the other hand, was looking to go old school, insisting on the Goonies. In the end, after a lot more searching (and arguing) they opted for The Sorcerer's Apprentice: a tale about a guy who has to learn magic from a wizard so they can both save a city from evil.

Throughout the movie, Archie kept thinking about Isabelle and the magic that she'd done. *No – no!* he thought, *it wasn't magic; it was just a trick, an illusion*. But he still couldn't work out how she'd done it. If it'd been something light – such as a piece of paper or even a pencil – then he wouldn't have been so impressed. But she'd been levitating a rock – and a heavy one at that. And then there was the van and how it'd been emptied so quickly *–twice!* Archie was even more bamboozled by this than the business with the rock. He just couldn't formulate a rational explanation of how this was possible.

His brother's words came back to him: Maybe a family of

wizards and witches has moved in next door ...

Archie shook his head, dismissing this ludicrous suggestion.

Tomorrow was Sunday. Archie didn't have any plans, so he decided that he would devote the entire day to being a sleuth. He imagined himself dressed like a hardboiled character from a detective novel: wearing a black trench coat, fedora, and sunglasses. This got him smiling.

'This movie isn't a comedy,' Oliver said to him. 'What's so funny?'

'Nothing,' Archie replied. 'I was just thinking.'

'Thinking about what?'

Archie tapped the side of his nose. 'That's for me to know and you to find out.'

'Stop talking, please,' Mrs Wiggins said. 'You know I can't stand it when you pair talk over a movie.'

Oliver gave his brother a sly look and then they both continued watching the movie.

Archie usually had a lie-in on a Sunday morning. Not today, though. At 8 am, he was up and raring to go. He was eating Cornflakes at the breakfast table when Mr Wiggins entered the kitchen.

'Off out somewhere, are you?' Mr Wiggins said. 'Off out with Ryan?'

'Yes,' Archie lied. He remembered that his father owned an item that he could find useful. 'Erm, have you still got that small monocular?'

'I most certainly have.' Mr Wiggins regarded his son with a quizzical expression. 'What do you want it for? Not bird watching, like me, I'm guessing?'

Archie did some quick thinking and said, 'Me and Ryan are, err ... going for a walk in the countryside and thought it would be a good thing to take with us. If we see something in the distance, we can check it out to see if it's worth going there.'

Mr Wiggins left the room and then returned with the monocular. He placed it on the table and said, 'It was expensive, so please be careful with it.'

Archie assured him that he would.

Inevitably, Mrs Wiggins also wanted to know where her son was going and why he was taking a monocular with him. She offered to make a packed lunch for him and he told her no thank you.

Fortunately, Oliver was still in bed, so there were no awkward questions from him.

Archie didn't want his parents to see where he was going, so he had to wait for the right moment to leave. A short while later, when they were busying themselves at the back of the house, Archie seized this opportunity and made for the front door. He shouted goodbye and was gone.

Across the street he went, to number 30 (the people who lived there were away on holiday, so there was no danger of anyone coming out of the property and accosting him for what he was about to do).

He looked around to make sure no one was watching him, then he ducked down the driveway and around the back of the trees. Crouching down, he squeezed in between two large bushes and tried to make himself comfortable. Sharp branches were poking him in the face and the ground was littered with rocks. He considered repositioning himself but decided not to. This was as good as it was going to get in terms of visibility and comfort. From this vantage point, he had an excellent view of the target house. He just hoped that nobody spotted him, because he couldn't think of one excuse for being a real-life Bush Camper (especially one with a monocular).

It was a nice day. The sun was playing peekaboo through the clouds and a light breeze was rustling the trees. A good day for a covert spy mission.

Across the street, at the big house, there were no signs of movement in any of the windows. *Probably still in bed*, Archie thought. *Exhausted from moving in yesterday*. But then he remembered how quickly they'd unloaded two vanloads and wasn't so sure that this would be the case.

Pulling the monocular from its sleeve, he sighted through the lens with his right eye whilst keeping his left eye firmly shut. The image was blurry, however, so he had to make adjustments.

It was as he was doing this that he heard the sound of approaching footsteps. He froze. Someone was walking past on the pavement. He heard the skitter, skitter of what could only be paws.

A dog walker ...

Not a problem.

Archie figured that all he would need to do was stay still and not make any noise. They would pass by and then he could continue doing what he'd been doing. But, of course, it was never going to be that easy.

As the dog passed, it showed an interest in the bushes where Archie was hiding. Through the branches and foliage, Archie could now see that it was a Jack Russell, being walked by an old lady, who Archie recognized as being Mrs Balham from number 36. The dog sniffed at the air and wagged its tail as it moved closer.

Oh poop, Archie thought, backing away as quietly as he could. *Oh poop-di-poop! This is all I need.*

A twig snapped under his foot. And that's when the Jack Russell went mad. It began barking and tugging at its lead, trying to get at Archie.

'Mr Chips!' Mrs Balham said, struggling to hold him back. 'What are you doing? Stop that! Stop that now – you *silly* mutt!'

Mr Chips took no notice. He continued to bark and tug at his lead. And Mrs Balham continued to struggle with holding him back.

'Mr Chips!' she said, remonstrating with him again (for all the good it did her). 'Come away from there, will you! What have you spotted, hmm? A rodent? A rabbit? Or a badger, perhaps?'

The way Archie saw things, he had two choices. One: he sat tight, hoped that the dog got bored and went away (which was not likely to happen). Two: he stepped out of the bushes and came up with a plausible explanation as to why he'd been in there. The problem was that he couldn't *think* of a plausible explanation (other than admitting to what he'd really been doing, of course). One thing was for sure, if he was going with choice two, he needed to do it ASAP, because Mr Chips was now going into overdrive with his barking and lead tugging. How long would it be before all this noise attracted other unwanted attention? Archie didn't want to find out ...

He put the monocular back in its sleeve, then tucked it into the rear of his jeans, out of sight. Then he stepped out of the bushes and began brushing himself off.

'Oh my!' Mrs Balham said, regarding him cautiously. 'Not a rodent or rabbit then. And certainly not a badger. What in the name of the Lord were you doing in there, young man?'

'I was ... looking for my ball,' Archie responded. It was the best he could come up with. 'I kicked it into this garden by accident and I can't seem to find it.'

'Well, that's most unfortunate. Apologies for my dog. He's just a bit overenthusiastic, shall we say.' A flash of recognition spread across Mrs Balham's face. 'I know you,' she said, glancing towards Archie's home. 'You live over there, don't you? And you know him too, Mr Chips, so I don't know why you're growling. You've let him stroke you before. Him and the rest of his family. Do you remember, you daft thing?'

Yeah, come on Mr Chips, Archie thought, smiling nervously at the dog, *take a chill pill*.

Although its barking had died down to teeth-bearing growls, Archie was still keen to get away from this situation. Any second now, he was sure that his mother's face would appear at the kitchen window and peer out at him. Either that or he would attract unwanted attention from the new neighbours.

Archie didn't want Mrs Balham to see the monocular, so he kept facing her as he backed away towards his house. 'Gotta go,' he said. 'Lots to do and not much time to do it all in. You know how it is, right?'

'I most certainly do. But what about your ball?'

'I'll find it later. I'll get my brother to help me search for it.'

Archie heard footsteps and then a familiar voice said, 'Oh dear, you haven't lost your ball again, have you?'

He turned to see Isabelle standing outside her house, holding a mountain bike. She chuckled to herself, shook her head, then climbed on the bike and rode away.

Not wasting a second, Archie raced back into his house and got the garage key from the kitchen.

'What's the rush?' Mr Wiggins asked him as she came out of the living room. 'You've only just left and you're already back. Why?'

'We've decided that we're going on our bikes,' he replied.

Unfortunately, by the time he'd got his BMX out of the garage and out to the pavement, there was no sign of Isabelle.

He asked Mrs Balham which way she'd gone and she replied, 'Left.'

Then he gave her and Mr Chips a smile as he took off down the road at a rate of knots.

Reaching the junction, he looked left and saw Isabelle at the bottom of the hill. With the wind in his face, blowing his hair back from his fringe, he raced after her, pedalling as fast as he could to close the gap. She paused at the next junction, waiting for a gap in the traffic, then she pulled out and disappeared from view. This made Archie pedal even faster.

'Woo-HOOO!' he said, gripping the handlebars tightly.

Fortunately, Isabelle wasn't in a hurry to get wherever she was going, so Archie caught up with her quickly. When he was about a hundred meters behind her, he slowed his pace to match hers. He just hoped that she wouldn't glance over her shoulder at some point and recognize him. That would take some explaining. Archie didn't want to be accused of being a stalker, so he dropped back even farther – but not so much that he would risk losing her.

Five minutes later, they were on the main road, heading out of town. *Where* are *you going?* Archie thought, more intrigued than ever.

He passed a road sign: Kerfuffle – 12
Harwood – 7
Bucklechurch – 3

Archie hoped that it was Bucklechurch that they were heading for and not one of the other places. As things turned out, that's exactly where they were going. It took them twenty minutes to get there and Archie's legs were beginning to ache by the time they reached the town centre.

Archie had passed through Bucklechurch quite a few times on the bus, but he had never been tempted to visit. It was a small town with an uninteresting array of retail outlets (mostly antique and charity shops).

Not once during the journey had Isabelle looked over her shoulder, which made Archie suspicious. He suspected that she knew she was being followed and was leading him on some sort of merry dance. Every time she disappeared around a corner he expected to lose her. But this turned out not to be the case. It was on a street named Tiddlywink Road that Isabelle finally reached her destination: a shop called The Enchanted Cove. From a safe distance, Archie watched as she left her bike outside and disappeared through the front door.

A short while later, she exited with a small carrier bag and began cycling towards Archie. Panicking, he pushed his bike down an alley and hid as best he could. He breathed a huge sigh of relief when he saw her pass by without so much as a glance in his direction.

Leaving his bike down the alley, tucked out of sight, Archie went to investigate the shop. He stopped outside and marvelled at the display in the window, which was filled with unusual items. *This is a magic shop*, he thought, eyeing up an assortment of different-sized cauldrons on one of the shelves.

A bell above the door jingled as Archie entered. There was no one behind the counter, so he browsed the narrow aisles, taking in all the weird and wonderful things on display. He took particular interest in some broomsticks lined up by the far wall.

'The broomsticks always garner so much attention,' someone said from the back of the shop. 'Those and the wands, of course.'

A short, plump woman with blonde, scraggly hair appeared before Archie. She was dressed in long, flowing, colourful robes, which draped behind her as she shuffled towards him.

'People must love sweeping floors,' Archie said.

The woman did not reply immediately. She looked at Archie for a few seconds, as if weighing him up. And then, when she was happy with her assessment, she spoke: 'How may I help you?' she asked.

'I've just come in to browse, if that's okay?'

'It most certainly is. Call me if you need assistance.'

Archie assured the woman that he would.

She sat on a stool behind the counter and began reading a book.

Archie noted the title: *Potions for the Inquisitive Mind*. He picked up a similar book titled *Concoctions from Beginner to Advanced* and skimmed through the pages. A potion for good luck on page 42 caught his attention. *Now this sounds like it could be a useful one to mix*, he thought. He grimaced at some of the things on the list of needed ingredients: spider's legs, salt, toe of frog, nettleweed, earwax ...

Archie snapped the book shut and put it back where he'd got it from.

On a shelf marked **DIVINATION**, he saw some purple stones in a bowl. They had strange yellow markings. Scooping some up, he wondered what they were used for and what divination could be.

As if reading his mind, the woman said, 'They're runes. And they can be used to tell the future.'

'Really?' Archie said with a sarcastic edge to his voice. 'Seriously?'

'Yes, seriously.'

'My dad says that anyone who can tell the future should be running the country.'

'Your father sounds like a wise man.'

Archie opened his mouth to say something, but the jingle of the bell above the door announced the arrival of another customer. He saw Isabelle coming toward him and his mouth dropped open in surprise.

'Back so soon,' the woman said to her. 'I'm guessing that you've forgotten something, yes?'

'Not exactly,' Isabelle replied. She stared at Archie. 'I must admit, I didn't expect to see *you* in here,' she said. 'Come here often, do you?'

Archie was lost for words for a few seconds. His mouth opened and closed like that of a fish. And then he managed to formulate a lie: 'I ... was just cycling by and thought I'd pop in for a look around. This shop looks cool from the outside and it's even cooler on the inside.' Archie picked up a wooden, webbed hoop, which had feathers and beads hanging from the bottom. 'I mean, how cool is this? I've always wanted one of these to hang over my bed.'

'And over your bed is exactly where that should be,' the woman said. 'Do you know what it's used for, young man?'

'Erm ... to stop nightmares,' Archie said.

'That's not a bad guess,' the woman said. 'That's a dream catcher you're holding. And it does exactly what the name suggests. And it lets the nightmares pass through.'

'Ah ... yes,' Archie said, smiling. 'I knew it was something like that.'

Isabelle rolled her eyes at him and then turned her attention to the woman. 'I'm sorry to bother you again, Mrs Hickinbottom, but do you have any more bograt's blood?' she asked her. 'My dad just rang me and told me to get as much as I can.'

'Bograt's blood!' Archie exclaimed. 'What the heck is a bograt?'

Both of them ignored him.

'I have,' Mrs Hickinbottom said, answering Isabelle's question, 'but not much, because you took most of it when you first came in.'

Mrs Hickinbottom told her the price and Isabelle produced a wad of notes from her pocket and handed them over. Mrs Hickinbottom smiled as she took the cash and then disappeared through a door at the rear, out of view.

'How come you've got that much money?' Archie asked Isabelle. 'Are your parents rich, or something?'

She tapped the side of her nose and told him to mind his own business. 'I don't like being followed,' she said to him, 'so please don't do it again.'

'I haven't followed you,' Archie protested. 'I was just passing by here and dropped in for a look around, as I explained before.'

'I didn't believe your lie the first time you said it and I don't believe it now.'

'I'm not lying!'

Mrs Hickinbottom returned with a small glass vial. She handed it to Isabelle, who thanked her and made for the door.

'Due to the limited uses and defensive nature of bograt's blood,' Mrs Hickinbottom said, 'I do feel an obligation to ask if your safety is at risk. I can close the shop and talk to you in private, if you like? It's no problem at all. I should have asked you the first time you were in here.'

'That won't be necessary,' Isabelle responded confidently, 'as there is no risk to my safety. Thanks for your concern, though.'

The bell above the door tinkled as she exited.

Archie went to leave as well ...

'Ahum, aren't you forgetting something,' Mrs Hickinbottom said, gesturing towards the dreamcatcher, which Archie was still holding. 'You need to pay for something before you can remove it from the shop, I'm afraid.'

He apologized and placed it back on a shelf. 'I'll get it next time,' he said, 'when I've got more cash.'

When he stepped outside, Isabelle was waiting for him with her arms folded across her chest. She did not look happy. Not happy at all.

'What's that in your back pocket?' she demanded to know. 'Show it to me.'

'I haven't got anything in my back pocket,' he lied.

'I saw it when you came out of the shop. Looks like some sort of miniature telescope. Have you been using that to spy on me?'

Archie had forgotten all about it and cursed himself for his stupidity. 'It's not a telescope,' he said. This wasn't technically a lie.

'You just told me that don't have anything in your pocket and now you're telling me it's not a telescope. Not a very good liar, are you?'

Archie was lost for words. 'I ... err ...' he stammered.

'I don't like being stalked,' Isabelle said, scowling at him. 'Please don't do it again, otherwise I'll tell my father. And you don't want *that* to happen.'

'I'm not stalking you. I was just passing this shop and dropped in for a look around, that's all.'

'Oh, please!' Isabelle said, rolling her eyes.

She'd left her bike propped against the shop window. She mounted it and pushed off, to cycle away ...

'I know what you are,' Archie said, bringing her to a halt, 'and I intend to prove it.'

Isabelle scowled back at him. 'And what exactly is it that you think I am?'

A woman passed by, wheeling a pushchair, so Archie waited before he replied. When she was a safe distance away, out of earshot, he let a single word slip from his lips: 'Witch.'

Isabelle's scowl disappeared. She gave Archie a mocking look. 'So, because you saw me doing a trick in my garden, making a rock float,' she said, 'you've jumped to a wild conclusion and made yourself look pretty damned silly in the process.'

'Well, how about you tell me how you did that trick and I might begin to believe you. And I don't think I'm being silly. Not only did you make that rock float, you're also here at this magic shop, buying something called "bograt's blood", which is probably an ingredient for a potion you'll be mixing, I'm guessing. That woman was concerned about why you want it, due to its "defensive nature". So are you in some sort of danger? Is your family in danger? Is that why you've moved house? Is someone after you? Is the bograt's blood to protect you from them?'

Isabelle's mocking look had changed back to a scowl. 'My, my, you are a little Sherlock Holmes, aren't you?' she said. 'I tell you what, let's assume that you are right and that I *am* a witch.' She reached inside her jacket and produced her wand. 'How about I change you into a slug? How would you like *that*?'

Archie backed away a few steps, his eyes wide with fear.

'Just leave me alone,' Isabelle said, 'and don't follow me again!'

Then she cycled away and didn't once look back.

When Archie returned home, he considered telling his brother about what'd happened, but he decided against this. What was the point? Oliver wouldn't believe him. *He'd probably laugh at me if I told him about the threat*, Archie thought dismally. He couldn't be certain that she'd be able to turn him into a slug, but the possibility that she might be able to was giving him cold shivers.

Crashing out on the settee in front of the TV seemed to be the best course of action, as far as Archie could see. Logging into his Netflix account, he noticed a new release in the movie recommendations: a fantasy romp that would take his mind off things for a few hours.

He was fifteen minutes in when Mrs Wiggins began quizzing him. She came through from the kitchen and said, 'Are you okay? You've been quiet ever since you came back? Is everything all right? Not feeling under the weather, are you?'

'No, I'm fine,' he replied, trying to sound chirpy. 'Just a bit ... tired, that's all.'

Mrs Wiggins nodded towards the TV. 'How long is this on for?' She checked the clock above the mantelpiece. 'You need to be in bed by ten, because it's school in the morning, remember?'

School? This got Archie thinking about Isabelle again. There was only one secondary school in the small town of Waddington, which meant that she would be attending the

Darkcoat Academy, just like him. What if he bumped into her in one of the wood-panelled corridors, or on the playground? What if she came to the wrong conclusion and turned him into a slug? Archie had decided that the safest, most sensible course of action was to put as much distance between him and her as possible (which wasn't going to be easy, given that she was living next door to him). Would she be in the same year as him? He estimated her age to be about the same as his. What if she was in some of his classes? There would be no avoiding her then ...

Mrs Wiggins clapped her hands together, pulling him out of his thoughts. 'Erm, I asked you a question, young man,' she said, 'and I'm still waiting for an answer.'

'I'll watch some of it tonight and some tomorrow,' Archie replied, putting his hand over his mouth to cover a fake yawn.

Mrs Wiggins seemed happy enough with this response, so she left him alone.

Archie couldn't get into the movie, though. His thoughts were racing too much for him to follow any storyline, so he gave up and went to bed.

He was about to turn the bedside lamp off when a strong feeling of curiosity washed over him. He went to the closed curtains and peeked through. Inevitably, his attention was drawn towards next door: to where the strange new girl lived. The bulb in the street lamp across the road had blown, so Archie couldn't see as much as he would have liked. The big, black Mercedes was outside the house: a dark lump in the gloom. There was no light being cast upon the front lawn, which suggested that the house was in darkness, everyone tucked up in bed. Archie was about to move away and climb into his bed when a flash of movement caught his eye. He leaned forwards, pressing the side of his face against the cold glass so he could get a better look. *Is someone moving around down there?* he thought. Another flash of movement caught his eye. Yep! Someone was definitely in the front garden. All he could see was a dark figure moving along the boundary line, near the fence which separated the gardens. The figure appeared to be spreading something from a container that he or she was holding. Reaching the corner of the garden, the figure continued with the spreading, all along the front boundary and then down the far side, until he or she disappeared from view.

What was that all about? Archie wondered. He figured it could be slug repellent or some other gardening-related activity, but who did that sort of thing in the dead of night?

'Weird,' Archie muttered to himself, shaking his head. 'Just ... weird.'

Then he remembered what'd happened in the magic shop – and the woman's words came back to him: due to the limited uses and defensive nature of bograt's blood, I do feel an obligation to ask if your safety is at risk. Putting two and two together, Archie figured that the bograt's blood may have been used to make whatever had been spread along next door's boundaries. He figured that it could form some sort of protection for the house. Protection from what, though?

He lingered at the window to see if the person would come back or if anything else would happen. When nothing did, he finally gave up and went to bed. Darkness sucked in around him as he turned off the bedside lamp and pulled the covers up to his chin.

What strange thing would Archie see happen next? Would someone go whizzing over the rooftops on a broomstick, or disappear in a puff of smoke? And what would happen to an intruder if they crossed the boundary line of the property next door? Would they be vaporised? Turned to a frozen statue? Or turned into a slug?

The last one made Archie's arms break out in gooseflesh. He shuddered and shook his head, trying to banish this thought.

His mind was racing as he processed everything that'd happened in the short time the new neighbours had been next door. He didn't think he would be able to get any shuteye. He envisaged himself in the early hours of the morning, still lying under the sheets, staring up at the ceiling. But twenty minutes or so later his eyes slowly closed and he fell into a deep, dreamless sleep.

In the morning, after eating a hearty breakfast of sausages, bacon and toast, Archie set out for school with his bag slung over his shoulder. It was a cloudy, cool day with a light breeze.

Inevitably, as he passed the house next door, he glanced towards the windows and took a keen interest in the boundaries. He couldn't see any evidence of anything having been sprinkled amongst the weeds and overgrowth. And he didn't linger too long, because he didn't want Isabelle to think that he was stalking her.

When he was a bit farther up the road, he heard hurried footsteps closing in behind him. He turned just in time to see his brother bearing down on him with a big grin on his face.

'Ah, damn! I was gonna put the frighteners on you then,' Oliver said, coming up next to him and giving him a playful punch on the arm instead.

'You'd need to be stealthier than that.'

'I don't normally have to. You look a bit on edge, bruv. Why is that? Someone at school giving you problems? All you have to do is let me know and I'll sort them out, you know that, don't you?'

'No one's giving me problems.'

'Are you sure?'

'Yes, I'm sure! And I don't need you to fight my battles for me. I'm more than capable of standing up for myself, thanks.'

'So what's wrong with you then? You don't normally leave before me, so why are you today? What's your issue?'

Archie shrugged. What was the point in telling him the truth? Oliver would only scoff and chastise him for being silly. *But if I don't offer him an explanation he'll keep pestering me for one*, Archie thought.

So he stopped, turned around and nodded towards number 25. 'That's my issue,' he said. 'The people who've moved into *that* house! There's something strange about them and I think I've figured out what it is. They're a magical family. The girl and her mother are witches and the dad is a wizard.'

Archie expected his brother to burst out laughing, but he didn't. He just stood there with a blank expression on his face. And *then* he burst out laughing. His shoulders hitched up and down as he descended into hysterics, tears forming in his eyes, then rolling down his cheeks.

'It isn't that funny,' Archie said. 'Isabelle, the girl, threatened to turn me into a slug.'

'What?' Oliver said, laughing even harder. 'Why?'

'Because I followed her yesterday.'

'Why did you follow her?'

'I wanted to figure out what was going on with her and her family, so I tailed her on my bike.' Archie explained about the magic shop in Bucklechurch. He told Oliver about the bograt's blood and its defensive nature. 'And I saw someone last night, sprinkling powder along the borders of next door's garden.'

'So what's that got to do with anything?' Oliver said, trying to get himself under control.

'I think the bograt's blood was used to create whatever it was that was being sprinkled,' Archie said, beginning to get very annoyed by his brother's reaction. 'I think they've created some sort of magical perimeter to protect them from someone – or something.'

Oliver's laughter had been beginning to die down, but now he was back in full swing again. And he was clutching at his stomach as well because he was struggling to breathe.

'Please quit it, will you!' Archie said. 'If you don't stop, I'm just going to walk away and I won't speak to you for the rest of the day.'

Straightening himself up, Oliver made another effort to get himself under control. He pursed his lips together to stop the laughter.

And that's when Archie saw her. Coming down the street towards them, dressed in her school uniform with a satchel slung over her shoulder.

'Uh-oh,' Oliver said, following his line of sight. 'Here she comes. I'd getting running if I was you – before she turns you into a slug.'

'Keep your voice down,' Archie said, 'she might hear you.'

He tried not to stare as she approached. Oliver, on the other hand, just couldn't help himself.

'Well hello there, neighbour,' he said, offering her a smile. 'How's things going?'

'Not too bad,' she replied, offering back a smile of her own.

Archie noticed that this wasn't directed at him.

After she'd passed by and was out of earshot, Oliver said, 'D'you think I should walk with her to school? I could show her where to go when she gets there.'

'Yeah, I suppose. Just don't annoy her, though. And if you do insist on annoying her – which would be *really* dumb in my opinion – then run as fast as you can if she pulls out that wand.'

Oliver gave his brother a strange look, then took off after Isabelle.

Archie was quite confident that she wouldn't entertain the idea of walking with Oliver. But that turned out not to be the case. Archie watched as they began talking to each other and then disappeared around the corner.

What an idiot I've been, Archie thought. *I could have learned a lot more about her if I'd made friends with her rather than stalking her. And what am I supposed to do now? Trail behind them like some spare part*?

He wasn't keen on doing that, so he stayed where he was for a short while to get some distance between him and them.

As Archie walked along the main road he saw them in the distance, talking to each other and smiling. He wondered what they could be saying. *Nothing negative about me, I hope*, he thought, hoping that he wasn't the reason for their laughter.

Ahead of them, the school loomed large and imposing: an old Gothic-style building with a grey slate roof and red brickwork. The double door arched main entrance always made Archie think of a large gaping mouth, ready to swallow him as he stepped inside. The place had always given him the creeps.

Ghost stories surrounding its history were many, but the one that creeped him out the most was that of Margaret Smallwood – known as the Lady of the Stairs – who was said to haunt the classrooms and corridors – along with the north stairwell, which seemed to be a hotspot. She'd been a teacher at the school some fifty years before. Apparently, she'd got in an argument with some kids who were mucking about on the stairwell and one of them, a girl called Massey Greenwood, had shoved her. Margaret had tumbled to the bottom, hit her head against the wall and not survived. According to the legend, she'd been haunting the school ever since, wanting vengeance – and to punish any misbehaving kids.

Archie had never seen any ghosts at the school, but there'd been many instances where he'd felt like he was being watched when there was no one else around. With regards to the north stairwell, he usually tried to avoid that area. It was always cold around there and the feeling of being watched was at its strongest (which fit in quite conveniently with the legend). Archie wasn't sure whether his imagination was playing tricks on him or not. He liked to think that that was the case, but the voice of reason in the back of his mind told him that it wasn't.

Later on, when Archie caught up with his brother at break-time, he quizzed him about what the two of them had talked about.

'Well, she didn't confess to being a witch, if that's what you're wondering,' Oliver replied, whilst doing some kick-ups with a football.

'So what did she say then?'

'She told me that you've been stalking her with a telescope.'

'It wasn't a telescope; it was Dad's monocular and I didn't even use it to spy on her. Did you ask her about the rock and how she made it float? What about the removal van? Did you ask her about how her parents had managed to unload it so quickly and make the journey south and back in an impossibly fast time? And let's not forget the person who was out late last night spreading some mysterious powder along the garden borders. Did you mention *that* to her?'

'No, I didn't ask her about anything like that.'

'Why?'

'Why?' Oliver said, mimicking him. 'Because I don't want her to think that I'm an idiot. You need to get a grip. Isabelle is a definite improvement on our previous neighbour. In fact, I'd probably go as far as to say that she's pretty damn cool.'

'She's in my form. She sat on her own and didn't talk to anyone.'

'That's because she's new and hasn't got any friends yet.'

'Carly Weathers and her mates were giving her dirty looks, so I think there's going to be some trouble there. The last girl that Carly took a disliking to ended up being hung from a coat peg by her knickers. If she tries that with Isabelle, she could end up being turned into a slug.'

Without a word of warning, Oliver bounced the ball off his brother's forehead and then caught it deftly with one hand.

'*Oi!*' Archie said, glaring at him. 'What did you do that for?'

'I'm trying to knock some sense into you,' Oliver said, giving him a look of pity. 'Although I think it'd take a lot more than a football to do *that*.'

'I'll get you back for that!'

'I'm sure you will. So who's this Carly? Is that the tall, skinny girl with the big nose who's always hanging around the bike sheds with her two cronies, harassing anyone silly enough to go near them?'

'That's her, yep. She's a nightmare. All three of them are – but Carly is the worst.'

'I wouldn't worry too much about Isabelle. She comes across as the sort of girl who can handle herself.'

I'm not worried about her, Archie thought. *I'm worried about what she'll do to Carly, Laura and Ruby if they push her too far*.

'If there's any trouble, you can intervene and save her,' Oliver suggested, giving him a wink. 'You can be her knight in shining armour, yeah?'

Archie could feel himself blushing. 'I don't want to be anyone's knight in armour, thank you very much.'

One of Oliver's friends called out to him from the other side of the playground, wanting him to pass the ball.

'Later, bruv,' Oliver said, taking off across the tarmac whilst dribbling the ball.

Then someone tapped Archie on the shoulder from behind, startling him. He turned to see Ryan's grinning face in front of him.

'Please don't do that again,' Archie said. 'You know I *hate* it when you do that.'

'Sorry,' Ryan said, running a hand through his wavy, brown locks, 'I just couldn't resist.'

'Have you really been in the toilet all this time? You went at the start of break and now it's nearly the end. Why does it always take you so long? What do you do while you're in there? Read a novel? Take a nap?'

Ryan shrugged his bony shoulders. 'It takes as long as it takes. I can't say any more than that.' He offered an apologetic smile, which then became a toothy grin.

Archie was just about to tell him about everything that'd happened since the new neighbours had moved in, but the bell rang, calling an end to things.

Mr Bloom, the science teacher, appeared from around the side of the building and began telling everyone to get to their lessons.

'I've got something I need to talk to you about at dinnertime,' Archie said to Ryan, 'so don't go disappearing into the toilets for the whole break.'

'Dinnertime is an hour long. Like I'm going to stay in the bog for that amount of time.'

'I really wouldn't put it past you,' Archie said as they both made for the entrance.

'Why don't you just talk to me about it now,' Ryan said.

'There isn't enough time,' Archie said.

'Is this juicy information?'

'Yes. Very juicy. Although you might not believe me. In fact, you probably *won't* believe me.'

'Ah, c'mon, you can't say that and then not even give me an inkling of what it's about, otherwise I'll spend the next lesson playing guesswork and won't be able to concentrate on anything.'

Archie shook his head, but then said, 'Look, it's about my new neighbour and some strange things that have been happening with her.'

'Strange things? What sort of things?'

'If I answer that question, you'll then bombard me with a load more questions, so I'm not saying any more until dinner.'

'Stop talking and get walking!' Mr Bloom said to them.

The two boys scurried along with the teacher's words ringing in their ears. They passed through the entrance and went to go their separate ways.

'This better be worth waiting for,' Ryan said as he backed away down the corridor to the left.

'It is,' Archie assured him. *And you really won't believe me*, he thought.

Archie's next lesson was Spanish (his least favourite subject (boring!)). He made his way up to the first floor. In the classroom, he took his seat at the front. He liked to sit at the front so he could get as much distance between himself and the troublemakers as possible (the troublemakers being Carly, Laura and Ruby). This was another reason why he hated Spanish. He couldn't remember a lesson that they hadn't caused trouble in. Mr Callum, the teacher, couldn't control them. He couldn't control anyone who was playing up, never mind Carly and her cronies. Quite often, his lessons would descend into chaos and the headmistress, Miss Burrows, would be called in to deal with the situation. She was at the opposite end of the spectrum where controlling the students was concerned. If she told someone to do something, they did it. No questions asked. She was a bulldog of a woman, with a menacing air about her. Even Carly was wary of her. But that still didn't stop Carly from causing trouble at school and terrorising other kids.

Her current target was a girl named Sally Green. Carly and her friends were sitting behind her, pinging balled-up pieces of paper off the back of her head. Sally, to her credit, was doing her best to ignore them. But Archie could see that she was getting more and more frustrated by the look on her face. Until three or four hit her at once and she finally snapped.

She turned on her seat and glared at them. 'Why don't you just all grow up!' she said. 'Haven't you got anything better to do, you bunch of saddos!'

Mr Callum had been too busy sorting through some papers on his desk to notice what was happening. But he was noticing now.

'What's going on back there?' he said, making his way towards the trouble. 'What's all this noise about?'

Carly shrugged. 'Dunno, sir,' she said, struggling not to smile. 'We was just sitting here, minding our own business, when this nutjob,' she angled her head at Sally, 'began yelling at us.'

'They weren't "minding their own business",' Sally explained, 'they were throwing paper at me.' She pointed to the balled-up bits on the floor.

Mr Callum did his best to look angry, but he just couldn't muster the intimidating aura that was needed for the situation. 'Now how many times have I warned you lot about misbehaving in this class? I want you on your knees, picking this all up – otherwise it's off to the headmistress's office with you.'

'First,' Carly said, 'I don't get down on my knees for anyone. And second, what proof do you have that it was us who threw the paper? Did you see us do it?'

'Well ... no,' Mr Callum was forced to admit.

'And have you got any witnesses?' Carly asked him, knowing that no one would speak out against her and her friends.

Mr Callum looked around the room, waiting for someone to speak up – but no one did. A small part of Archie wanted to side with Sally. But the larger part – the bit that controlled his mouth and common sense – was telling him not to get involved.

'So it's just her word against ours,' Ruby said smugly as she glared at Sally.

Mr Callum was about to reply, but the door opened and a latecomer entered the room. Archie turned to see Isabelle standing in front of him with an apologetic look on her face.

'Sorry I'm late,' she said, 'but it's my first day and I got a bit lost.'

Carly said something to her friends and they both giggled.

Isabelle glared at them.

'It's a big school,' Mr Callum said to her, 'so I can understand you getting lost. I still get lost myself sometimes and I've been working here for ten years.' He chuckled to himself as though he'd told a particularly funny joke. Then he looked around the room for a free seat. The only one was next to Sally, so that's the one he beckoned her to take. 'Make yourself comfortable.'

Oh my God, Archie thought, *he couldn't have put her in a worse place*. *This is going to be interesting …*

He watched as Isabelle seated herself and took her pencil case out of her bag.

Mr Callum warned Carly and her friends not to cause any more problems, then he went back to his desk and continued sifting through his papers.

Inevitably, it didn't long for things to escalate again. A balled-up piece of paper hit Sally on the back of her head and a millisecond later one hit Isabelle. And then came the giggles …

'Very mature,' Isabelle said, turning on her seat to look at them. 'How old are you? Twelve … or *seven*?'

Sally turned in her seat as well. 'Mentally,' she said, 'I'd say about seven.' She reconsidered. 'Actually, that's a bit of an insult to the seven-year-olds I know, so I'm going to go with five.'

This got a few giggles from around the room, which annoyed Carly and her friends.

'Perhaps I should throw something heavier next time,' Carly said, looking from one girl to the other, marking them with a death stare. 'Something that'll *hurt*.'

'Oh, so you're admitting that you threw these bits of paper at me,' Sally said, pointing towards the mess around her desk. 'You're actually admitting that, yeah?'

'She's not admitting anything,' Laura said, doing her best to look mean and moody, 'she's just warning you what'll happen if you don't stop being lippy.'

'It's you who's being lippy,' Isabelle said. 'Why don't you just leave us alone and we'll leave you alone – how does that sound?'

Carly balled up a piece of paper and threw it at Isabelle, who ducked and watched it sail over her head.

'Err, I saw that!' Mr Callum said, stomping towards them, making a real effort to appear authoritative. 'Now what are you playing at, young lady?'

'She was provoked!' Ruby said in her defence.

'The only one doing any provoking is you lot,' Sally said. 'We're just trying to mind our own business.'

'I've tried to be patient with you,' Mr Callum said to Carly, 'and look where it's got me. You disrupt every lesson and I'm sick of it. Get yourself to Miss Burrows's office. She can deal with you.'

Carly was gobsmacked. 'But ... I was provoked! If you're going to send me to the headmistress's office, you need to send them as well,' she seethed, nodding towards Sally and Isabelle. 'Otherwise I'm not budging.'

'We're not going anywhere,' Sally said, 'because we're not the trouble causers.'

'I'm well aware of that,' Mr Callum told her. He focused his attention back on Carly. 'Now, are you going to get up and leave of your own volition – or do I have to get Miss Burrows to come to you? And she won't like that, I can tell you. It will exasperate the situation.'

Archie had no idea what exasperate meant, but he knew that this would not be good for Carly. *Way to go, Mr Callum!* he thought. *Showing some backbone, at last!*

A look of defiance spread across Carly's face as she considered her options. For a second, Archie thought that she wouldn't move – but then her chair scraped across the floor as she got up and stormed across the room. She slammed the door on her way out.

Clearly relieved to be rid of her, Mr Callum said, 'Looks like somebody hasn't had their Weetabix this morning.'

This got a few giggles.

'Right, class,' Mr Callum said, making his way towards the door, 'I'm just going to check that she hasn't gone AWOL. I'll be no more than five minutes. And I don't want any more trouble while I'm gone. I think we've already had enough for one lesson, thank you very much.'

After he'd gone, Laura had a warning for Isabelle and Sally: 'Carly's gonna get you for that. You know that, don't you?'

Isabelle and Sally looked at each and both shrugged at the same time.

'That's what I'd expect,' Isabelle said.

'Me too,' Sally said.

Archie didn't see Carly again until dinnertime. The sound of chit-chat and laughter echoed throughout the hall as he queued to get his food. He chose pepperoni pizza for his main and lemon cheesecake for afters. Then he took a seat at a table in the corner. Ryan joined him a few minutes later, plonking his tray of food down on the table next to him.

'You opted for pizza as well,' Ryan said as he seated himself. 'And the cheesecake. Great minds think alike, eh?'

'They're the only things on offer that look appetizing.'

Archie told Ryan about what'd happened in the Spanish lesson. 'Isabelle is my new neighbour. She and her family have moved into the kooky old house next door.

'Ooh, there'll be more trouble there then,' Ryan said, taking a bite of his pizza. 'Carly won't let that slide.'

Archie nodded towards the other side of the room. 'She's in the queue, look – with her two buddies,' he said. 'Let's hope they don't plonk themselves down next to us.'

'Ha-ha! Yeah, that'd make for an uncomfortable dinner break. But I've got a feeling they'll be sitting over there,' Ryan said, doing some nodding of his own.

Archie followed his line of sight and saw that Isabelle and Sally had seated themselves in the opposite corner of the room. 'They're trying to stay out of the way,' he said. 'I don't blame them.'

'Somehow, I don't think that's going to work. They need a magic spell to make them invisible. Hey, there was something you wanted to talk to me about, so what is it? Curiosity has been eating away at me since the first break.'

'I don't think now is a good time,' Archie said, gesturing towards Carly and her friends, who had got their food and were now making their way towards Isabelle and Sally. 'It's about to kick off again.'

Ryan grinned as he downed another mouthful of pizza. 'D'you think we should sit closer? Get a ringside seat, yeah?'

Archie shook his head, but then changed his mind. 'There's a table free that's close to them,' he said, picking up his tray of food. 'C'mon, let's go – before someone else takes it.'

They reached the table just as Carly and her friends were passing. Archie and Ryan seated themselves, then watched as events began to unfold.

'Do you mind if we sit with you?' Carly asked Isabelle and Sally.

'I'm not sure that would be a good idea,' Isabelle responded.

'We're not here to cause any trouble,' Ruby said, plonking her tray down. 'We're just trying to be friendly, is all.'

'We want to make amends,' Laura said with a grin that suggested otherwise.

'So can we sit with you?' Carly said, repeating her original question.

Sally glared at all three of them. 'As Isabelle said, I'm not sure that would be a go –'

Carly and her friends didn't wait for her to finish her reply. They seated themselves opposite the two girls, then began smiling at them.

'Awkward,' Ryan said to Archie.

'Yes,' he replied, '*Very* awkward. I'll give it less than two minutes before all hell breaks loose.'

'Really?' Ryan said. 'That long? I'd say less than one.'

'You're probably right.'

Archie sat up and began looking around the room.

'What are you looking for?' Ryan asked him.

'I'm just seeing if there's any teachers around. And there isn't.'

'That's not good news for Sally and her new buddy. Mr Bloom was hanging around near the door about five minutes ago, though.'

'Well, he's not there now.'

Archie and Ryan heard a commotion and saw Sally stand up with a look of thunder on her face.

'You *bitch!*' she said, glaring at Carly. 'You absolute *BITCH!*'

Carly held up her hands as if claiming her innocence. 'It was an accident,' she said with a mischievous glint in her eyes. 'Sorry.'

'What happened?' Archie asked Ryan. 'What did she do?'

'I didn't see. But the front of Sally's skirt is soaking wet, so I'd say that Carly just knocked her drink over her.'

'You did that on purpose!' Isabelle said, standing up as well.

'No, she didn't,' Ruby said.

'Yes she did!' Sally said.

'No, she *didn't!*' Laura said.

'Yes she *DID!*' Isabelle said.

Carly rose to her feet and the back of her legs hit her chair, causing it to fly across the floor. 'It was an *ACCIDENT!*' she repeated. 'An AC-CID-ENT! What part of that don't you understand?'

Ruby and Laura rose to their feet as well.

Everyone else in the hall had stopped what they were doing so they could watch the entertainment unfold. Some boys on a nearby table started up a chant: '*Fight! ... fight! ... fight! ...*' and then lots of other kids joined in as well: '*FIGHT! ... FIGHT! ... FIGHT! ...*'

A crowd began to gather.

'Three to two,' Ryan said. 'I don't like the odds.'

'What is your problem?' Sally said to Carly. 'Why are you targeting us?'

'Miss Burrows has contacted my dad and arranged a detention for me this evening,' she responded. 'I'd say that was reason enough, wouldn't you?'

'That's your fault,' Isabelle said. 'If you hadn't been throwing stuff at us, you wouldn't have *got* a detention.'

'It was just bits of paper,' Laura said.

'It's not like they hurt you,' Carly added with a snarl.

'Yeah, well, this won't hurt you,' Isabelle said, picking up her drink and attempting to soak her with it. Carly stepped to the side, however, and most of it missed.

But a roar of approval still rang out around the hall as all the spectators jostled to get a better look.

And that's when a voice echoed across the hall, telling everyone to move out of the way.

Archie turned to see the students parting to make way for Miss Burrows, the headmistress. She was accompanied by Mr Bloom, who looked tiny next to her.

'This is not a good start for your new neighbour,' Ryan said.

'That's a bit of an understatement,' Archie said.

'What in the blue blazes is going on here!' Miss Burrows said, putting her hands on her hips as she glared at Isabelle.

'Why did you just throw your drink over this girl?' She nodded toward Carly.

'Because she just threw her drink over Sally!' Isabelle replied.

'It was an accident!' Carly said. 'I didn't mean to do it, miss. Honest, I didn't.'

'Yeah, she didn't do it on purpose,' Laura said.

'She just caught the cup with the side of her hand as she was reaching for the sauce,' Ruby added.

'Shut up, you pair!' Miss Burrows said to them. 'I didn't ask for your input, so don't give it.' She focused her attention back on Isabelle. 'Whether or not it was an accident, you shouldn't have reacted the way you did, young lady. Throwing your drink over someone on your first day is not a good way to start, now, is it?'

Archie could see that Isabelle was desperate to protest her innocence, but she kept her mouth shut and nodded in agreement with the headmistress (which Archie thought was the right thing to do).

Carly had a smug grin playing at the corners of her mouth.

'I don't know what you're looking so happy about,' Miss Burrows said to her. 'You've already got yourself one detention and now you've just got yourself another.'

'What!' Carly said, aghast. 'But why?'

'Why?' Miss Burrows said, talking to her as though she were the biggest idiot imaginable. '*Why?* Because ever since you came to this school three months ago, you've caused nothing but trouble. Almost every time there's an incident of misbehaviour, you're involved. I don't believe for one second that you knocking that drink over was an accident. You did it as an act of revenge for the detention you received from me.'

'But it was an accident!' Carly said, looking to her friends for backup.

'Yeah, she didn't do it on purpose,' Ruby said.

'Definitely not on purpose,' Laura added.

'I don't believe a word out of your mouths,' Mr Bloom said, finally getting in on the conversation.

'And neither do I,' Miss Burrows said. 'And if I hear one more word from the pair of you, you'll be punished as well.'

She focused her attention back on Isabelle. 'And as for you, young lady, you can join Carly for detention this afternoon. After the last bell rings. In room 34. I'll contact your parents to let them know.'

This gave Carly something to smile about.

'I have some papers I need to go over, so I shall personally host your bout of punishment,' Miss Burrows informed both girls, who looked very disappointed to receive this bit of information. Then she told Sally to go and clean herself up. 'And you can help her,' she said to Isabelle. 'It'll get you two groups of girls apart from each other, which can only be a good thing.'

As Isabelle and Sally were gathering up their things to leave, Miss Burrows turned to address the crowd of student onlookers. 'Okay, the show is over,' she said, clapping her hands together, 'you can get back to what you were doing now!'

'I can't believe that Burrows just gave the new girl a detention,' Ryan said, scoffing his pizza. 'That's *so* unfair.'

'It's because she tried to drench Carly,' Archie explained.

'Yeah, I know that – duh! It's still unfair, though.'

'Life's unfair. I heard my mum say that once.'

'Sounds about right. I'd love to be a fly on the wall in room 34 this afternoon. There's going to be such an atmosphere.'

'You don't need to be a fly on the wall. Just get yourself in enough trouble and you can join them in person.'

'Oh, right,' Ryan said, giving his friend a sly smile, 'so what do you suggest?'

'I dunno. You could ... smear pizza in Carly's face. That'd be enough.'

'I'll take a pass on that one. Why don't you give it a try?'

'Funnily enough, I'm going to take a pass, too.'

Archie finally began tucking into his pizza, making it disappear quickly.

'Hey, are you going to tell me what it is that you keep meaning to talk to me about, or what?' Ryan inquired, staring at his friend with raised eyebrows.

Archie opened his mouth to speak, but then he had second thoughts. What if Ryan didn't believe him? What if he thought that it was all just some big joke? *My brother didn't believe me*, Archie thought, *so why should my best friend?* And there was the promise to consider. He'd given his word that he wouldn't tell anyone ...

'Do I have to tickle it out of you?' Ryan said, raising his hands and wriggling his fingers to show that this was no idle threat.

'In the dinner hall? Seriously?'

'Yes, seriously,' Ryan said, wriggling his fingers again, with a big grin spreading across his face.

There had already been one big disturbance in the hall. Archie did not want there to be a second (especially one involving him), so he said, 'It's about the new girl, Isabelle. My next door neighbour ...' Archie bit down on his bottom lip, whilst trying to think of some way that he could say what he wanted to say without it sounding like a windup.

Ryan gestured for him to carry on talking. 'Break is only an hour long, you know,' he said. 'So spill it, yeah.'

'You won't believe me.'

'I will.'

'No, you won't.'

Ryan shrugged. 'Okay, so maybe I won't. But you can't just get me all intrigued like this and then not tell me.' He raised his hands again, threatening a tickle attack. 'Spill it, Wiggins! Just talk!'

Right, okay, here it goes, Archie thought. He told him about how Isabelle had made the rock float in the air with her wand. He mentioned the unbelievably quick trips back and forth in the removal van. He admitted to having followed Isabelle to the magic shop. He detailed what she'd bought and what he suspected that it'd been used for. Last but not least, he told him about the threat she'd made: to turn him into a slug, if she caught him following her again.

Ryan had kept a straight face while Archie was talking, but that last bit had seemingly been too much for him. Covering his mouth with his hand, Ryan did his best to stifle a giggle.

'And there we go!' Archie said, looking away in disgust. 'I knew you'd laugh.'

'I'm sorry,' Ryan said, trying to get himself under control. 'But if things were reversed – if I'd been the one saying what you just said – you'd be laughing at me. And you know you would.'

'Yeah ... maybe,' Archie had to admit.

'Are you being serious? Or is this a windup?'

'It's *not* a windup.'

'Have you told anyone else about this?'

'Just my brother. And, yes, he laughed as well.'

'So what, you think this girl is some sort of witch or something?'

'That's *exactly* what I think she is.'

'Look, the trick with the wand and rock will be just that ... a *trick*,' Ryan said. 'The rock was probably held up with some super thin wire that you couldn't see.'

'There was no wire. I checked. And the rock wasn't magnetised either. It was a real one. I picked it up and held it. It was *real!*'

'And as for your neighbour spreading something around the borders of her garden, that's easily explained. It was probably slug or ant repellent or some other powder used for gardening. Although putting it down late at night is an odd thing to do, I must admit.'

'I think you're right about it being a repellent, but I think it's to ward off something more sinister than slugs or ants.'

'Like what?'

Archie shrugged. 'I dunno. Your guess is as good as mine.'

'Hey, maybe it was ground up garlic,' Ryan suggested, tongue in cheek. 'Maybe they're trying to keep some *vampires* at bay.' He moved on to the next point he wanted to address. 'As for the quick trips in the van,' he said, 'maybe they lied about where they moved from. Perhaps your neighbours moved from somewhere closer, somewhere not too far from here.'

'That's possible. But why would they lie? And it wasn't just how fast they made the trips, it was the speed with which they unloaded the van as well. It was filled from top to bottom twice and they unloaded it in less than ten minutes on both occasions. So how do you explain that?'

'How many was doing the unloading?'

'Two: the mum and dad.'

Ryan gave this some thought. 'Erm ... they're both hard workers?'

'They could be the hardest workers in the world and they *still* wouldn't be able to unload that van in that space of time.'

'So ... what? They magicked all stuff into the house? And you didn't see any of it?'

'No,' Archie was forced to admit. 'I got distracted on both occasions.' He brought his fist down on the table in frustration.

Some kids at a nearby table gave him a strange look

'Wow! You're taking this seriously, aren't you?' Ryan said to Archie.

Archie pushed his plate away. 'I've lost my appetite,' he said.

'Well,' Ryan said, tucking back into his pizza, 'I don't think there's anything in life that should ever cause someone to lose their appetite. Especially something as daft as *this*. Hey, if you don't want your food, can I have it?'

'D'you know what, I knew telling you would be a mistake,' Archie said, pushing his plates towards him. 'Can you really manage two pizzas and two slices of cheesecake?'

'I dunno. But I'm gonna give it a good try,' Ryan said, grinning through a mouthful of food.

Archie felt a bit grossed out by this spectacle.

He sighed, then looked over towards Carly and her friends. A dinner lady had cleaned up the spilt drinks, so they were now eating their food and having a good laugh amongst themselves.

'She seems happy considering she's got another detention,' Ryan said, following Archie's line of sight.

'It's a normal day-to-day thing for her. They're probably plotting their next move against Isabelle and Sally. Thinking of ideas to humiliate them.'

'If what you're saying is true about Isabelle being a witch, then I wouldn't want to be Carly or any of her friends. Did you say that she threatened to turn you into a slug? And that was just for following her. Imagine what she'll do to someone who's really annoyed her. Good job she isn't *actually* a witch, isn't it?'

Archie had heard enough. He got up and walked away.

'Oi! Wait up!' Ryan said. 'I haven't finished my food yet!'
Ignoring him, Archie headed for the door.

In the playground, he sat crouched against the fence on the far side. He shielded his eyes from the sun with his hand as he watched other kids play.

It was five minutes later when Ryan came over to him.

'If you're just going to make fun of me then go away,' Archie said.

'I'm not going to make fun of you,' Ryan said, crouching next to him.

They sat in silence for a while, watching a game of dob. It was Ryan who eventually broke the silence.

'So let's say you are right,' he said. 'Let's say that she is a witch. What do you plan on doing about it?'

'I don't plan on doing anything. I just want to prove that she's one, so I can show you and my brother that I'm not going mad.'

'And how are you gonna prove it?'

'I have no idea.'

'It's a shame you didn't film her levitating that rock. I'd like to have seen that.'

'Why? So you could tell me again that she was using a piece of wire or some other sort of trickery?'

'No. I'm not gonna do that. If you wanna try and prove that she's a witch then I'm with you on that. The only question is, how do we go about it?'

Archie looked sideways at his friend, waiting for him to crack up laughing or at least be sporting a smile. But Ryan was doing neither. He was deadly serious.

'We could try staking out her house,' Archie suggested. 'Although that didn't work out too well for me last time.' He told him about how he'd hidden in a bush across the street and been discovered by Mrs Balham and her dog.

'You've turned into a real-life bush camper,' Ryan said, chortling. 'Ha-ha! I like it.'

'There is that threat to turn me into a slug to consider as well.'

'That was probably just an idle threat. I'm sure she wouldn't do something as extreme as that just for following her. She'll probably turn you into a goat instead, or a dog, or an alpaca, or ...'

'Yeah, okay, I get the point.'

The bell to end dinner break sounded.

'Look, we'll talk about this again when we've got a bit more time, yeah?' Archie said, excited about the prospect of discussing tactics with his best friend. 'What's your next subject?'

'Physics. What's yours?'

'Geography. With Sally and Carly and her friends, so that's going to be fun. I don't know if the new girl will be there, but it'll make things even more explosive if she is.'

'If she's in my class, I'm going to be keeping a very close eye on her.'

'Ditto.'

'Surely even Carly wouldn't be stupid enough to cause more trouble now she's got another detention ... would she?'

They both looked at each other and said 'Yes' at the same time.

Much to Archie's surprise, the geography lesson passed without any further incidents of significant attempts at bullying. Perhaps Isabelle not being there had helped ease tensions a little, or maybe Carly wasn't as stupid as Archie and Ryan had taken her for. Whatever the reason, this was an unexpected and welcome break from the nastiness for Sally. Giggling and dirty looks were the worst she had to endure, which had to be preferable to having things thrown at her, Archie figured.

It was in the next lesson when trouble flared up again, which was kind of surprising – considering that neither Carly nor any of her friends were there. Cooking was Archie's favourite subject. This was not something he'd ever admitted to anyone – and he had no intentions of ever doing so either. The only negative thing was the teacher, Mrs Tippings, who was an abrasive, busy bee of a woman, always either buzzing around the classroom or hovering at people's sides, constantly giving out advice.

Ryan was excited to see that Isabelle was also in this class. And he got even more excited when Mrs Tippings told everyone to form groups of three.

'We need to form a group with Isabelle,' he said to Archie as he began edging towards her.

'What?' Archie said. 'Why?'

'You want to find out whether she really is a witch, don't you?' Ryan said in a low voice.

'Err, yeah, but ...'

'No buts, just come on.'

Archie was still reluctant to follow his friend, but he found himself doing it anyway because the curious part of him thought that it was a good thing to do.

'Is it okay if we join up with you?' Ryan said, presenting himself in front of Isabelle with a smile on his face.

Isabelle seemed okay with the idea – until Archie edged in on the situation.

'I think I'll pass,' Isabelle said, scowling at him.

Archie turned to walk away, but Ryan grabbed him by the arm.

'Look, my friend is sorry about what happened between you two,' Ryan said. 'He didn't mean to follow and stalk you; he was just curious about you, that's all.'

Archie felt his cheeks flush red with embarrassment. He looked around to see if anyone was listening in on the conversation. Fortunately, all the other kids were still busy forming groups. Something that was beginning to annoy Mrs Tippings.

'Please hurry up and get in threes,' she said, pacing back and forth impatiently. 'This lesson is only an hour long. We haven't got all day, you know!'

Isabelle began looking around the room.

'You won't find anyone better at cooking than us,' Ryan said to her. 'I'm on a par with Gordon Ramsay and my friend here is even better than, erm ...' he clicked his fingers together, 'Henston Flumenball, or whatever his name is.'

'It's Heston Blumenthal,' Isabelle said with a roll of her eyes. 'And you pair don't even look like you could cook toast without burning it.'

'That's a little harsh,' Ryan said, pretending to be offended.

'It's probably true though,' Archie said, 'in your case.'

'I'm not *that* bad,' Ryan said.

'I remember being at your house and you asked me if I wanted pizza to eat,' Archie said. 'I told you pepperoni and you came back with plain cheese. Cooking doesn't get much more basic than that – and you *still* got it wrong.'

Ryan glared at him as if to say: *whaddaya playin' at, buddy!*

'You're not exactly selling yourself as a great pair to join up with, you know,' Isabelle commented as she looked around again for another group to join.

'Okay, so we're both terrible at cooking,' Archie admitted, 'but it looks like we're the only ones left that you can pair up with, so ...'

Mrs Tippings, who now seemed happy to progress with the lesson, clapped her hands together and said, 'Okay, class, turn to page 221 of your textbooks to see what you'll be cooking today. I think you're going to like it.'

Excitement filled the classroom as they all discovered that they would be baking chocolate cakes.

'*Ooh!*' Ryan said, rubbing his hands together in anticipation. 'We need to make sure we get this right.' He looked at Isabelle. 'So, how's your cooking? Please tell me you're a whiz in the kitchen.'

She could probably make some appear out of thin air, Archie thought, *if she used that wand of hers*.

'I'm sure we'll bake some lovely cakes,' Isabelle said, dodging the question, 'if we concentrate on what we're doing.'

The first thing to do was measure out all the ingredients. The next thing, according to the instructions, was to beat together the correct amounts of butter and sugar in a bowl. Isabelle assigned this task to Ryan. She told Archie to find a tin and grease it while she perused the instructions to see what needed to be done next.

Ryan attempted to make small talk with Isabelle, trying to find out things about her, but her responses were guarded, mostly yes and no answers. Then he asked her about the Enchanted Cove ...

'Is it a good shop?' he said in a nudge-nudge, wink-wink kind of way. 'Do they have anything that you'd recommend for me and Archie?'

Isabelle gave him a sideways look which suggested a no, but then she said, 'They sell some nice musky incense candles. I like to have one burning while I'm in the bath. It's very relaxing. You should try it.'

'That sounds great,' Ryan said, 'but I was hoping you'd recommend something a little more magical than a candle.'

'Why don't you go and take a look for yourself,' Isabelle said. 'I'm sure the shopkeeper will be able to answer your question better than I can.'

Archie did not like where this conversation was heading, so he kicked his friend in the shin and glared at him.

'What did you do that for?' Ryan said to him.

Archie continued to glare, conveying a very clear message.

'What?' Ryan said, glaring back at him. 'You want to know as much as I do, so there's no point in beating around the bush, is there?'

'Honestly, if I could join another group now, I would,' Isabelle said.

'Okay, look,' Ryan said to her, 'my friend and I want to know how you made that rock float in mid-air. Archie seems to think that you're an actual witch, but I must admit that I'm not as convinced as him (what with me not witnessing what happened). So we'd be very appreciative if you could just enlighten us one way or another.'

For a few seconds, Isabelle just stared at Ryan with a blank expression on her face. Then she said, 'I'm a witch. A *real* witch. Are you happy now you know the truth? Can we get on with what we're supposed to be doing?'

Neither of the boys knew what to make of this response. But before they could say anything else, Mrs Tippings walked past and inquired how things were coming along.

'You should have everything mixed and ready to go in the oven by now,' she said, casting a critical eye over their efforts, 'but that clearly isn't the case, now, is it?'

None of the children knew what to say in response.

'I'm going to check on everyone else now,' Mrs Tippings said in a no-nonsense voice, 'and by the time I come back, I want you lot up to speed. Are we clear on that?'

The three of them gave back grunted replies.

'I need more enthusiasm from you than that,' Mrs Tippings said.

'Yes miss!' they all said in unison.

'That's more like it,' Mrs Tippings said.

After she'd moved along, Isabelle took charge of the situation and told the boys what was needed.

Everything was going well, getting back on track, until Ryan decided that it would be a good idea to flick some flour in Archie's face.

'Don't do that,' Archie warned him.

'It's just a bit of flour,' Ryan said, flicking some more towards him.

'Please don't do *that*!' Archie warned him again.

'Are you losing your sense of humour?' Ryan said, blowing more in his face.

And that was when Archie lost it. He snatched the bag, grabbed a big handful and threw it at his friend. Unfortunately for Archie, Mrs Tippings had come back to see how they were getting on. And even more unfortunate was the fact that Ryan ducked out of the way - and the white stuff hit Mrs Tippings smack in the face.

For a second there was silence in the classroom - and then all the onlookers, the other kids, burst out laughing.

'Oops!' Ryan said.

'Looks like you might be joining me in detention this evening,' Isabelle said, rolling her eyes at Archie.

'He *is* going to be joining you in detention!' Mrs Tippings said, glaring at him. She grabbed a tissue from her pocket and began wiping the white stuff from her face. 'What are you staring at?' she hissed at the rest of the class. 'Get back to what you were doing! Get back to what you were doing *NOW!*'

Everyone got back to what they were doing.

'I'll have Miss Burrows contact your parents to inform them about what's happening,' Mrs Tippings told Archie.

Great, he thought. *That's just ...* great.

After class, Archie had a go at Ryan as they were walking down the corridor to their next lesson: art.

'I've got a detention now because of you,' Archie said. 'Thanks for that - *friend!*'

'How is that my fault? I threw a bit of flour at you as a joke, then you got mardy and threw a load back at me. How was I supposed to know that the teacher would be behind me?'

'Well, if you hadn't been fooling around in the first place, then none of this would have happened? And why did you have to ask Isabelle whether she's a witch or not? I mean, it's not like she was going to give you an honest answer, is it?'

Ryan pulled him to one side and told him to keep his voice down, whilst kids moved past in both directions, en route to their lessons.

'It's not like she's actually one anyway,' Ryan muttered under his breath.

'So you just lied about believing me? You were just humouring me, yeah?' Archie didn't wait for a reply. 'I knew it. I knew you didn't believe me - I just *knew* it.'

'Part of me wants to believe you,' Ryan said, giving him an apologetic look. 'But another part of me - the common sense part - tells me that you need to get a grip.'

Archie wanted to storm away and stamp his feet, just to show how annoyed he was. But he took a few deep breaths and calmed himself. 'My parents are not going to be happy with me,' he moaned. 'They'll probably punish me as well. They'll probably ground me.'

'Yeah, probably,' Ryan had to admit. 'But it's gotta be kind of worth it, in a way, though, don't you think?' he said with a smile slowly spreading across his face. 'The stunned look on Mrs Tippings's flour-covered face has to be just about the funniest thing I've ever seen in my life.'

'That's easy for you to say when you're not the one who's in deep trouble,' Archie said. But he couldn't help but sport a smile himself.

For a few seconds, they just looked at each other, communicating without speaking. All positive stuff.

Then Ryan said, 'Look, if you still want to try and prove that Isabelle is a witch then I'm with you on that one.

Although you getting grounded could be a bit of an obstacle where *that's* concerned, don'tcha think?'

'Yeah ... yeah, it will be.'

Farther along the corridor, Mr Langford, the art teacher, poked his head out of the classroom door and noticed them. 'Are you pair coming in, or are you going to stand there talking all day?'

'We're going to stand here all day if that's okay with you?' Ryan said, offering up a big, goofy grin.

'Ha-ha-ha!' Mr Langford said, pretending to laugh. 'Forever the joker, eh, Jackson? And I bet you would stand out here too, if I let you. Anything to avoid having to do your work. Well, whether you want to do your work or not, you still need to be in class – so get a move on – chop, chop!'

Archie and Ryan did as they were told.

Isabelle wasn't in this class, but her new friend Sally was. Unfortunately, Carly and Ruby were also here, which made for an uncomfortable hour for Sally. They didn't cause any trouble with her as such. Much like in geography earlier in the day, the worst she had to endure from them were nasty looks and the odd giggle.

As everyone was seating themselves at their desks, Archie was surprised when Carly called out to him: 'Hey, Wiggins, I heard about what happened in cookery,' she said. 'How you chucked flour all over Mrs Tippings. I wish I'd been there to see it. Must have been hilarious!'

Bursts of laughter filled the room as all eyes fell on Archie, who wasn't sure how to respond.

'Please tell me that you meant to do it and that it wasn't just an accident,' Carly said.

Archie was about to reply, but Mr Langford's voice boomed across the room, telling everyone to sit down and shut up. 'I'm sure it was an accident,' he said. 'It would take a *very* brave person to do something like that to Mrs Tippings on purpose.' He clapped his hands together. 'Come on, you lot! Get your backsides on a seat now. And when I say now, that means *NOW!*'

Everyone did as they were told.

At the end of the lesson, as Archie was making for the door, Carly appeared beside him and asked him if he'd got detention for what'd happened in cookery.

'Eh, yeah,' he replied, 'I'm going to be joining you and Isabelle for an hour of fun with Miss Burrows.'

'Cool!' Carly said, giving him a smile. 'We can walk there together, yeah?'

'Eh ...' Archie said, trying to think of some way that he could avoid this ...

'Can I talk to you about something?' Ryan asked him as he came to his rescue.

Nodding enthusiastically, Archie said, 'Sure, sure, sure.'

Archie was hoping that this would get rid of Carly, but it didn't. She just lingered there with a big, goofy grin on her face.

'A little privacy would be nice,' Ryan said to her.

'Oh, right, okay,' Carly muttered, looking slightly offended as she walked away. Just before she disappeared through the doorway, however, she stopped and said, 'I'll see you there then, Archie, yeah?'

'Yeah,' Archie said. He was smiling on the outside, but inside he was cringing.

After she'd gone, Ryan said to Archie, 'Looks like you've got a new best friend there, mate.'

'Really?' he replied, aghast at the idea.

'She's obviously impressed by your antics in cooking. She probably thinks you did it on purpose.'

'Great,' Archie said. 'This is all I need.'

Sally walked past and gave him a look he couldn't judge.

'Shall I come to your house about six o'clock?' Ryan suggested. 'You'll have had your dinner by then and we can discuss tactics about you know who.'

'Sure. You may not be able to come in the house though as I'll probably have been grounded by then.'

'Not a problem. I'll just bring my school bag with me and tell your parents that I'm helping you out with some maths homework.'

'My dad will believe that but my mum might smell a rat. She's got an in-built lie detector, I'm sure of it.'

'Yeah, my mum's the same. We'll give it a go though. I don't see how she can say no.'

'Are you pair going?' Mr Langford said from behind his desk. 'Or are you just going to stand there talking for the rest of the day?'

The boys made for the door.

In the corridor, Archie said, 'Right, I better go. I don't want to be late for the detention. That wouldn't go down well.'

'I wouldn't want to be you for the next hour, stuck in a room with those three.'

'Oh, it's going to be a riot of laughs,' Archie said sarcastically.

By the time he arrived at room 34, the two girls were already seated at desks. Isabelle was to the left and Carly to the right, as far apart as they could be. Fortunately, Miss Burrows hadn't shown up yet, so she wasn't there to chastise Archie for being slightly late.

Both girls watched Archie as he made for a desk in the centre.

'You should sit near me,' Carly suggested, pointing to a nearby desk.

'I don't think Miss Burrows will allow you to sit together,' Isabelle said.

'I didn't ask him to sit next to me,' Carly snapped at her. 'I asked him to sit *near* me. There's a difference.'

She smiled at Archie and he gave a half-hearted smile back.

'I better go in the centre,' Archie said. 'I'm pretty sure Miss Burrows will tell me to move if I go anywhere else.'

'That's exactly what I'll do,' she said from behind him as she entered the room. She had three laptops tucked under her arm and was carrying a large black bag with the other. 'Apologies for being late, but it was unavoidable.' Her bag went down with a thud as she let it drop to the floor by her desk.

By this time, Archie had seated himself and was looking on eagerly, ready to get on with things.

Miss Burrows handed out the laptops and then said, 'I want you to write an essay. Pick whatever subject you like. One thousand words: which is about three pages, give or take.'

'That's a lot of words!' Carly exclaimed.

'It most certainly is,' Miss Burrows agreed.

'This detention is for one hour,' Carly said, 'so what happens if we haven't written that many by the end?'

'You'll have to take it home on a thumb drive, finish it and hand it in tomorrow,' Miss Burrows explained. 'You've got plenty of time. As long as you crack on with it, you should finish by four thirty-five, no problems.' She sat down at her desk and then looked at all three of them. 'Well, what are you waiting for? The sooner you get started, the sooner you'll be out of here.'

Archie stared blankly at the wall, trying to think of a subject he could write about. Miss Burrows challenged him about this, but then he remembered that he had a reasonable knowledge of British history, so he decided to go with that.

Isabelle and Carly were already typing. Archie wondered which subjects they had chosen. *How to be a great bully*, he thought. *Now* that's *something that Carly knows a lot about. She could write a book about* that.

'Ahum!' Miss Burrows said, getting Archie's attention. She pointed to the clock on the wall above her head. 'Time is ticking away, Mr Wiggins, so I suggest you crack on.'

Archie got typing.

Twenty minutes later, he'd barely filled half a page. He kept struggling to think of what to write next and how to word things. Every minute that passed made him feel more and more anxious. He didn't want to take the essay home. He wanted to finish it now and be done with it.

Carly, on the other hand, had been tapping away furiously the whole time.

Archie thought: *she's going to finish before us, then walk out of here with a big smile on her face while we're still sat here like fools.*

And another twenty or so minutes later, that's exactly what happened. Carly put her hand in the air and told Miss Burrows that she'd finished.

'My, my,' Miss Burrows said, surprised, 'you didn't hang around, did you? Although bear in mind that if you've written a load of drivel, you'll have to do it all again.'

'It's not a load of drivel,' Carly said.

Inspecting her work, Miss Burrows read the title: 'Makeup and nail care,' she said with a funny expression. 'This isn't quite the sort of topic I was hoping you'd cover, but then I did say that you could write about any subject you liked.' She checked through the work, reading some bits and skipping others. 'And you've certainly gone into some detail here, so I must commend you for your efforts. I'm sure this will make for a riveting read.'

'Can I go now?' Carly asked her.

'Yes,' she replied.

As Carly was leaving, she looked at Isabelle and smiled.

'Oh,' Miss Burrows said to Carly, 'don't forget that you have another detention on Friday. Same time. Same place.'

That wiped the smile off her face. She swept from the room, yanking the door shut behind her.

Archie had forgotten about the second detention. At least that gave him something to grin about.

'Remember,' Miss Burrows said, 'the sooner you finish, the sooner you can leave.'

Archie set to work again.

But then a few minutes later, Miss Burrows got up from her desk and said, 'I've just remembered something that I need to do. I'll be gone a short while: five minutes, tops.'

Isabelle raised her hand and opened her mouth to speak, but Miss Burrows had already shut the door behind her.

Archie and Isabelle listened to the sound of her footsteps fading away down the corridor.

A few seconds of silence followed as the two remaining

children looked over at each other. Then Archie asked Isabelle how she was getting on.

'I've done six hundred words,' she replied, shifting uncomfortably in her seat.

'Oh, right. You're doing better than me then; I've only done four hundred. Do you think you'll get finished in time?' Archie glanced at the clock on the wall. 'There's only seventeen minutes left, so I'm pretty sure I'll be taking a thumb stick home with me.'

'Yeah, well, if you get on with it now, you'll have less to do later, won't you?' Isabelle said, shifting uncomfortably again. She pulled a funny face.

'Are you okay?'

'No. I need the toilet – and I need it now. I was about to tell Miss Burrows, but she shut the door.'

'Number one or number two?'

Isabelle scowled. 'What difference does it make? Honestly, just when I'm sure you can't get any dafter than what I already think you are, you say something like *that*.' Her scowl morphed into a look of pure discomfort.

'If you're so desperate, why didn't you ask her sooner?'

'Sometimes the urge just hits me out of the blue. And don't go asking me if there's a spell or a potion that can help me with that, because there isn't.'

'I had no intentions of asking you about anything to do with magic. And I'm sorry that Ryan asked you about it earlier. He didn't believe me when I told him that I think you're a witch, but he just had to go and ask you anyway. He's a bit silly like that, I'm afraid.'

'Have you told anyone else that you think I'm a witch?' Isabelle rolled her eyes towards the ceiling, still clearly in discomfort.

'No,' Archie lied. Then he backtracked and decided to tell the truth. 'Actually, I mentioned it to my brother and he didn't believe me either. He thinks you're just a trickster, just like the YouTubers he watches that can make stuff disappear or appear out of nowhere. I just want to know one way or another whether you are a witch or not. I won't tell anyone else, if you are. You have my word on that. Not that anyone would believe me anyway.'

'Your word means nothing. You made a promise before and you broke it.'

Before Archie could apologize, Isabelle's seat scraped across the floor as she got up and hurried towards the door.

'Where are you going?' Archie asked her.

'To the toilet.'

'Shouldn't you wait for Miss Burrows to come back so you can ask permission?' he asked her.

She didn't reply. She just opened the door and disappeared off down the corridor.

Archie sat there for a few seconds, the silence sucking in around him. He didn't like being left on his own. Not in this school, with all its ghost stories – especially that of the Lady of the Stairs. It was an old building full of creaks and tapping noises. Archie knew that those noises were to do with the clunky, outdated radiators and the draughty corridors, but any sound that broke the silence unnerved him.

His mum's voice spoke up in his mind: *the best way to deal with this is to just crack on with your work, you know that, don't you?*

Sound advice. And, after taking a deep breath, he tried to do just that. He got a few more sentences down, but then the radiator behind him pinged and caused him to jump a little. *I wish they would just hurry up*, he thought, glancing at the clock. He was sure that Miss Burrows had been gone for longer than five minutes. *Why do people always take longer than what they say they're going to take?* Archie wondered. *Why does five minutes always end up being more like fifteen or twenty?*

Archie's eyes fell upon Isabelle's bag, which was tucked underneath her desk. Other than school books and stationery, he wondered what else could be in there. Some mysterious, magical items, perhaps? Or maybe even her wand? He figured that she probably wouldn't risk bringing any such items into school, but there was only one way to be sure.

He hurried across the room, knelt by Isabelle's desk and pulled her bag towards him. Something inside of him was telling him that this was the wrong thing to do, but another part – the curious, mischievous part – was urging him on. His fingers hovered over the zip as he battled with himself internally.

Footsteps.

Approaching quickly ...

Archie pushed the bag to where it'd been and then raced back across the room. Before he could get to his desk, however, Miss Burrows appeared in the doorway. Placing her hands on her hips, she gave Archie a searching look and asked him what he was doing.

'I was, erm ... just checking to see how many words Isabelle has done,' he lied.

'You don't leave your seat unless I tell you that you can leave it.' Miss Burrows took a few steps forwards and studied Isabelle's empty seat. 'Where has she gone?'

'I'm here,' Isabelle said, appearing from behind her. 'I'm sorry, miss; I was desperate for the toilet and just couldn't wait.'

Miss Burrows gave her a searching look, as if she doubted the validity of her story. 'I don't care how desperate you are,' she said, 'you do *not* leave this classroom without my permission. Do I have to explain the health and safety implications to you? Or are you smart enough to work it out on your own?'

'But ... I would have weed myself,' Isabelle said with an edge to her voice.

'I told you that I would only be gone for a short while,' Miss Burrows said, beginning to lose her temper. What part of that didn't you get? I'm sure you could have held it in for a bit longer.'

Isabelle explained about not being able to hold her bladder very well (with even more of an edge to her voice this time).

'I doubt very much that you have a weak bladder,' Miss Burrows said, glaring at her. 'You do what I tell you to do and how I tell you to do it! You're new at this school, so you don't understand that yet. But you will understand it soon enough, if you keep looking at me like you are now, young lady! Now get back to your seat and finish your work.'

Isabelle was furious. But she did as she was told. Back at her desk, she seated herself and began tapping away on her keyboard again. She started normally, pressing the keys down with the usual amount of force. But then she began prodding them harder with each letter she typed.

'If you break that,' Miss Burrows said, 'your parents will have to pay for a replacement. And you'll also earn yourself an extra detention. They wouldn't be too happy about that, now, would they?'

Isabelle eased off a little with the prodding, but then began jabbing harder again as Miss Burrows made her way back towards her desk.

'Stop doing that,' the headmistress said.

Isabelle ignored her. She stared dead ahead, a blank expression on her face, as she continued to prod away.

'Stop doing that!' Miss Burrows said again (this time with some real bass to her voice).

Isabelle ignored her. And then began prodding even harder.

Wow! Archie thought as he watched all this unfold. *Looks like someone's got temper tantrum issues.*

'How *dare* you ignore me!' Miss Burrows said, storming across the room towards Isabelle. 'When I tell you to stop doing something, you stop doing it! And that means NOW!'

Isabelle stopped tapping.

Then a look of thunder spread across her face as she focused her hatred on something else: a bookcase on the other side of the room. The next thing Archie knew was that a large, hardback book was winging its way towards him, travelling through the air at blurring speed. No time to duck. Only wince and close his eyes and tense up and get ready for the impact.

But the book didn't hit him. He opened his eyes expecting to see that it'd either sailed past him and perhaps hit the wall or skidded across the floor. What he did see, however, took his breath away. The book was floating in front of his face, no more than six inches from his nose. The title was blurry, but he could still make it out: Success with Intermediate Geometry.

His whole body tense as a longbow string, he turned his head and looked at Isabelle. 'Well, that was close,' he said, giggling nervously. 'Good job you had a change of heart at the last second.'

'I didn't have a change of heart,' Isabelle said. 'I didn't stop the book.' She nodded at the headmistress. 'She did.'

The book dropped on Archie's desk – *thud!* – as both children focused their attention on Miss Burrows.

'Ah,' she said, smiling nervously at them, lost for words. 'Now this could take a little explaining.'

'Not to me it won't,' Isabelle said.

Miss Burrows gave her a curious look.

'Thanks for stopping me from being hurt,' Archie said, pushing the book away. 'And I can't wait to hear an explanation for this.'

'I don't suppose there's any point in telling that it was a trick, is there?' Miss Burrows said. 'A trick of the eye? An illusion? That you didn't see what you thought you just saw?'

'That would be one heck of a trick,' Archie said. 'A bit like making a rock float with a wand,' he said, glancing at Isabelle. 'Although stopping the book in mid-air trumps that, I'd say – given that a wand wasn't needed.'

The heels of Miss Burrows' shoes tapped on the floor as she walked across the room and closed the door. 'Okay,' she said, turning to face her students and looking from one to the other with a measuring expression, 'it seems this bout of punishment has veered in an unexpected direction and an explanation is indeed in order. I won't insult your intelligence with lies. I did use magic to stop that book in mid-air. And I would do the same again if a similar situation were to arise.'

'But that risks exposing what you are,' Isabelle stated, 'which is exactly what you've just done.'

'I'm well aware of the risks and what I've just done,' Miss Burrows said, 'but I cannot stand by and watch a student – or anyone else – get hurt when I can prevent that from happening.'

What is going on here? Archie thought. *Have I dozed off in class? Am I dreaming this?*

Any second now he was sure that Miss Burrows would wake him up, either with a yell of her voice or a stiff prod on the shoulder. Deep down, however, he knew that wasn't going to happen. He knew that he was sitting in a room with two witches. And one of them just happened to be the headmistress of the school, for crying out loud!

Miss Burrows folded her arms and shook her head. 'What a most unfortunate position I've put myself in,' she said, looking from one child to the other. 'The only question now, of course, is what I'm going to do about it?'

'Well, you don't need to worry about me,' Isabelle said, reaching into her bag, pulling out her wand and holding it up proudly. She nodded towards Archie. 'He's the problem.' Isabelle pointed her wand in his direction. 'Motus Moblata!'

Archie cringed – and then watched in amazement as the book was raised to his eye level and then floated in front of his face. This was the same spell that he'd witnessed her doing the first time he'd met her.

'That's very impressive,' Miss Burrows said. 'And if you can put it back on the shelf, where it belongs, I'll be even more impressed.'

Isabelle gave a confident smile and then did just that,

slotting it exactly where it'd been before.

'Okay, so somebody knows their magic,' Miss Burrows said, 'but you shouldn't be bringing your wand into school – unless an afterschool class has been arranged.'

'An afterschool class?' Archie said, gobsmacked. 'As in ... a magic class?'

'Yes,' Miss Burrows said.

I really am dreaming, Archie thought. *I must be!*

'Do I need permission from my parents to attend?' Isabelle asked the headmistress.

'Yes, you most definitely do,' she replied.

'Great!' Isabelle said, beaming. 'I'll be at the next one, for sure.'

This was the first time Archie had seen her smile and it was a welcome sight.

'Although, I must admit,' Miss Burrows said, 'I'll have to consider whether your appalling behaviour will exclude you from any after-school activities. Skilled witch or not, a detention on your first day at Darkcoat Academy is not the best start, now, is it?'

Isabelle's smile slowly faded from her face.

Archie had tuned out to what the headmistress had just said. He was too busy thinking about the fact that she was a witch and that there was a magic class which had been taking place at his school that he knew nothing about. Until now.

He had so many questions boiling up inside of him. He blurted one after another: 'So how many kids attend the class? How many witches and wizards are there at this school? Can anyone do magic, or is it only certain people? And how – '

'Whoa! *Whoa!*' Miss Burrows said, holding a hand up and cutting him off. 'One thing at a time, please. Let's answer the most important question first: can anyone do magic? No. Only those gifted with the power. With regards to how many wizards and witches there are at the school, it's not many: about a handful (all of which attend the after-school class).

And now you're going to ask me where you can get a wand, aren't you? Well ...'

'That wasn't going to be my next question,' Archie said. 'I know where I can get one. I just don't know whether I'll need one. How do I find out whether I've been "gifted with the power"? Can you tell just by looking at me?' he asked the headmistress. 'Or is it something you can sense?'

'I can't tell by looking at someone,' Miss Burrows informed him. 'And with regards to sensing, there are certain wizards and witches who have that ability, but I am not one of them. There is one sure-fire way of finding out, though ...' She placed her wand on the desk in front of Archie. 'Don't be too disappointed if nothing happens. The odds of there being two magical students in this room at the same time are quite slim, just so you know.'

Archie looked at the wand in awe. And then he picked it up. It felt light in his hand, a tingling sensation pulsing in his fingers. Was that a good sign? He figured it must be ...

'Now, which spell shall we have you try,' Miss Burrows said, clicking her fingers together in contemplation. 'Something simple, obviously.' And then it came to her. 'Ah, yes, a simple force push should do the trick. That's about as easy as it gets.'

'Force push?' Archie said. 'Will I be training to be a Jedi?'

'No, you will not,' Miss Burrows said, not getting the joke. 'Whatever one of *those* is.'

'You don't know what a Jedi is?' Archie said. 'Seriously?'

Ignoring him, Miss Burrows grabbed a plastic paper tray from her desk and placed it in front of Archie.

She said, 'Relax. And with a relatively firm grip, level the wand at this tray and then, as you're saying the magical words – Momentus Potentia! –, imagine it moving away from you and it may just be so.' She gave him advice on pronunciation. 'Give some bass to the men in Momentus and draw out the O in Potentia.'

Archie tried to compose himself. Then he said the magical

words and ... nothing happened. His shoulders slumped in disappointment as he looked at Miss Burrows.

'Give it another try,' she said, offering him an encouraging smile, 'and this time remember to draw out the O in potentia.'

'And relax,' Isabelle advised. 'You look *wayyy* too tense.'

Archie tried to do just that, but he wasn't finding it easy being the centre of attention. He steadied himself, took a deep breath, then once again attempted to cast the spell. And this time he was successful. He watched in amazement as the container went flying across the room and smashed to pieces against the door.

'Whoa!' Miss Burrows said, impressed. 'You were only supposed to move it across the desk.'

'Sorry!' Archie said. He cringed – but inside he was beaming. He had just cast a spell – a *real* spell – which meant that he was a wizard. He wanted to get up and dance a jig, but he resisted the temptation.

'Well, two new magical kids discovered in one day and both in detention,' Miss Burrows said. 'What are the odds of *that*, I wonder?'

'There you go,' Isabelle said to Archie. 'I knew you could do it.'

'You did?' he said, giving her a curious look. Something occurred to him. 'I needed a wand to cast a spell,' he stated to Miss Burrows, 'but you managed to stop that book *without* a wand.' He looked at Isabelle. 'And you didn't need one either when you made the book fly across the room.'

Isabelle said, 'Like me, Miss Burrows has obviously been doing magic for some time. After a while, it rubs off on you, seeps into you. And then you can do basic things like ... stopping a book from hitting somebody.'

'You must not tell anyone about the class,' Miss Burrows said to Archie with an especially stern voice. 'And don't tell anyone about what you've seen and learned here. Not your friends, or your family. No matter how tempted you may be. The magic class consists of a small selection of pupils who can be *trusted*. I'm sure I don't need to explain why it's important to keep the class and everything you learn in it a secret.'

'You certainly don't,' Archie said. Something else occurred to him. 'You told us that we need permission from our parents to attend the magic class. But how am I supposed to get permission from them if I can't tell them about it?'

'Well, you won't be telling them that it's a magic class,' Miss Burrows said. 'As far as they're concerned, you'll be playing draughts.'

'Draughts?' Archie said. 'What the heck is draughts?'

'It's a board game,' Isabelle explained. 'A bit like chess, but not as complex.'

'Erm, I'm not sure my brother will believe me when I tell him I've signed up for something like *that*,' Archie said. 'And I'm not sure my parents will either. Are any of the other teachers who are wizards or witches? Or are you the only one?'

'There is one other,' Miss Burrows said, but she did not mention a name.

Who could that *be*? Archie thought ...

'Good job Carly isn't still here,' Archie said. 'Don't think your secret would be safe with her, somehow.'

'Yes,' Miss Burrows said, 'it would have been most unfortunate if *she* had witnessed me stopping that book. I think a memory wipe would have been in order.'

'There's a spell to erase people's memories?' Archie said, wondering if there was anything that couldn't be done with magic.

'Yes,' Miss Burrows said simply.

'It might be a good idea to use it on you,' Isabelle said to Archie.

He opened his mouth to ask her why, but Miss Burrows spoke up, cutting him off.

'What's happened?' she said. 'Is there something I should know about?'

Isabelle gave Archie a sly sideways look. 'Well, let's just

say that "someone" has been spying on me and following me around so they can prove that I'm a witch. And he told his friend about me, too. They were trying to get me to admit to being a witch in the cookery lesson, which is when it all went wrong and Mrs Tippings got covered in flour.'

'It wasn't me who was quizzing you!' Archie said in his defence. 'It was Ryan and I was trying to stop him.'

'Who else have you spoken to about this?' Miss Burrows asked him.

'Just my brother,' Archie replied. 'But he didn't believe me – and neither does Ryan. He was just quizzing Isabelle to humour me.'

He did not like the way the headmistress was looking at him right now: through slitted eyes, as if she was weighing him up, assessing him.

'Please don't wipe my memory!' Archie begged. He wondered what would happen if the spell wasn't cast correctly. What if all his memories were erased so he didn't even know who he was? The thought of that happening to him made his legs quiver. 'I'm not going to tell anyone about what's happened. You can trust me! Honestly, you can!'

Miss Burrows was still giving him that look: weighing him up, assessing him.

'I will have to think long and hard this evening about whether or not you'll be suitable to attend magic class,' she said. 'Your recent behaviour goes against you, but you are normally well behaved, so there's that to consider.' She turned her attention to Isabelle. 'I will also have to consider whether you are suitable or not as well. As I stated before, your behaviour on your first day has been quite appalling and hardly inspires confidence in me that you'll be a good student. And you need to be more careful with your magic. More conspicuous. You can't just go flaunting it in front of people. Archie must have witnessed you casting a spell, or performing a charm, otherwise why would he have had suspicions of you being a witch?'

'Flaunting it?' Isabelle replied. 'I wasn't flaunting it; I was in my garden, which is overgrown and well-shielded on all sides, when he,' she hooked her thumb towards Archie, 'appeared out of the bushes, trespassing, looking for his ball. I didn't tell him that what I was doing was real magic; he just got it into his head that it was. And as for my behaviour being appalling, I haven't done anything wrong. That Carly girl has been trying to bully me and all I've done is stick up for myself, which I think I'm entitled to do.' Isabelle raised her chin as a show of defiance. Her grip on her wand tightened.

'My, my, you have got a bit of a temper on you, haven't you?' Miss Burrows said. 'A bad temper and the ability to do magic is not a good combination. It can result in ... unfortunate things happening. Don't go getting any ideas about casting a spell on Carly – turning her into a slug or something equally as disgusting – because that really will get you in trouble with me.'

'I'm not going to be casting spells on anyone, no matter how tempted I might be,' Isabelle said, lowering her chin slightly and loosening her grip on her wand. 'I've never done anything like that before and I'm not about to start now.'

'That's good to hear,' Miss Burrows said, giving her an appreciative nod. She looked towards the clock on the wall, noted the time and added, 'Okay, I think we need to knock things on the head. Your parents will be calling me up, wanting to know where you are if I keep you here any longer.'

'Speaking of our parents,' Archie said, 'didn't any of them think that it's a bit odd that you kept us back this evening? Detentions are usually arranged for a later date after the offence, so that people can make arrangements around it, yeah? I mean, what if I'd had plans for after school? What if Isabelle or Carly had had plans? What then?'

Archie could see Isabelle looking at him out of the corner of his eye. He didn't need to turn his head to know that it wasn't a favourable look.

'Our headmistress is a witch,' she said. 'If she wants to

arrange something for this evening, then that's what she'll do. It's not something that'll be a problem for her, I can assure you.'

'You're always such a fountain of redundant questions, Archie,' Miss Burrows added. 'Let's just hope that's not the case during magic class (assuming you're accepted of course).

'I haven't finished my work,' Isabelle said, steering the conversation back on track.

'I haven't finished mine either,' Archie said. 'I've still got three hundred words to do.'

'Normally I'd tell you to finish it at home,' Miss Burrows said. 'But given the revelations that have taken place – and the time we've spent discussing those revelations – I don't think any extra homework will be needed. So pack your things away and I'll see you tomorrow.' She smiled and then motioned towards the door. 'I shouldn't have to remind you not to discuss anything you've learned here today, but here I am doing it again, just to be on the safe side.'

Archie pressed his fingers together and ran them across his lips, making a zipping gesture. 'The secret is safe with me,' he said. 'I won't tell anyone.'

'And me neither,' Isabelle said. 'Obviously.'

'I'm sorry for asking so many questions,' Archie said to Miss Burrows, 'but I'm really curious as to how you managed to form a class for magic in the first place. How did you know which kids are wizards and witches? Is there a spell you can cast for that, or have you got some sort of in-built detector?'

'There is no spell,' she replied. 'But you're on the right lines in thinking of an in-built detector. Except that it's not me who has that capability; it was a friend of mine (who I got to walk around the place, identifying those with magical potential). She sadly passed away a few months ago and is sorely missed.' Miss Burrows took a moment to compose herself and then continued: 'I first had the idea for a magic class when I came to this school a year ago. Statistically, I knew the chances were good for there being around twenty to thirty or so witches and wizards here and I thought it would be great if I could get some of them under my wing and give them proper tuition to harness their powers. My friend identified twenty-six candidates, from which I selected five who I believed could be trusted. Some knew that they're magical and some did not. It's been one of the best things I've ever done, forming the group, and I've not regretted it for a second. I've found some real talent at this school.'

'So there's quite a lot of kids here who have the power but don't even know that they have it?' Archie said.

'That's right,' Miss Burrows confirmed.

'There are lots of people around who have the power that don't know they have it,' Isabelle added. 'And most of them will die not knowing what they were capable of.'

'Wow! How depressing is that for them?' Archie said. He looked at Miss Burrows. 'I'm guessing that there's a few teachers at this school capable of doing magic but only the one you mentioned can be trusted, yeah?'

'That's right,' she confirmed.

'Did your friend miss me out when she did her walk around?' Archie said. 'Or did she tell you about me and you decided not to offer me a place in the group for one reason or another? Maybe because I wasn't suitable?'

Miss Burrows gave this a little thought. 'Hmm, that's a fair point,' she said. 'I don't remember her identifying you at all. I can't imagine that she'd have missed you, so I can only assume you must have been absent that day for one reason or another.'

Yeah, knowing my luck I probably was, Archie thought.

As he followed Isabelle towards the door, he had one more question for the headmistress: 'How long will it be before we find out whether we're eligible or not?'

'I will not be rushed,' she replied, 'but I'm sure I'll come to a decision quickly enough.'

'Oh, right ... right,' Archie said, lingering in the doorway.

'Thank you for considering me.'

'Save your thanks for when I've made my decision,' Miss Burrows said. 'And try not to get in any more trouble, because that really won't sit well in your favour.'

As Archie left the room, he caught sight of Isabelle disappearing down the corridor. He caught up with her on the south stairwell.

'Hey, wait up!' he said, hurrying along behind her.

But she didn't wait up. She reached the bottom of the stairwell and headed for the exit, her shoes tapping on the floor as she moved briskly along.

'Hold up, will you!' Archie said. 'What's the rush?'

'My parents will already be angry with me for getting a detention,' Isabelle said. 'I don't want to make them even angrier by rocking up later than expected.'

'Can't you just magic yourself home?'

'Oh my God, you have got a lot to learn about what you can and can't do with magic.'

Out of the building they both went, with Isabelle setting an impressive pace across the playground.

'Do you think she'll let us attend the magic class?' Archie said, struggling to match her pace.

'How should I know? Do I look psychic to you?'

'Nothing would surprise me, given everything that's happened in the last few days – and especially the last hour or so. Miss Burrows told me that she wouldn't make us wait long before she gives us a yay or nay, so that's good, isn't it? Can you *please* slow down a little? I don't think a few minutes here or there is going to make much difference where your parents are concerned.'

'You don't know my parents.'

Archie was getting the impression that half the reason Isabelle was in such a hurry was to distance herself from him, so he dropped back and let her surge ahead.

'You could at least apologize for making that book fly towards my head!' he said loudly.

'I wasn't aiming it at you!' she called back to him. 'That's just the direction it took!' She turned so she was walking backwards. 'I am sorry, though,' she said, looking sincere.

Before Archie could reply, she turned back around and continued her hurried walk.

When he arrived home, Mrs Wiggins pounced on him as soon as he was through the front door. She wanted to know what on earth had happened and how he'd managed to get himself in so much trouble.

'Didn't Miss Burrows tell you when she rang you up?' Archie asked her.

'Yes, of course she did. But I want to hear *your* version of events.'

Mr Wiggins appeared from the living room, holding a newspaper in one hand and a steaming cup of coffee in the other. He didn't look angry. Just concerned.

'Basically, I was mucking around in cookery and I threw some flour over the teacher instead of Ryan,' Archie explained as he let his bag slump to the floor with a thud. 'It was an accident. A one-off. It won't happen again.'

Mrs Wiggins pretended to look confused. 'An accident!' she said, screwing her face up in annoyance. 'An *accident?* Please tell me how you can "accidentally" throw flour over a teacher? Honestly, I've never been so embarrassed when I took that call from the headmistress. I hope you apologized to Mrs Tippings. The poor woman must have felt humiliated. And I hope you apologized to the headmistress as well.'

'Go easy on him,' Mr Wiggins said to her. 'He says that it's a one-off and that it won't happen again, so let's take him at his word.'

'Oh, I might have known that you'd take the softly-softly approach,' Mrs Wiggins said, 'because that's all you ever do, isn't it?'

'We agreed that shouting and raving about this wouldn't help, didn't we?' Mr Wiggins said to her. 'What's done is done.

It's in the past. Let's move on now and forget about it. He's had detention for what he did, so he's been punished.'

'Did anyone else get a detention?' Mrs Wiggins asked Archie. 'Or was it just you?'

'A girl named Carly was there. But she was in trouble for something else. She's always in trouble.' Archie didn't mention Isabelle because he didn't want his mother to think badly of her.

'Well, you don't want to be mixing with the likes of her, now, do you?' Mrs Wiggins said.

Too right I don't, Archie thought.

Mrs Wiggins folded her arms across her chest and blew a wisp of hair away from her fringe. 'Honestly, I expect better from you, Archie,' she said, appearing to calm a little. 'Throwing flour over a teacher ...' she tutted and shook her head. 'That's the sort of thing your brother would do. Get yourself off to your bedroom. I'll call you down when I've had a chance to think about whether to impose any further punishment.'

'Isn't the detention enough?' Archie said, hoping that it would be.

Mrs Wiggins did not reply. She just waved him impatiently away.

When Archie reached the top of the stairs, Oliver greeted him with a smug smile.

'I knew you'd be earwigging,' Archie said, gesturing for him to move out of the way.

'Throwing flour over a teacher,' Oliver said, shaking his head. 'Everyone at school knows about that, you know. My mates think it's one of the funniest things to ever happen at that school and I have to agree. I wish I could have been there to see it. Just to see the look on Mrs Tippings's face. And the look on yours when you realized you'd mucked up.'

'Why don't you just go back and play on your XBOX. Haven't you got a dub to catch or something?'

'Catching dubs is what I do. But there's no way I was ever

going to miss out on an opportunity to pull your leg about this, bruv.'

'Well, you've done it; you've pulled my leg. Now can you just get out of the way, please?'

Oliver stayed rooted to the spot, with a smug smile on his face.

Archie tried to push past him, but his big brother wouldn't move.

'This way's blocked,' Oliver said. 'You should find another way.'

'Ha-ha! Very funny. And how am I going to do that? Should I climb the wall outside and get in through my bedroom window? Or shall I just magic myself past you?' *Which I might just be able to do soon enough*, he thought, *if Miss Burrows gives me the green light to attend magic class*.

'Maybe Isabelle will help you with that magic. I mean, she is a witch after all – according to you.'

'*Please* get out of my way,' Archie said with an edge to his voice. He was gearing himself up to go for a shin scrape (probably not the best idea, but frustration was beginning to boil inside of him). Then Oliver stepped to the side and beckoned him to pass.

Archie was about to do just that, but he hesitated, fearing a trap.

'Go on,' Oliver said, beckoning him again, 'what are you waiting for?'

'Erm, a tickle attack, or worse.'

'Oh for crying out loud,' Oliver said, rolling his eyes and then disappearing into his room.

'Idiot,' Archie said under his breath.

In his bedroom, he crashed out on his bed and stared up at the ceiling with a grin on his face. The fact that his brother had just bullied him didn't bother him at all (it wasn't the first time and wouldn't be the last). Being in trouble with his parents wasn't getting Archie down either. He had just found out that magic was a *real* thing and that he was a wizard, who might soon be learning how to cast spells and mix potions. He wondered which spells he might cast, which potions he might concoct. He marvelled at the fact that a magic class had been taking place at *his* school and he knew nothing about it – until now. He marvelled at the fact that his new neighbour was a witch and that the headmistress of the school was also one, too. Miss Burrows had told him that one of the teachers was also magical. He gave some thought as to whom it would be. He gave some thought as to whom the handful of students would be. Ten minutes later, he was still lost in his thoughts – still awed by the revelation that he was a wizard –when Oliver stuck his head around the door and asked him if he was deaf.

'What's up?' Archie said, propping himself up on his elbows to look at him.

'Mum's calling up to you,' he said, 'asking you to go downstairs. I had my headset on and even I could hear her.'

'Ah, right,' Archie said, springing up off the bed. He moved towards the door, but Oliver remained where he was, once again blocking his way.

'Oh come on,' Archie moaned, 'not this again!'

This time, however, Oliver did not have a smug grin on his face.

'Look,' he said, seeming a little uncomfortable with what he was about to say next, '... I'm sorry for blocking your way when you came up the stairs. It was a crappy thing to do. I was in a mood because I'd lost a game of Fortnite. I was in the last two and got taken out by a bot. He got lucky with some 'nades.'

'Lucky?' Archie said, unable to resist a chance to wind up his brother. 'Are you sure about that?'

'Yeah, I'm pretty sure,' Oliver said, not biting.

Then Mrs Wiggins' voice echoed up the stairs: 'Archie, get down here now, will you! Please don't make me ask again! You're in enough trouble as it is!'

Oliver moved out of the way. 'Go on, squirt,' he said,

nodding towards the landing. 'Before she loses her rag.'

Archie took off past him and found Mrs Wiggins at the bottom of the stairs looking less than impressed. She didn't say anything, however; she just turned and led the way into the living room. Archie followed behind sheepishly.

Mr Wiggins was sitting in his armchair in the corner, his newspaper folded on his lap. He was sporting a sombre expression, which was not an encouraging sign. It looked out of place on his usually jovial face. Mrs Wiggins had her hands on her hips, which was also not an encouraging sign.

'So how long am I grounded for?' Archie asked, getting to the point.

'Who said anything about anyone being grounded?' Mr Wiggins said.

'I just assumed ...' Archie began.

'Well, we're a long way from happy with you,' Mrs Wiggins informed him, 'make no mistake about that. But you have had detention for what you did and you've never been in trouble at school before. Taking everything into consideration, we feel that grounding you as well would be harsh (given that you didn't throw that flour over the teacher on purpose.'

Archie was delighted. This was not how he'd envisaged this conversation playing out. He did his best not to look too happy, though, as he knew that it would not go down well with his parents (and they could always change their minds, after all).

'But make no mistake,' Mrs Wiggins said, levelling the dreaded finger at him, 'if you get in any more trouble then you *will* be grounded – for a week. Am I making myself clear here?'

'Crystal,' Archie replied, not liking the sound of *that*.

'Think yourself lucky that we're being lenient,' Mr Wiggins said, 'and learn from this experience, Archie. You're a clever lad, so I'm confident you will.'

Archie assured him that he would.

'Now go and find yourself a chore to do,' Mrs Wiggins said.

'Anything that'll keep you out of mischief for a bit.'

With his shoulders slumped, he went to the back door and looked out towards the garden. Noticing a spade and some other tools near the edge of the lawn, he quizzed Mrs Wiggins about them: 'It's beginning to get dark out there,' he said. 'Do you want me to put those away?'

'That'll earn you some brownie points,' Mr Wiggins said.

Mrs Wiggins waved Archie away with a flick of her fingers. 'Yes, yes, have at it.'

Not wasting a second, he went outside and began putting the tools in the shed. It was as he was coming back up the steps that he heard voices next door. He went to investigate, positioning himself next to the tall boundary hedge which separated the two gardens near the house.

'I'm not sure I can live like this,' a woman said. 'Not knowing from one day to the next whether one of them has tracked us down. I will be suspicious of every stranger I see on the street. Every knock on the front door will send shivers down my spine. I know what you're going to say – that they won't find us, that they *can't* find us – but that isn't going to help dampen the fear that's welling up inside of me.'

A man said, 'We are safe here, Kelly. We wouldn't be here if I didn't think we were. Trust me, you have *nothing* to worry about. You and Isabelle mean the world to me and I will protect you both with my life, if it comes to it. We've set the Bubble Barrier around the house, so it's not like anyone can just waltz up to the front door.'

'Oh you don't think they'll have anticipated something like that,' Kelly said, her voice shaky with fear. 'And it can only hold them off for so long, you know that. Moving to another country – perhaps Australia – would have been wiser. We're only renting this house, so it wouldn't be a problem.'

'There is our daughter to think of. We've only just arrived in Waddington. She wasn't happy when we told her that we were moving here and you want to tell her that we're moving again. And to the other side of the world. I'm not sure how that would go down with her.'

'It wouldn't have to be Australia. France would do.'

Archie had concluded that he was earwigging a conversation between Mr and Mrs Lockhart, Isabelle's parents.

Archie moved a little closer so he could hear better. And that's when he trod on a twig – *snap!*

Silence from the other side of the hedge ...

Then Mr Lockhart spoke up: 'Hello? Is someone there?'

Archie didn't reply. He stood still, as if he'd been frozen by a spell.

'Hello?' Mrs Lockhart (Kelly) said. 'Is anyone behind this hedge?'

Archie remained still.

'It's probably just a cat or a squirrel,' Mr Lockhart suggested.

'Hmm, maybe,' Mrs Lockhart replied, not sounding convinced. 'But let's continue this conversation in the bedroom – just to be on the safe side.'

Archie heard footsteps moving away. A door opened and closed, but he stayed where he was until he was certain that they'd gone. And then he went back inside and ate his dinner – bangers and mash – which Mrs Wiggins had left on the dining room table.

So I was *right about what that person had been doing in the front garden the other night*, he thought as he tucked into a sausage. He took huge bites, savouring every mouthful. *But who have they fled from? And why?* He wondered what would happen to someone who breached the protective barrier that'd been placed around the house. Was it a defence against certain people or any stranger? Archie imagined the postman stepping over the boundary and shuddering as if he'd been electrified. *Just certain people, then*.

'Why are you grinning?' his brother said as he was passing through the room. 'You've just had a good telling off by Mum and Dad, so what have you got to smile about?'

Archie shrugged. 'Life's not all bad at the moment.'

'Really? Explain. I'm all ears ...'

But Archie did not say another word. He resumed eating his food with Miss Burrows' cautionary words echoing in his mind: *don't tell anyone about what you've seen and learned here. Not your friends, or your family. No matter how tempted you may be.* Archie had given his word that he wouldn't and he intended to keep it.

His phone pinged. A text message from Ryan: soz m8 can't cum this evo as sumthins cum up. We'll talk about Isabelle at skool tmoz, yeah?

Archie thumbed a reply: no probs.

Later that evening, when he was tucked up in bed, he didn't know how he'd be able to sleep. His mind was buzzing with the possibilities of all the magical things he might learn to do. He visualised himself waving his wand and making things float. He visualised himself making Carly disappear in the bat of an eyelid. He fantasised about soaring up towards the clouds on a broomstick. But none of these things would happen, of course, unless he was given the nod by the headmistress. *Please let me attend the class*, he thought, saying a silent prayer. *Please, please, PULEEEEZE!*

It was forty-five minutes later when his eyes slowly began to shut and he drifted off to sleep.

He got up early the next morning, dressed like it was a race between him and some invisible person, then he went bounding down the stairs for his breakfast. In the hallway, he nearly bumped into Mrs Wiggins who put her hands out and brought him to an abrupt halt.

'*Whoa! Whoa!*' she said dramatically. 'What's the rush? Why are you in such a hurry?'

'I'm ... err, hungry ... eager to get some food down my neck,' was the best answer he could come back with.

'I was hoping you'd say you were eager to get to school.'

'I am. But first I need some Weetabix.'

Mrs Wiggins managed a weak smile as she moved aside to let Archie pass.

'Best behaviour today, remember?' she said. 'I don't want the embarrassment of another call from the headmistress while I'm in the office. Being a PA to a demanding boss is stressful enough as it is, thank you very much.'

'Yeah, yeah, best behaviour, of course,' he replied, trying to sound as enthusiastic as possible.

After he'd wolfed down his breakfast, he went back upstairs and waited by his bedroom window. He looked down the street, keeping an eye on next door's driveway. Any second now she would appear; he was sure she would. But five minutes past, then ten. No sign of Isabelle. *Perhaps she left really early for some reason*, he thought.

Mrs Wiggins called up to him: 'You better leave soon, or you'll be late! You don't want another black mark against your name, now, do you?'

He was just beginning to think that he would have to abandon any idea of walking with Isabelle when she appeared in view. With her satchel slung over her shoulder, she began walking down the road at a brisk pace.

Archie was out of the house in the blink of an eye. As he passed next door's garden, he couldn't help but glance towards the protective borders surrounding the place and wonder what would happen if he stepped over one of the overgrown flowerbeds. An image of the postman being electrified once again popped into his head, making him shudder.

Archie had to jog to catch up with Isabelle. Upon hearing his approach, she glanced over her shoulder, but she didn't stop.

'Hey, wait up!' Archie said as he closed the distance. 'Hold up, will you!'

Isabelle kept walking.

Archie caught up with her and said, 'Is it all right if I walk with you?'

'Late as well, are you?' she replied, not even bothering to look at him.

'Yeah,' he said, knowing that he'd been rumbled. 'I had a late night. Didn't get enough shut-eye. Couldn't sleep because I was too excited, thinking about magic. What's your excuse?'

'I was watching a TV series in my bedroom and one episode led to the next. Before I knew it, I glanced at the clock and it was 2 am. You know how it is.'

'I do. Do your parents let you stay up that late?'

'Of course not. I just keep the volume low on my telly and listen out for them. If I hear them coming, I turn everything off and pretend to be asleep.'

'That sounds like something my brother would do.'

'I've only spoken to him once, but he seems okay, your brother.'

You should try living with him, Archie thought.

They rounded the corner and went up the hill which led to the main road.

'So ... do you think we'll find out today whether we can attend or not?' Archie said. 'To magic class, I mean?'

Isabelle shrugged. 'Miss Burrows said she'd give us a decision quickly, so I'd say there's a good chance that it'll either be today or tomorrow.'

'I hope it's today and I hope *so* much that it's a yes. I've never been so excited about something in my life.'

'There's nothing more exciting than magic. Nothing that comes even close. But you'll find that out soon enough. Assuming you get the nod, that is.'

Archie was still struggling to keep up with Isabelle, so he asked her if she could slow down, just a bit.

'No, I don't want to risk being late. And you shouldn't want to risk it either – for obvious reasons.'

Scurrying alongside her, Archie said, 'If I'm not accepted, do you think you could teach me some magic?'

The sideways glance that Isabelle gave him suggested the

answer was no.

They walked along the main road in silence for a minute or so, with Isabelle not easing on the pace and Archie continuing to struggle to keep up.

Not being one to tolerate uncomfortable silences, he said, 'I overheard your parents talking in the garden yesterday evening. They seemed very concerned that some people might find out where you live. That's why you moved, isn't it? Because you were in danger? Your family was in danger? And that's why someone – either your mum or dad – has placed that protective barrier around your house, isn't it?'

Isabelle stopped dead and gave Archie a cold, hard stare. 'You earwigged my parents' conversation?' she seethed. 'Wow, you really are a stalker, aren't you?'

'I wasn't earwigging,' Archie said in his defence, 'I just happened to be standing by the hedge while they were talking.'

'And how long were you standing there for?'

Archie shrugged. 'I dunno. A couple of minutes.'

'You could have walked away. Why didn't you?'

Archie shrugged again. 'I dunno. I was curious, I guess. You'd have probably earwigged too if you were in my position. A mysterious family moves in next door and strange things start happening, *magical* things. Of course I'm going to want to know what's going on. And if some nasty people are coming after you and your parents then that could put my family in danger. We live next to you, for crying out loud!'

'You're not in danger and neither is your family. The people who are after us are only interested in *us*. Perhaps I should hit you with a memory wipe. I think it would be justified.'

Archie backed away a few steps, aghast at the idea of having his memory wiped. 'You wouldn't,' he said. 'Miss Burrows would wonder why I'd all of a sudden forgotten about everything: about the magic class and the possibility of me attending. She'd put two and two together and point the finger in your direction.'

'Just stay away from me and my family,' Isabelle said as she began to walk away. 'If you know what's good for you, you'll mind your own business.'

'But I could help you!' Archie said.

'No, you can't!' Isabelle replied as she quickly put distance between her and him.

Archie watched her stomp away and then remembered that he was going to be late if he didn't get a move on. Even though he jogged the last part of his usual route, he still ended up being a few minutes late. Fortunately, his form tutor, Mr Godber, was too busy dealing with something on the far side of the classroom to notice Archie as he made straight for his desk.

Carly would have dropped him in it if she hadn't been so busy trying to bore holes into the back of Isabelle's head with a steely gaze. Laura and Ruby, seated on either side of Carly, in their usual places, were trying their hardest to look tough. Archie kept an eye on the situation as the session progressed, wondering if any nastiness would ensue.

As it turned out, nothing did. But it was obvious that Carly and her friends weren't done with Isabelle yet (or Sally, most likely). *They're probably waiting for the right moment to get revenge*, Archie assumed. *When the teachers and other witnesses aren't around*. The next step up from detentions was suspension. And even Carly wasn't stupid enough to put herself in a position where *that* could happen. Hence just the evil stares ...

'If only you knew what I know,' Archie muttered to himself as he glanced towards the terrible trio.

His timetable for the day looked like this: English – Science – Music – Maths – PE. Normally the fourth one would be of least interest to him, but today he couldn't wait for it – because this was the lesson being taught by Miss Burrows. Would she give him a yay or nay? Archie so, *so* hoped that it was the former.

At the end of the form class, Carly walked past Archie and didn't acknowledge him. His heroics with the flour from the previous day had seemingly been forgotten and he'd been relegated back to not being worthy of her attention; which was fine by Archie, because he didn't want anything to do with her anyway.

Cue Isabelle, who didn't want anything to do with Archie either, despite his best attempts at being apologetic. She ignored him, finding something of interest to look at on the other side of the classroom as she walked past.

In the English lesson, Ryan asked him how he'd got on in detention and he replied that it'd been okay, just boring. Archie did not mention what'd happened with the book and how the headmistress had stopped it in mid-air. He didn't mention magic at all. It was Ryan who brought up the subject.

'Made any progress on proving that your neighbour is a witch yet?' he said, leaning in close and whispering in Archie's ear.

'No,' he said, shaking his head vehemently. 'None at all.'

'So how are we going to prove it then?'

'Erm, we're not. I think my imagination has been getting the better of me and I need to concentrate on other things.'

Ryan gave him a quizzical look. 'Has something happened? Has Isabelle threatened to turn you into a slug again?'

'No, no,' Archie replied, shaking his head again. 'I've just realised that I've been being silly is all. I mean, come on, as if anyone could actually be a witch or wizard? Magic isn't real. You said that. And you were right.'

Ryan was still giving him the quizzical look. 'Are you sure something hasn't happened? You were adamant that Isabelle is a witch and now you're not. This is quite an abrupt u-turn. Are you *sure* she hasn't threatened you in some way? You can tell me. I'm your best friend. If you can't trust me then who can you trust, right?'

'She hasn't threatened me,' Archie said. He looked around

to see if anyone was earwigging their conversation. The rest of the pupils were too busy with their conversations to take any notice of them. Except for one person: Sally. She'd seemingly appeared out of nowhere and seated herself in her usual place, behind the boys. Archie gave her a searching look and she gave him one back. He wondered how much of their conversation she'd heard, if any at all.

And then the teacher's voice boomed out across the room, telling everyone to take their seats. 'Ruby, get your backside on some plastic now,' he bellowed, spittle flying from his bulbous lips. 'Don't make me ask you again!'

Without Carly around, Ruby wasn't so brave, so she did what she was told sharpish.

The rest of the lesson dragged, with Archie clock-watching even more than usual. Then the rest of the day dragged, with lots more clock-watching in science and music.

When it was time for maths, Archie was first in line at the classroom door. And when Isabelle showed up, he gave her a smile which she returned with a roll of her eyes. And then when Miss Burrows arrived, Archie stood to attention as if he were a soldier awaiting inspection from a sergeant major.

Miss Burrows opened the door and all the kids piled in behind her. Carly and Laura were first, as always.

As Isabelle was passing Archie, she said, 'Try not to look so desperate, will you. It isn't going to help.'

'I'm just trying to maximise my chances,' Archie replied as he followed her through the door.

'Be patient,' Isabelle said without even a backwards glance.

As Archie took his seat, he noticed Carly glaring at Isabelle again. *She is* definitely *not done with her*, he thought.

Once everyone was settled, Miss Burrows proceeded to hand out some textbooks. When she got to Archie, he smiled up at her, blinking furiously with nervous excitement.

'Got something in your eyes, have you?' she said as she

placed a book in front of him.

'No, miss,' he replied.

A few chuckles of laughter filled the room. Archie didn't need two guesses as to which direction they'd come from.

His shoulders slumped and disappointment set in as Miss Burrows continued handing out the books. He looked over the other side of the room and saw Isabelle watching him with raised eyebrows. She was clearly trying to convey a message and her last words echoed in his head: be patient. He was about to smile at her, but then she must have remembered that she hated him and looked away accordingly.

Archie glanced back at Carly and noticed that she was still glaring at Isabelle.

At the end of the lesson, Archie lingered in his seat as everyone else filed out of the room. He was hoping that Miss Burrows would tell Isabelle to remain behind as she walked past the headmistress's desk, but this turned out not to be the case. It wasn't until all the other students had gone that Archie began packing away his stuff. He kept glancing toward Miss Burrows as she arranged papers on her desk.

'I will not be rushed on a decision,' she said, not even looking at him.

'Oh, I wasn't ...' Archie began.

'I know exactly what you're doing,' Miss Burrows said, cutting him off. 'I told you that I'd give you a quick decision and that is what I will do. Please be patient.'

'I ... erm ... sorry,' Archie said, zipping up his bag and vacating the room as quickly as possible.

He felt so angry with himself as he made his way to his last lesson. *I should have just left with everyone else*, he thought. *What a fool! What an absolute fool!*

PE was something that Archie either liked doing or didn't, depending on what was being taught. On this particular day, he and the other students had been charged with doing a lot of jogging, which was about as boring as it could get, as far as Archie was concerned. And to make things even worse, it began raining halfway through the lesson: lightly at first, then a bit heavier as Archie began the second lap. Everyone overtook him. Ryan was enjoying himself, though. He jabbed Archie with his finger as he lapped him.

'Thanks for that!' Archie said.

'Come on, slowpoke!' Ryan said as he surged ahead. 'Get a move on, you snail!'

Archie wondered if there was a spell that could make him run quicker.

Then Carly also jabbed him with her finger as she passed. This caused him to slip in the mud and slide to his knees.

'Ha-ha!' Carly said as she carried on running.

Archie remained there for a few seconds, feeling sorry for himself – until Sally and Isabelle appeared next to him, looking down at him.

'Come on, get up,' Sally said, holding out a hand to him, 'before Mr Gibb notices and starts yelling at you.'

Archie took the offered hand and allowed himself to be yanked to his feet.

And then Mr Gibb did notice him. He noticed all of them and began scowling at them from the other side of the field. 'Why have you stopped?' he said. 'You don't take a break until I tell you it's time to take a break! Get those legs moving! NOW!'

'Charming as ever,' Sally said as she resumed her running.

'Has Miss Burrows said anything to you yet?' Archie asked Isabelle as he began to jog alongside her.

'Nope. Has she said anything to you?'

'No.'

'Better just be patient then,' Isabelle said as she surged ahead to catch up with Sally.

I wish people would stop telling me to be patient, Archie thought. But he knew that that was all he could do.

By the end of the lesson, Archie was cold, dripping wet and exhausted. Never in his life could he remember being so relieved to take a hot shower. He was enjoying it so much that he didn't realise that everyone else had finished and was dressing themselves. By the time he'd dressed himself, all the other kids had gone, apart from Ryan – who was heading for the door.

'Hold up and I'll walk with you,' Archie said as he slipped on his shirt.

'I need to go,' his friend replied. 'I've just remembered that my mum told me to get home as soon as possible because we're going somewhere in a bit.' He raised a hand and was gone before Archie could say another word.

Mr Gibb was standing on the other side of the room with his arms folded across his barrel chest. 'When I was at school and it was home time, you wouldn't have caught me lingering around like this,' he said, his voice echoing off the white tiled walls. 'As soon as that bell rang, I was out of there. Gone like a shot, as they say.'

'I'll be out of your way in less than a minute,' Archie said as he began putting on his shoes.

Mr Gibb gave him a nod and then disappeared from view. The door banged shut as he left the changing area, the sound of it echoing into the emptiness of the room. Not hanging about, Archie quickly finished tying his laces, slung his bag over his shoulder and headed for the door. The tip-tap of his shoes echoed into the emptiness of the corridor as he headed for the exit. But then he stopped and looked behind him, sure that he'd heard a noise. No one appeared to be there, so he kept moving. Then he *definitely* heard a noise. Spinning around, he turned to see a figure looming in front of him, looking down at him. He breathed a sigh of relief when he got over the initial shock and realised it was Miss Burrows.

'Oh my God, you scared the heck out of me,' Archie said.

Miss Burrows looked down her pointed nose at him and then handed him two pieces of folded paper. One was a permission slip and the other Archie read with a sense of wonder welling up inside of him:

One Wand (Willow, Oak, or Hazel)
One Cauldron
Amethyst Gems
Beginner to Intermediate Potions by Charlie Pepwick
Entry Level to Intermediate Spells by Miranda Clutterbuck
One Broomstick (Grade 1, preferably)

'The next class is on Thursday,' the headmistress said. 'It's in room 56 and starts at 3:45. Do *not* be late.'

Archie's eyes were wide as dishes and his mouth had dropped open as he continued to scan the list. 'Will I need to have all these things before then?' he said. 'How much do they cost and where will I get them from?'

'Everything you need can be obtained from the Enchanted Cove in Bucklechurch. Some of the items are more expensive than others. Just get what you can. I can supply you with the rest, for now. Mrs Hickinbottom, who runs the place, will give you a discount on your initial purchases if you tell her that you're one of my students. The most expensive thing will be the wand, but it's the one thing you should prioritise getting above all the other things. You'll want to get used to using the same wand so you can get a feel for it and it can get a feel for you.'

'How much will one cost? And how much will it cost for everything?'

'You should be able to pick up a good wand for around a hundred pounds (minus the discount I mentioned). And everything else on the list should run to no more than a few hundred (again, minus the discount).

'That's three hundred in total,' Archie said in despair. 'Where am I going to get that sort of money?'

'Just get the wand and then worry about the rest later. Get the other bits and bobs when you can. Even if it takes you a long time, it doesn't matter. Only you can see what it says on that note. To everyone else it is a blank sheet of paper.'

Another voice spoke from down the corridor, behind Archie: 'Hopefully you'll put in a little more effort with your magic than you did with your running today. And hopefully you'll have more talent for wand-waving.'

Archie turned to see Mr Gibb standing there with a rare smile on his face.

'You're a wizard!' Archie exclaimed, shocked by this revelation.

'Yes,' Mr Gibb confirmed. 'And a ruddy good one at that. Why do you look so surprised?'

Archie shrugged. 'I ... erm, I dunno. You're the last person I would have suspected, I guess.'

'Witches and wizards come in different shapes and sizes and from all sorts of backgrounds. You've heard of the saying "don't judge a book by its cover". Well, I'm a prime example of that.'

'Mr Gibb teaches the magic class when I'm not available,' Miss Burrows informed Archie.

Oh, he thought, not sure how he felt about that. Miss Burrows was strict but Mr Gibb was even stricter.

'You have an amazing time ahead of you,' Miss Burrows said as she joined Mr Gibb and they both began to walk away, down the corridor. 'Just remember my warning about not telling anyone about this. The last thing I want to do is perform a memory wipe charm on anyone you'll have blabbed to.'

Archie opened his mouth to assure her that that would not be necessary, but the pair of them disappeared through the double doors before he could get a word out.

'I'm not telling anyone,' he said to himself. 'I wouldn't risk my spot in that class for anything, or anyone.'

A big grin spread across Archie's face. He exited the building and began skipping across the playground in an excited jig. *I'm going to attend a magic class*, he thought. *I'm actually going to attend a* real *magic class!* The rain had stopped, so that was something else to be happy about.

On a whim, he decided to use the gate on the far side, which took him past a copse of trees to the right. His excitement continued until he was about halfway past the copse. Then he stopped and listened, sure that he'd heard someone talking, a giggle of laughter. He stayed put for a few seconds, his head cocked to one side, still listening. When he was sure that it'd been just his imagination, he kept going. But then he stopped again when he heard another giggle.

Through the trees, he saw a group of kids: one standing to the left and three to the right. As Archie moved closer, he recognized all of them and immediately knew what was happening.

'You got me two detentions!' Carly said, jabbing her finger at Isabelle. 'And now you're going to pay for it!'

'Yeah, you're gonna pay for it!' Laura said, backing Carly up.

Ruby cracked her knuckles menacingly.

'You don't scare me,' Isabelle said, standing her ground.

'There's three of us and one of you,' Carly said, edging forwards, 'so shouldn't you be running away? Wouldn't that be the wise thing to do? Unless you're itching for a beating, of course? We can oblige there, can't we, girls?' she said to her friends.

'Oh, yeah,' Ruby said, cracking her knuckles again as she advanced as well.

'It'd be a pleasure,' Laura added. She let her bag drop to the ground as she joined the other two.

Archie had seen and heard enough. He strode into view, raising a hand to get everyone's attention.

'Why don't you three just bog off!' he said to Carly more than the other two. 'Haven't you got homes to go to?'

Carly looked at him as if he were something she'd scraped off her shoe. 'You'll go away and mind your own business,' she said, 'if you know what's good for you.'

'I'm not going anywhere,' Archie responded. He didn't

want to get involved in this but felt obliged to even the odds. 'It's three plays two now, so I think you're the ones who should go home, don't you?'

'Going to hit a girl, are you?' Ruby said.

'No, I'm not,' Archie replied. 'And neither are you.' He stood next to Isabelle.

Carly eyed both of them with a fierce look on her face. For a moment, Archie thought that fists would be thrown and that all hell would break loose, but then Carly and her friends began to back away.

'Maybe next time your guardian angel won't be around to save you,' Carly said, looking at Isabelle. 'It's only a matter of time.'

'Oh, just get lost, will you!' Isabelle said.

'Get lost, will you!' Ruby said, imitating her whilst pulling a funny face.

'How very mature,' Isabelle muttered under her breath.

Archie watched as the three bullies continued to back away. They shouted insults as they disappeared behind the trees, out of view.

'Thanks for standing with me,' Isabelle said to Archie. 'God knows what would have happened if you hadn't turned up.'

'There would have been a fight,' Archie said, 'and you'd have probably lost.'

He heard a whooshing sound and turned to see a stick flying through the air, heading for Isabelle. He tried to warn her – but it was too late. The stick pinged off the side of her head, impacting hard enough to knock her off balance. She went down sideways, letting out an '*Ooomph!*' of surprise as she sprawled in the leaves.

Laughter echoed throughout the trees.

The look on Isabelle's face changed from one of surprise to anger in the blink of an eye. Scrambling to her feet, she let her bag slip off her back and drop to the ground. She unzipped the top and then reached inside to grab something ...

Guessing what it would be, Archie moved to stop her. He reached her just as she was about to pull out the wand.

'That'll get you in a *lot* of trouble,' Archie said, looming over her, 'and they aren't worth it.'

'It *would* be worth it!' Isabelle replied through gritted teeth. But she kept the wand in her bag, though – and then zipped it back up and got back to her feet with some assistance from Archie.

The sound of laughter faded amongst the trees as the bullies moved away.

'Their time will come,' Archie said.

'You bet it will,' Isabelle said, brushing herself down

'You have a red mark on your cheek. That could take some explaining to your parents.'

Isabelle ran her fingers across her skin. 'It's nothing,' she said. 'It'll probably have faded by the time I get home. I could have handled those girls without you.'

'Could you?' Archie said, sounding highly sceptical.

'I need to get home,' Isabelle said, ignoring him and walking away at a brisk pace. 'My parents will be wondering where I've got to.'

Archie took off after her.

'If you're going to have a go at me about what just happened, save your breath,' she said when he caught up with her, 'because I'm not interested.'

'Miss Burrows told you not to bring your wand into school unless it's a magic class day,' Archie said.

'Yes, I know what she said.'

'She's not one to be ignored, you know; she'll confiscate it if she catches you with it. She seems to like confiscating things.'

'She won't catch me with it,' Isabelle said as they left the copse and began walking along the main road.

Okay, Archie thought, *if you say so*. 'Hey, did Miss Burrows say anything to you today about magic class? She caught up with me after PE and gave me a list of things I'll need.' Archie produced the note from his pocket and showed it to Isabelle. 'I don't know how I'm going to afford all of this stuff. She told me that the wand is the most important thing to get, but that alone will cost me a hundred pounds.'

Isabelle stopped walking. Despite what'd just happened, she managed a smile as she said, 'Our headmistress is happy to give me a chance, despite my "appalling behaviour"'. Then she produced a note of her own, which appeared to have nothing written on it. 'Only you can see what's on your note (as I'm sure Miss Burrows will have told you). But it'll be the same as what's on mine. I can help you out with some of the things on your list, but there's one condition. You stop stalking me.'

Archie opened his mouth to say that he wasn't stalking her, but then he thought better of it. Isabelle was offering to give him some of the stuff he needed and he didn't want to risk her changing her mind.

'No more stalking,' he promised. 'Like I said, it's the wand I need the most, but with one costing around a hundred pounds, I'm guessing that you haven't got a spare one of those knocking around. And even if you have, your parents aren't going to let you just give it away.'

'I've actually got four wands. And my parents won't know if one's disappeared from my collection. Honestly, I could make our cat disappear and they wouldn't notice for a week; they're just not that with it.'

'You have a cat? I haven't noticed any new ones around since you arrived.'

'Well, her name's Bella. My mum's been keeping her in because she's worried she might go out and not be able to find her way back home, what with us being new to the area and all. Bella's jet black and isn't keen on strangers, so I'd keep your distance when we do finally let her out.'

Isabelle resumed walking and Archie scurried to match pace with her.

'If I see her I'll walk the other way,' Archie said, chuckling to himself. 'Hey, are you aware that Mr Gibb, the PE teacher, is a wizard?'

'Yes, of course. I'm a vampire, remember? I know who all the magical people are at our school. Plus, Miss B told me.'

'He was with her when she gave me the note. Honestly, he's the last person I'd have suspected. I just can't imagine him with a wand in his hand, doing anything remotely magical.'

'There's a lesson to be learned there for you.'

'Yeah, Miss Burrows said something similar to that.'

They walked for a few minutes without saying a word. It was Isabelle who broke the silence as they rounded the corner onto Salt Road.

'Thanks for standing up for me back there. But you didn't need to do it. I really could have handled those girls just fine without you.'

You would have handled them, all right, Archie thought. *You'd have probably made them disappear into another dimension or something.* 'I'll keep my distance next time I see anything taking place between you and those girls,' he promised. 'You have my word.' He looked at Isabelle, studying the side of her face.

'I take it the red mark hasn't faded yet,' she said.

'Actually, it has. I probably wouldn't be able to see it if I wasn't looking for it.'

'Oh, well, at least that's some good news. Let's hope my parents won't be able to see it either.'

They stopped outside of Isabelle's house and looked up at the large Victorian property.

'My brother and I have always been scared of your house,' Archie said. 'We're convinced that it's haunted, even though we've never seen any ghosts or ghoulies twitching the curtains.'

Isabelle smiled. 'Well, I haven't come across any ghosts or ghoulies yet, but if I do I'll let you know. And if you come into your garden about six-thirty, I'll have a few surprises for you.'

Archie wondered what they could be and then realized. 'Oooh, I can't wait,' he said, filling with excitement. His gaze went to the garden and he remembered the powder that'd been sprinkled around the borders. He had been so occupied with finding out that he was going to be training as a wizard that he'd forgotten about the potential dangers that Isabelle and her parents were facing.

'See ya later,' Isabelle said as she trotted off down the path towards her house. 'Oh, and thanks again for helping me out. You're a knight in shining armour, Archie, you really are.'

'No problem,' Archie replied, raising a hand as she disappeared through the large oak front door.

He stayed where he was for a few seconds, looking up at the old building, its roofline silhouetted against the cloudy skyline – until a large shadowy figure appeared in one of the upstairs windows, looking down at him.

Archie scurried away, towards his own house.

In the hallway, Mrs Wiggins asked him why he was so late. 'Where have you been?' she said.

Archie cursed himself for not anticipating this question. 'I ... erm ... I got talking to Ryan on the way home and we lost track of time. Sorry. It won't happen again. Honest.'

'Am I detecting a hint of sarcasm in your voice, Archie Wiggins,' Mrs Wiggins said, placing her hands on her hips and giving him one of her no-nonsense stares, 'because you know how I feel about sarcasm.'

'No, no, no – I am *definitely* not being sarcastic,' Archie replied, even though he was. Just a bit. He decided that a change of subject was in order, so he produced his permission slip and asked Mrs Wiggins to sign it.

'Draughts?' she said, giving him a curious look. 'Do you even know what it is that you're signing up for here, kiddo?'

'Yep. I know perfectly well what I'm signing up for. I want to give it a try.'

'Fine. But I don't think it'll be to your tastes, just so you know,' Mrs Wiggins disappeared into the kitchen and then returned with the slip all signed and done. 'You never know, you might actually like it.'

Oh I'm going to love *it,* Archie thought. 'Erm, is there any chance that I could have my pocket money early?'

'Number one, what do you want it for? And number two, what makes you think that you're even getting any this week after what happened at school?'

Archie's shoulders slumped, even though this was the response he'd expected. 'I'll understand if I can't have it,' he said, ignoring the first question.

'If you can tell me what you want it for, it will probably go some way to influencing my decision one way or another.

Again, Archie cursed himself for not anticipating such a question. 'I ... I've seen a football top that I like. It's on offer at the sports shop in town. Half price. They only had half a dozen or so left when I was in there at the weekend, so they might all be gone.' He tried to look dejected at the prospect.

'You hesitated before answering my question. Why?'

'I was about to lie and tell you that I was going to buy a book. I realised you wouldn't believe me, so I told the truth.' Archie looked his mum in the eye and didn't blink. He knew that if he couldn't hold her gaze, she would know he was telling fibs ...

'Okay,' Mrs Wiggins said, satisfied with his response. She disappeared into the kitchen, returned with her purse and handed over a crisp £10 note. 'Honesty will always get you a long way with me. I think you're finally beginning to realize this, at last.'

Na, mum, I'm just becoming a better liar, Archie thought. He decided to push his luck. 'Erm, I still don't think I'll have enough with this. Any chance of a double advance?'

'Okay, now you are pushing your luck,' she said. But she produced another tenner and handed it to him. 'And you can wipe that wounded rabbit look off your face because it's not needed anymore.'

'Thanks, Mum, you're the best,' Archie said, throwing his

bag in the cupboard and skedaddling upstairs as if his pants were on fire.

'Dinner's in five minutes,' Mrs Wiggins called up after him, 'so don't get comfortable up there!'

In his bedroom, Archie emptied his savings jar on his bed and groaned at the disappointing amount. He now had £23.46, which included what he'd received from his double advance. He pulled the note from his pocket and scanned the list, wondering if it would even buy one of the things he needed.

'It might just get me the books, if I'm lucky,' he mumbled to himself.

He wondered if there was any other way he could get more money together. He briefly considered asking his brother and then thought better of this. Oliver always spent his pocket money straight away and this would lead to a load of questions about what Archie wanted it for. Better to just not bother. There was Ryan to consider. Archie didn't even know whether he got any pocket money from his parents, but he was always skint, so it was pointless asking him either. Archie let out a moan of frustration at his lack of options.

Later that evening, at six-thirty on the dot, Archie snuck out of the back door and made his way into the garden. He waited by the fence, just as Isabelle had told him to. A few minutes passed and there was no sign of her. He got on his tiptoes and looked over. He called out to her a few times, but there was no response. Where was she? Had she forgotten about their meeting? Or was she playing some sort of prank on him, getting his hopes up just so she could dash them?

Nobody could see Archie from the downstairs windows because of the bushes obstructing the view, but anyone looking down from upstairs would be able to see him clear as day. And then there would be questions ...

Archie heard movement on the other side of the fence, the sound of twigs being trampled underfoot. Then came the voice:

'Are you there?' Isabelle called out to him.

'Yes!' Archie replied excitedly. 'Blumin' 'eck, I was beginning to think you'd forgotten, or something.'

'I couldn't get away from my dad. He insisted on striking up a conversation with me just as I was about to go out of the back door. Anyway, here's what I could rustle up.'

A hand appeared above the fence, holding a wand.

Archie stared at it in awe, his fingers twitching with excitement.

'Are you going to take it, then, or what?' Isabelle said.

Archie took it.

He wondered if this was all she'd managed to get for him, but then her hand appeared again, clenched in a fist. He opened his hand beneath hers and she dropped something into his palm. He stared at the small object, wondering what it could be. It looked like a miniaturized version of ...

'A cauldron,' Isabelle said. 'One that'll fit in your pocket.'

The "cauldron "was no bigger than a thimble. Archie wondered how he could mix any potions inside of it – and then he figured it out. 'There's a spell to make this thing bigger, isn't there?' he said. 'And it's small so I can smuggle it into school, yeah?'

'Key-rect!' Isabelle confirmed.

Her hand appeared over the fence again: once more, clenched in a fist.

Archie took what was offered and stared at the small, violet gems in his palm, trying to fathom what they could be used for.

'Amethyst gems,' Isabelle said. 'That's most of the main things you'll need. The books can be gotten from the Enchanted Cove for less than thirty pounds, I'm guessing. Which will just leave you with the broomstick to get. But they're quite expensive, I'm afraid.'

'I only have twenty-three pounds.'

'That may be enough after the discount is taken off. Oh,

and don't try doing any magic with that wand yet. I'm sure I don't need to explain why it would be a bad idea.'

'I don't know any spells, so there's no chance of that happening.'

'I better get back inside before my parents notice I'm missing. I'm meant to be in my bedroom doing homework.'

'Okay. Thanks for all this stuff. You can't even begin to understand how happy this has made me.'

'No problem.'

'Hey, are you going on the school trip tomorrow?'

'Hmm, now let's see. Am I going to the zoo or staying at school, bored out of my skull? Which one do you think?'

'The second one.'

'Key-rect.'

'Did your parents say anything about the red mark? Or was I right about it having faded enough not to be noticeable?'

'You were right; they didn't notice. Okay, gotta go. See ya!'

Archie heard her move away. 'Bye,' he said.

He stared at the items he was holding with a big grin spreading across his face.

And that's when someone banged on one of the upstairs windows, scaring the heck out of Archie. He looked up and saw his brother staring down at him with an inquisitive expression on his face. Archie put the wand behind his back and slid it up his sleeve. He pocketed the other items. He wondered how long Oliver had been standing there and how much he'd seen.

Spying the football to his right, Archie dribbled it a bit and then buried it in the back of the goal. Then he looked up at Oliver with raised eyebrows, asking a question without saying a word. Oliver responded with a shake of his head and by showing his XBOX controller, which was the answer that Archie had been hoping for. He didn't want to play football at the moment when he could be admiring his newly-acquired magical items.

Oliver looked at his brother through slitted eyes and then disappeared from view. *He's going to drill me with questions when I get inside*, Archie thought. *He saw everything that happened and he's going to grill me about what was handed to me over the fence*. Deciding that he may as well get it over and done with, Archie went back inside and hid his magical items under his bed covers, then he knocked on Oliver's bedroom door.

'Go away!' came the response.

Archie ignored him and entered anyway.

Oliver was busy playing Fortnite. He'd just jumped out of the Battle Bus and deployed his glider. 'Are your ears not working?' he said, shooting an irritated glance in Archie's direction.

'You gave me a funny look while I was in the garden. I just wondered why.'

'You were standing there, holding a stick. I was just curious as to what you were doing with it.'

Archie felt relieved. Oliver hadn't witnessed the handover otherwise it would have been the first thing he'd have mentioned.

'I was mooching around,' Archie explained. 'You know what it's like when you're bored. Anything can look interesting. Even a stick on the ground.'

'You need to get yourself an XBOX. And you also need to get out of this room. If I die because of you, I'm gonna be *so* miffed.'

Archie left him to it.

In his bedroom, he looked for somewhere he could hide his magical items. He opted for under his bed, behind a boxed Scalextric set which was covered in dust because it hadn't been moved in months. He figured they would be safe there from his mother's prying hands.

Later that evening, just before Archie retired to bed, he knelt down, reached behind the Scalextric set and pulled out his magical items. He stared at them in wonder, then waved the wand around, pretending to cast spells. He heard the creak of floorboards, footsteps on the landing. Not wasting a second, he re-hid everything and waited to see if anyone had come to speak to him. Archie heard a door close – and then nothing. *Just Oliver going to bed*, he thought, relaxing a little.

But then Archie went to close his curtains and noticed a dark, shadowy figure in the street. The figure was standing opposite next door's house, looking up at the old, kooky place. *Who the heck are you?* Archie thought. He blinked and the figure was gone, leaving Archie to wonder whether he'd imagined the person.

'Hmm,' he said to himself, 'am I seeing things?'

Mr Wiggins poked his head around the door. 'Talking to yourself is the first sign of madness, you know,' he said. 'And what is it that you think you didn't imagine?'

Archie decided to tell the truth. He told his dad about the shadowy figure, about how he'd blinked and the figure had disappeared, as if like magic. And that's when Archie once again remembered the protective barrier that'd been placed around next door's property.

'Are you all right, son?' Mr Wiggins said. 'All the colour has just drained out of your face, like you've seen a ghost.'

Archie took a second to compose himself and then answered: 'It was probably just a shadow that I saw, or maybe I did imagine it.'

Mr Wiggins gave him a searching look. 'Is there anything you want to tell me?' he said. 'Is anything bothering you?'

'No,' Archie assured him, whilst trying to look as unbothered as possible, 'I'm all right. I just thought I saw someone, that's all. You don't often see people lingering around on our street, late at night.'

Beckoning Archie to move out of the way, Mr Wiggins cupped his hands to the side of his head, then pressed his face against the glass, looking left and right. 'Well, I can't see anybody, but you've always got to be cautious about these sorts of things,' he said. 'It could be someone casing out next door for a burglary.'

'Or it could have just been a shadow or my imagination.'

Mr Wiggins seemed satisfied that the street was currently clear of potential interlopers. 'I'll keep an eye on things,' he said, making for the door. 'And if I notice anything untoward I'll ring the police. It's getting late, so get yourself in bed and get some sleep. I'm sure there's nothing to be concerned about, but I'll double-check that all the doors and windows are locked before I retire, just to give us peace of mind. Oh, and don't forget that it's your school trip tomorrow. Your mum's afraid that you'll leave without your packed lunch and go hungry.'

Archie assured him that he wouldn't, then he closed the curtains and slid under the bedcovers. He turned off his bedside lamp and watched as his dad closed the door. He didn't think he would be able to sleep due to a mixture of excitement and concern. He was excited because of the wand and other magical items beneath his bed and concerned because of the shadowy figure he may have seen in the street. It was about thirty minutes later when his eyes began to close.

When he woke, it was still dark. His bedside clock glowed with the time: 02:45. Normally, once he'd fallen asleep, that was it – he wouldn't wake until his clock chimed out its alarm in the morning. And yet here he was, now wide awake, staring up at the ceiling, wondering why he was awake. His eyes went towards the curtains and curiosity got the better of him. Making his way across the room, he poked his head through, then he looked left and right. There was no one around, as far as Archie could see. He focused his attention on the spot across from next door's house where he thought he'd seen the shadowy figure and ... his heart missed a beat as he saw a flicker of movement.

Bracing himself, he watched to see if anyone would step

out of the shadows.

And then something did ...

Archie relaxed a little as a black cat came into view and sauntered casually across the pavement, illuminated by the glow of a street lamp.

Concluding that he may have just imagined the whole shadowy figure thing, he went back to bed and was once again asleep in less than ten minutes.

In the morning, Archie made sure that he took his packed lunch with him as he left the house. He set off at the same time as the previous day in the hope that he would time it right and be able to walk with Isabelle again. But there was no sign of her as he went past her house and down the road.

He got a chance to speak to her after the form session.

'Hey!' he said, catching up with her in the corridor. 'Can I just talk with you for a second?'

'Sure,' Isabelle said.

They both moved to the side, away from the hustle and bustle of kids passing, so they could hear each other speak. Then Archie told her about what he'd seen (or what he thought he'd seen) the night before.

The look on Isabelle's face suggested that he'd done the right thing. It also suggested that she was concerned – *very* concerned.

'You say you "think" you saw someone,' Isabelle said, studying Archie carefully with her big brown eyes. 'So did you see someone or not?'

'I'm ... not sure,' Archie replied. 'It looked like someone was there – and I blinked and there was no one there. Then I thought I saw someone later on in the night when I woke and peeked through the curtains, but it was just a black cat.'

'So it could have been a cat you saw the first time then?'

Two girls came past, screeching as one chased the other.

Isabelle looked as though she could happily have magicked them away to the other side of the country.

'It could have been, yes,' Archie said, answering her question. He felt annoyed with himself that he couldn't be certain, one way or another. 'I was in two minds as to whether to tell you or not.'

'You did the right thing.'

Archie looked at Isabelle, asking a question with his eyes.

Isabelle exhaled deeply and then said, 'I'll tell you everything later. After the trip, after school.'

'I'm going to the Enchanted Cove after I get back. D'you want to come?'

'Sure. Why not. We'll cycle there, yeah? And *then* I'll tell you everything. We'll find somewhere to stop on the way back, somewhere quiet where we won't be interrupted.'

Archie nodded enthusiastically. 'It'll be good to go with someone who knows their way around a magic shop.'

He heard a familiar voice echo down the corridor towards them and rolled his eyes. 'Uh-oh, here comes trouble,' he said. 'If she says anything to you, just ignore her.'

'How's your head!' Carly yelled as she passed them with her two usual friends: Laura and Ruby. They were laughing it up (no surprises there).

'Your time's coming,' Isabelle muttered as she and Archie watched them disappear around the corner to the right.

'Don't do anything silly,' Archie warned her.

'I won't,' Isabelle replied with a wicked grin playing at the corners of her mouth. 'When the time is right,' she whispered to herself, 'she's going to get it. Every lesson that me and Sally are in with her, she's making our lives hell, so she's going to get *it* good and proper. Sally was so angry when I told her about that stick that was thrown at my head.'

Archie had no idea what "it" could be, but he hoped he would be around to witness whatever retribution was planned. He had a sneaking suspicion that it would involve magic.

The corridor was emptying as all the students disappeared off to their lessons.

'We better get moving otherwise all the good seats on the

coach will be gone,' Archie said, beckoning Isabelle to follow him.

'So what makes a seat a good one?' she said in no rush to follow him.

'One that's not near Carly and her mates.'

'Oh, right, yeah,' she said, taking off after him.

Mr Gibb and Mr Godber were the main teachers in charge of the trip, so there weren't many instances of misbehaviour. On the journey there, Archie sat with Ryan and Sally sat with Isabelle, all at the front. Carly and her sidekicks were at the back (no surprises there). Everyone enjoyed themselves and loved seeing the animals (especially the giraffes). Even the weather was kind with no more than a scattering of wispy clouds to blight an otherwise flawless sky.

In the toilet block, however, Archie overheard an interesting conversation between two boys: Liam Wright (the naughtiest boy in the year) and Ben Eagles (his sidekick). Archie was in a cubicle, so they didn't know he was there.

'I'm telling you now,' Liam said, his voice echoing throughout the room, 'I saw her out the corner of my eye. It went really cold, my breath frosting the air, but when I turned around she'd disappeared.'

'Are you sure you didn't just imagine it?' Ben said.

'No. As I told you before; I did *not* imagine it.'

'So what did she look like?'

'I don't know. It was a glimpse – out the corner of my eye! Could you glimpse someone like that and then give a description?'

'Probably not,' Ben admitted.

'I'm not going anywhere near that stairwell again. It scared the heck out of me.'

Archie heard a tap running, the deafening sound of a dryer. The door opened – and then there was silence. *Just another spooky sighting at the Darkcoat School*, he thought. *No biggie*. He waited a minute or so for the boys to be clear of the block before exiting himself.

Archie mentioned this to Ryan while they were perusing the reptile house.

'Liam could have been pulling his leg,' Ryan suggested.

'He sounded pretty damn serious to me.'

Ryan shrugged as he marvelled at the size of a coiled-up boa constrictor. 'I'll believe in ghosts when I see one,' he said. 'Have you ever seen one?'

'Nope. But I have had a feeling of being watched loads of times while at school and then there's the sudden temperature drops to consider. You try hanging around the north stairwell for some time and see how you get on.'

'I go up and down there most days and I've never had a spooky experience. Every now and then someone tells a story about a ghostly sighting, which keeps the legend going. But that's all it is – just a legend (same with all the other ghost stories surrounding the school). As I said, I'll believe it when I see it. And I don't expect to see it anytime soon.' He prodded the glass that separated him from the boa. 'Hey, d'you think this thing could swallow one of us whole?'

'Why don't you go in and find out?'

'I think I'll pass on that, thanks. We should put Carly in there and see if it can swallow *her*.'

'It probably could, but then it'd throw her back up.'

Both boys laughed out loud at this. They soon shut up, however, when they saw her coming toward them.

With regards to the ghostly sighting, Archie thought it best to adopt Ryan's attitude of "I'll believe it when I see it myself". But Archie hoped that he would never experience anything of the kind. He wasn't sure his heart would be able to cope with it.

On the coach ride back to the school, Sally and Isabelle weren't so lucky with the seating. They were late joining the queue for the coach so they ended up sitting somewhere in the middle. Fortunately, Mr Gibb was close by so there were no attempts at bullying from the rear.

When they arrived back at the school, Archie and Ryan were the first ones to jump off the coach. Ryan began walking down the pavement, but he stopped when he noticed that his friend had stayed put.

'What are you waiting for?' he asked him. 'Come on, let's get going!'

'You go on without me,' Archie responded. 'I've, erm, got something I need to do.'

'What's this something you've got to do? We can do it together, yeah?'

Archie was about to formulate a lie – or at least attempt to – when Isabelle came to his rescue:

'He's coming to my house to do some studying,' Isabelle said, appearing next to him. 'We're going to help each other with our homework.'

Ryan pointed a finger at Archie. 'You're letting *him* help you with your homework?' he said, pulling a funny face. 'I'm not sure he's the best person for that ... unless, oh, I get it.' He gave both of them a sly look. 'It's okay, I understand.' He winked at Archie as he began backing away. 'I'll get out of your way and let you get on with your "homework".'

'No, it's not like that,' Archie said.

But Ryan had made up his mind and was already walking away. He kept glancing back with a grin on his face as he strutted down the street, which made things even worse.

'I'm sorry about my friend,' Archie said. He could feel his cheeks burning. 'He's just trying to embarrass me – and doing an excellent job of it, I might add.'

'It's okay, I know exactly what he's doing,' Isabelle said, smiling.

From behind, Sally tapped them both on the shoulder and said goodbye. 'I'll see you at school tomorrow she added as she made for a car which was waiting on the other side of the road.

Isabelle and Archie assured her that they would.

They saw Carly and her friends heading toward them.

'Come on,' Isabelle said, grabbing Archie by the arm and hustling him along the pavement, 'let's get going. There's a shop we need to get to and you're clearly very eager to get there.'

'That's somewhat of an understatement. I want to get there before it shuts because this is the last chance I'll have before the lesson.'

'It's open 'till five-thirty. I checked last night, so just chill out. There's plenty of time.'

When Archie arrived home, Mrs Wiggins inquired if he'd had a nice time at the zoo and he told her that he had. Upstairs, he pocketed the money from his savings jar.

On his way out of the house, Mrs Wiggins asked him the inevitable question: 'Where are you going?'

'Just ... off to the park with Ryan,' he lied.

'But you've only just come in.'

'I know. And now I'm off out again. I'll be there about an hour.'

Archie left before she could quiz him some more.

A few minutes later, he and Isabelle were on their bikes, heading down the big hill, towards the edge of town. She'd taken the lead and was setting a ferocious pace. Archie was struggling to keep up with her, even though he was pedalling as fast as he could.

'Hey, slow down!' he called out. 'It's not a race, you know!'

But Isabelle couldn't hear him. As she reached the bottom of the hill, she glanced left then right and was out across the junction before Archie was able to close the gap. And when Archie reached the junction he had to wait a while because of the traffic streaming past on both sides of the road. By this time, Isabelle was a long way ahead. It wasn't until she reached a set of traffic lights that Archie finally caught up with her.

'Crikey! What's the rush?' he said, pulling up next to her,

out of breath. 'You didn't even look back to see if I was still with you.'

'I wasn't aware that I was rushing,' she answered, not out of breath at all. 'You need to work on your fitness.'

The lights changed and off she shot again – this time with a big grin on her face.

'Oh, that's how you want to play it,' Archie said, taking off after her with a look of steely determination on his face.

But it didn't matter how hard he pedalled, how hard he tried, he just couldn't catch her. In the end, after Isabelle had disappeared off into the distance, Archie gave up and moved along at a pace that was comfortable for him. He just hoped that he would be able to find the shop when he reached Bucklechurch. He had only done the journey once before, but he was sure he would remember the route he had taken the last time he'd been trailing behind Isabelle.

Archie was more than ready for a rest by the time he reached Tiddlywink Road. Parking his bike next to Isabelle's, he entered the Enchanted Cove, the bell above the door tinkling to signal his arrival. The door clicked shut behind him as he took a few tentative steps down the nearest aisle, looking out for Isabelle. The smell of scented candles was strong in the air, almost overpowering.

Hearing voices, Archie made his way to the other side of the shop to find Isabelle talking to Mrs Hickinbottom. Isabelle was marvelling at a particularly fine-looking broomstick and inquiring about the price.

'That's the most expensive one I have at the moment,' Mrs Hickinbottom said, 'and would set you back three-hundred pounds, no less. That's a lot of pocket money you'd have to save up, hmm?'

'My birthday is only a few months away,' Isabelle replied, 'so I won't be needing any of my pocket money.'

'That'll give you something to look forward to,' Mrs Hickinbottom said. 'But in the meantime, is there anything else I can get you? Something a lot cheaper than three-hundred pounds? Some ingredients for a potion, perhaps? A good luck charm?' She picked up a silver bracelet from one of the shelves and showed it to Isabelle. 'This will look nice on your wrist, don't you think?'

'I'm not really into jewellery,' Isabelle said. 'And that thing isn't going to bring me good luck anyway. That's the sort of thing you sell to non-magical people who come in here for a browse. Good luck can only be obtained by a potion – and even then it's only temporary.'

Mrs Hickinbottom wrinkled her nose as she put the bracelet back. 'Well, you certainly know your stuff, don't you?' she said with a slight edge to her voice. 'But if you're just here to browse I'm going to leave you to it. I've got jobs I can be doing and time is a precious thing, as I'm sure you can appreciate.'

Archie advanced and presented himself. 'Ahum,' he said, coughing to get the woman's attention. 'Isabelle isn't buying today, but I am.' He reached into his side pocket and pulled out his money – notes and coins – to prove that he meant business.'

'And is there anything specific that you're looking for?' Mrs Hickinbottom said. 'Or are you just browsing like your friend?'

From his back pocket, Archie produced the note with the list of items he needed and handed it to her. 'Isabelle, my friend here, has given me a wand, a cauldron, and some runes, so it's just the other stuff that I need now.'

'You're students of Miss Burrows,' Mrs Hickinbottom said, nodding her approval. 'I hold your headmistress in very high regard. She has sent a lot of business my way over the years and she's a damn fine witch as well. Probably the most accomplished one I've ever met, if the truth be told. And it looks like you've got yourself a good friend here,' she said, raising her eyebrows at Isabelle. 'She's saved you a lot of money.'

'Yes, I owe her big time,' Archie said.

He smiled at Isabelle and she smiled back.

'How much have you got there, exactly?' Mrs Hickinbottom said to Archie.

He unclenched his hand and showed her his notes and coins.

'Hmm,' Mrs Hickinbottom said, not looking optimistic. 'I think you've got enough for the books (with the discount deducted) but not the broomstick.'

'Oh,' Archie said, lowering his head in disappointment. He wondered how he would ever be able to afford one (which Isabelle had said was quite expensive). He inquired how much a grade one broomstick would cost.

Mrs Hickinbottom said, 'The least expensive one I have at the moment will set you back about a hundred pounds (including the discount), I'm afraid. You'll have to start saving and doing chores. There's always your birthday, as well. You could ask for cash instead of presents.'

'That's not for nine months,' Archie said dejectedly. 'And how would I explain what I'd bought? My parents would want to see what I'd purchased with the money and I wouldn't be able to show them. And even if I did, they wouldn't believe that that's what I'd spent the money on. Not to mention the fact that they would want to know *why* I'd bought a broomstick.'

'That's all for you to figure out,' Mrs Hickinbottom said. 'The best I can do is give you another twenty per cent discount on your books. How does that sound?'

Archie felt disappointed about not being able to afford a broomstick, but he still smiled. The lady was being kind to him – she was offering him another discount (and a generous one at that) – so it was the least he could do.

'Thank you,' he said. 'I appreciate that.'

'Right, good-o!' Mrs Hickinbottom said. 'I'll go and get your books.'

She disappeared into a room at the back, then returned with a bag and handed it to Archie.

'Thanks,' he said, handing her the money. 'I really

appreciate your kindness.'

'That's okay,' Mrs Hickinbottom said. 'You just need to promise me that you'll study hard and be sensible with your magic.'

'I promise,' Archie said.

'Don't you need to buy the books?' he asked Isabelle. 'I'm going to guess that you've got a broomstick.'

'Oh, yes, I've definitely got a broomstick,' she confirmed. 'And I've got everything else I need. There isn't a serious book about magic that I don't own. I've got loads of ingredients for potions, so if you ever need anything, just give me a shout. Honestly, if I could buy everything in this shop, I would. I *love* buying magical things.'

'Well, I've got to admire your enthusiasm,' Mrs Hickinbottom said, 'but I'm going to have to ask you if that's all you'll be needing for today as I'm pushed for time. I've just remembered that I've got some business to take care of and will have to close up early.'

'I don't need anything else,' Archie said. He looked at Isabelle.

'Me neither,' she said.

They made their way towards the door.

'Oh, one last thing,' Mrs Hickinbottom said, focusing her attention on Isabelle, 'how did it go with the bograt's blood? When you were last here, I asked you if your safety was at risk. I also told you that you could talk to me in private. That offer still stands (although it would have to be tomorrow as I am pushed for time, as I stated).'

'My safety isn't at risk,' Isabelle assured her. 'I don't need to talk to anyone, but thanks for the concern.'

The bell above the door jingled as she made a hasty exit with Archie right behind her.

'I should be able to buy something without being quizzed as to why I'm buying it,' Isabelle said as she mounted her bike.

'She's just concerned,' Archie said as he mounted his and

hooked his carrier bag over the handlebars. 'And so am I.'

'I promised I'd explain everything to you and I will. But not here. We'll stop off somewhere on the way back. Somewhere quiet, just like I suggested earlier.'

Isabelle rode away and Archie followed.

Pulling alongside her, he said, 'Sorry, but I've got to ask – what in the blue heck is a bograt?'

'It's a rat that lives in a bog,' Isabelle replied, rather unhelpfully.

She accelerated away again, leaving Archie behind.

'Oh God, here we go again,' he moaned as he took off after her.

They were about halfway home when Isabelle finally slowed down and brought herself to a skidding halt. Archie was some way behind her at this point and wondered what'd caught her attention. By the time he caught up to her, she had already wheeled her bike away from the road and was heading for a playground a few hundred feet away. And by the time Archie reached the playground, Isabelle was already on one of the swings, going back and forth, trying to get as high as she could.

Resting his bike against Isabelle's, Archie seated himself on the swing next to her and tried unsuccessfully to get as high as her.

'Why'd you have to go so fast?' Archie said. He almost added: you didn't the first time I was trailing you, but he didn't want to admit to following her, so he left it at that.

'I wasn't going fast,' Isabelle replied, giving him a sideways grin, 'you're just slow.'

'I'm not the speediest, I'll give you that. But I'm not that slow, either. You could have waited up for me. All you had to do was pedal slower.' Archie said all this in an amiable tone.

And Isabelle replied in an amiable tone, too: 'I could have – but I didn't.'

Silence descended between them as they both continued

swinging back and forth.

Archie was tempted to say something, but he didn't. He waited for Isabelle to speak because he felt that it was the right thing to do.

'My dad killed someone,' she eventually said. 'And that's why we moved.'

'What?' Archie said. He brought himself to a sliding halt and stared at Isabelle, who was still swinging back and forth, but not as high now. 'Did I just hear you right? Did you just say that your dad murdered someone?'

'No, that's not what I said. I told you that he killed someone. When you murder someone, that's intentional. What happened with my dad was an accident. Someone was attacking him and he defended himself.'

Archie relaxed a little. He was less concerned now that he knew there wasn't a murderer living next door to him. Archie knew that what Isabelle was about to tell him would not be easy for her, so he waited patiently for her to continue with her story. And then she did ...

'When we lived down south in Staythorpe, my dad used to go to a pub called the Willows Arms. About three or four times a week he'd disappear for an evening and come home late, stinking of beer. He liked to play cards with his friends and anyone else who wanted to lay money down on the table and join in. And then one night, a stranger came in and wanted to play. There was a spare seat, so my dad and the other players were happy for him to take it. Everything was fine at first when the stranger was winning. It was when he began losing that the problems started. He accused my dad and the others of cheating. My dad was winning the most money, though, so it was him who got the brunt of the accusations.'

'Was this a magical pub?' Archie asked. 'One where wizards and witches gathered? And was the game of cards magical in some way?'

'No, no – and no,' Isabelle replied, annoyed. 'And please

don't interrupt me again while I'm telling you about this. It's hard enough to talk about as it is without you chiming in with a stupid comment.'

Ouch! Archie winced as if he'd been slapped. *I didn't think it was stupid*, he thought. 'Sorry, it won't happen again,' he assured her.

Isabelle resumed her story: 'Anyway, as I was saying, it was my dad who got the brunt of the accusations. But it wasn't until the end of the evening that things turned really nasty. By this time, the stranger was very drunk. He followed my dad and his friends into the car park and insisted on picking a fight with them. My dad offered to give him his money back, which he accepted. But that didn't stop the trouble. The stranger was intent on fighting with someone – and that someone was my dad. Punches were thrown and my dad managed to avoid all of them. But then the stranger went for a big haymaker and lost his balance. He fell sideways and cracked his head on a rock. He didn't get up.'

'I must admit, I'm a bit disappointed. I thought you were going to tell me that your father pulled out his wand and blasted the guy.'

'That would make for an entertaining tale, I'm sure. And my dad could have easily dealt with the guy if he had used his magic. But then my dad would have needed to do some explaining to his friends because most of them have no idea that he's a wizard. You can't just pull your wand out and start blasting when there's non-magical people around. That can get you into a lot of trouble, for obvious reasons. Thank God you were around when Carly threw that stick at me, otherwise I'd have been in a lot of trouble myself.'

'Is that what you'd have done to her? Blasted her into oblivion?'

'Not into oblivion, no. But I'd have given her enough of a shot that she knew not to mess with me again. You have to be careful where magic is concerned. It's a strange and wondrous thing that's full of seemingly endless possibilities that'll blow your mind, but it's also something you need to respect.'

'I don't think I could do anything but respect something as awesome as magic,' Archie said. 'So, were there plenty of witnesses to what happened with your dad and that stranger? I'm guessing that there were. Nothing draws a crowd like a bit of fisticuffs.'

'There were lots of witnesses. And not just my dad's friends. He didn't get prosecuted for what happened because it was deemed as self-defence. The problem wasn't so much the fact that he'd killed someone; it was *who* he'd killed. The stranger – a man named Garvin Huxley – turned out to be the brother of Barrick Huxley, who just happens to be one of the most powerful wizards in the country, if not *the* most powerful.'

'Oh,' Archie said. He guessed where the conversation was heading and now knew why there'd been a need for Isabelle and her family to relocate.

'Apparently, Garvin lives in France (or did do, when he was alive) and was in Staythorpe visiting his brother for a short break. After my dad was cleared of any wrongdoing, Barrick vowed revenge. He told my dad that he had taken something dear from him, so he vowed that he would do the same to my dad. Hence the need for us to move.'

'Oh,' Archie said again. 'And by someone dear, did he mean you or your mum?'

Isabelle shrugged. 'We have no idea and we didn't wait around to find out. Our house was rented, so moving quickly wasn't a problem.'

'Wow,' Archie said, taking all this information in and processing it. 'Yours and your parents' lives have been turned upside down because of one moment of madness. And your dad didn't even do anything wrong; he was just defending himself.'

'I was so annoyed at first because I didn't want to move. I didn't want to leave all my friends behind and go to a new school. But I knew that the safety of my parents was the most important thing to me and my safety was the most important thing to them, so there was no other option.'

'Did your dad try talking to this Barrick guy? Did he try reasoning with him?'

'Yes, he explained everything to him, but he was having none of it. You see, the problem isn't just that he's a powerful wizard; he also happens to be the biggest gangster in the south of England. He's infamous for making people who've betrayed or annoyed him disappear. And there's one more thing: he's a vampire as well.'

Archie was shocked to silence. He stared dead ahead, watching the cars go by in the distance, processing this new information. A wizard who's also a gangster – the biggest gangster in the south, no less – was potentially targeting his new friend. *And he's a vampire, too!* Archie thought. *Yikes!* Archie wondered how this might impact on him. Would this Barrick target him for being friends with Isabelle? Would his family be in danger?

'I'll understand if you don't want anything more to do with me or my family after this,' Isabelle said. 'I'd be wary about being around me if I was in your position.'

Archie gave things some more thought before he spoke. 'I know we've only just become friends,' he said, giving her a reassuring look, 'but friends don't abandon each other when the going gets tough. Without you, I wouldn't have a wand, or a cauldron, or Amestiff stones (or whatever they're called). I'll help you in any way that I can.'

'Thanks,' Isabelle said, giving him a warm smile. 'But I don't expect you to put yourself in any danger. If you could just keep an eye out for anything suspicious, especially on our street, then I'd really appreciate that.'

'Anything suspicious? As in like shadowy figures? After everything you've told me, I feel even more annoyed with myself for not being able to tell you whether I saw someone or not. Have you got a description for this guy? And is there anyone else I should look out for? The thugs who're working for him?'

'The people who work for him wear black suits, always black. And as for Barrick himself, he's very tall and slim with blue eyes and fiery red hair. Distinctive looking. Not hard to miss, which is good. And his car isn't hard to miss, either: a big American one with lightning bolts down the side. He obviously doesn't like being inconspicuous. Oh, and you know how I told you that he's a vampire, don't go getting the idea that he's going to try and suck your blood or something. He's not *that* type of vampire; it's your power he'll be after. That's what he'll drain away, so he can make himself stronger. Magical vampires are not very common. Of all the wizards and witches I've met, I only know of one other.'

'And who is that?'

'Me,' Isabelle said.

Archie stared at her with his mouth open.

'Don't worry, I'm not going to suck the magic out of you. Vampires don't need to draw power from anyone to stay alive or anything; it's just people like Barrick that you need to be concerned about. He's just a power-hungry maniac who'll do anything to be at the top of the heap. And you should know that vampires can detect the magic within someone – along with their levels of power – so there's no hiding from him once he's been near you.'

Archie took a few seconds to process the consequences of what he'd just been told. 'That means that you knew I was a wizard as soon as you came near me,' he said. 'And yet you didn't want anything to do with me when we first met. Why? I'd have thought you'd have been itching to be my best friend.'

'I come across magical people all the time, so meeting you was no big thing for me. And besides, I wasn't in the best mood when we first met. I'd just moved house when I didn't want to and there was all the other stuff that's been going on. I just wanted to be left alone, to be honest.'

Something else occurred to Archie: 'Hey, if you can detect who's magical, then that means that you know who the wizards and witches are at our school. You know who'll be at the class tomorrow.' He looked at Isabelle with raised eyebrows, waiting for her to spill ...

'I do know,' she confirmed, smiling mischievously and blinking at him in a way which suggested that she wasn't about to divulge such information.

'And?' Archie said.

'I don't want to ruin the surprise for you. The suspense of not knowing is an exciting thing. I don't want to take that away from you, so you're just going to have to be patient. Sorry.'

'Be patient? Are you kidding me? Come on, spill the beans. Just tell me – yeah! Tell me!'

Isabelle communicated a clear message to him with another mischievous smile.

Archie waited to see if she was pulling his leg. But when it became apparent that she wasn't, he said, 'Seriously? You're just going to leave me hanging like this?'

Isabelle said nothing.

'Tell me that Carly's not a witch? *Please* tell me that she isn't?'

Once again, Isabelle said nothing.

'Oh, right, okay. Well, I'm now more curious than ever. But if she is a witch then that would just about be the worst news ever.' Archie pulled his phone out of his pocket. 'Look, we should exchange mobile numbers so we can contact each other in an emergency. Give me yours and I'll drop you a text.'

'Good idea,' Isabelle agreed, producing her own.

After the exchange, Archie once again tried to prize out of Isabelle who the magical people were at the school, but she just wouldn't tell him.

She veered the subject in a different direction: 'I'm not sure whether to tell my parents about your shadowy figure sighting. Part of me feels as if I should because I want them to be prepared for any danger that could be coming our way. And part of me doesn't want to panic them unnecessarily. My mum will confine me to the house if she gets a whiff of danger. And we'd probably end up moving again, which I *really* don't want to do; especially now I'm beginning to settle in at school and make new friends. What would you do?'

Archie gave it some thought. 'If it was me I'd ... probably not tell them, if I'm honest,' he said. 'I don't think I could cope with being confined to home. And the idea of moving somewhere new would be a scary prospect. I would just be super-vigilant from now on. Suspicious of everything and ready for action if it came to it. That said, I don't want you to take my advice and it be the wrong advice. I don't want to be responsible for any harm coming to you or your family.'

'I'll do what you've suggested. But that's my decision. I'm not going to blame you if it all goes wrong.'

Even so, Archie knew that he *would* feel guilty if it were the wrong decision. 'My mum's going to wonder where I've got to,' he said, checking the time on his mobile phone and then standing up. 'I told her I was going to be about an hour and that was an hour and a half ago.'

Isabelle sprang off her swing and mounted her bike. 'Best get back quickly then,' she said. 'And that means not dawdling along at five miles an hour. Try to imagine that Barrick is chasing you and that might speed you up.'

Without another word, she took off towards the road and was out of sight before Archie could even mount his bike.

'Ah, man, not this again,' he said as he took off after her.

Archie didn't catch up with Isabelle. No matter how much he tried, no matter how hard he pedalled, he just couldn't close the distance (even with imagining a wizard gangster chasing him).

About fifteen minutes later, when he arrived back on Salt Road, Isabelle was sitting on the kerb outside her house, waiting for him.

'I thought you'd at least make it competitive this time,' she said, smiling at him.

'You had a head start,' he said, laying his bike down next to hers.

'Next time I'll let you have the head start. And I'll still win.'

'We'll see.'

Archie looked towards Isabelle's house, then her garden. 'So what would happen to me if I stepped over that boundary?' he asked her.

'To you?' she replied as she stood up. 'Nothing. Unless you're a wizard or witch with bad intentions towards me and my family, you've got nothing to worry about.'

'And what will it do to a wizard or witch who has bad intentions?'

'Well, it's not going to blow them up, if that's what you're thinking. But it will slow them down. And it'll give them a nasty shock as well, if they touch it.' Isabelle grinned at the idea of this.

'So it's like an invisible electric fence?'

'Ahuh,' Isabelle confirmed.

'But what if they arrive on broomsticks and land on your roof?'

'It's a Bubble Barrier that's surrounding our house. You can try to go over or under it, but the result will be the same.' Isabelle widened her eyes and began to shake as though someone had plugged her into the National Grid.

Archie grinned and said, 'But if this Barrick is as powerful as you say he is, surely your barrier isn't going to keep him at bay for long.'

'You're right; it won't. But it'll be long enough for us to at least get ourselves together and decide what we're going to do.'

A face framed by straight brown hair appeared at one of the bottom windows, looking out.

'That's my mum,' Isabelle said, rolling her eyes. 'Great,

now I'm going to have to answer a load of questions about what I've been doing with you.'

'Just tell her and your dad the truth. Perhaps they'll be impressed to know that there's a wizard-in-the-making next door.'

'That'll lead to a load of questions and a lot of warnings about what we might get up to together. I'll just tell my parents that we've been to the park. It's not a lie. I better go in now. I'll see you tomorrow.'

Isabelle began pushing her bike down the driveway, past the black Mercedes.

'We can walk together to school in the morning, if you like?' Archie said.

'Sure, I'll be leaving around quarter past eight, assuming I get myself out of bed on time,' Isabelle said as she disappeared around the side of the house.

Archie looked towards the window to see if her mother was still watching him, but there was no one there.

Okay, now I just need to get in my house without someone noticing this, he thought, unhooking the bag containing his books from the handlebars.

This turned out to be easier than expected. If Mrs Wiggins had been in the kitchen, then it would have been a problem. She would have been in Archie's face before he could close the front door, wanting to know what was in the bag. Fortunately, she was in the living room with Mr Wiggins, having a conversation about where they could put up a new shelf.

'Archie, is that you?' Mrs Wiggins called out.

'Yes, it's me!' he replied.

And then he disappeared up the stairs before she could quiz him.

Oliver was busy gaming in his room, so no problems there.

In his bedroom, Archie closed the door and emptied his books on his bed. He picked up the one titled *Entry Level to*

Intermediate Spells and began perusing the pages. He found the levitation spell that Isabelle had most likely used to make the rock float and this brought a smile to his face. Retrieving his wand from under the bed, he laid it next to the book. The text and images made the spell look easy enough to cast, so he considered whether to give it a go. He figured he could use something light, like a plastic toy car. That way, if it dropped or went flying across the room for whatever reason, it wouldn't be a disaster. If Mrs Wiggins came snooping, he would just tell her that he'd dropped something. What could go wrong with a simple levitation spell? Nothing, he figured, as long as he pronounced the words correctly. But when he picked up the wand, he noticed that his hand was shaking. If *I'm nervous about picking up the wand*, he thought, *then I'll be nervous about saying the words. And if I get that wrong ...*

Archie didn't want to contemplate what could happen, so he stowed the wand back underneath his bed, along with his new purchases. Apart from the book of spells. He wanted to have a good look through that, so he sat cross-legged on his bed and began thumbing through the pages. He found a spell that could disarm an attacker, which he thought would be useful, given what Isabelle had told him about the gangster that had it in for her family. There was one to start a fire (definitely not a spell to practise at home, that). A human statue spell was another that he was sure would be useful for self-defence (and against Oliver when he was being annoying). Archie continued flicking the pages and being amazed by all the weird and wonderful things he would be able to do when he began learning magic.

But then Mrs Wiggins called up to him: 'Archie! Your dinner is in the microwave! Are you going to come down and eat it or what?'

'Yeah, yeah!' he called back, snapping the book shut in frustration. 'I'll be there in a minute!'

He made sure to hide it before leaving his room.

Later that night, before Archie retired to bed, he poked his head through the curtains and checked the street for interlopers. There were no shadowy figures across from Isabelle's house and no suspicious vehicles parked anywhere (only the usual ones). Archie even glanced skywards to see if he could spot anyone riding a broomstick, but he saw nothing but the twinkling stars which dotted the black velvet sky. Satisfied that all was as well as it could be, he retired to bed and soon dozed off to sleep.

In the morning, Archie walked to school with Isabelle and they talked about magic. He told her that he'd been tempted to do the levitation spell and she told him that he'd done the right thing by not attempting it.

'You only have to wait 'till this evening and you'll be doing plenty of magic,' Isabelle said as they walked along the main road with a brisk wind buffeting them from the east.

'I know, I know,' Archie said, 'but there's some weird and wonderful spells in that book. And that's just the one for beginner to intermediate. What's the advanced book going to be like? What sort of spells will *that* contain? And I skimmed through the potions book this morning. There's one in there for re-growing hair. You should show it to your dad.'

'My dad has been doing magic for a long, long time now. If he wanted hair on his head, I think he'd have it by now, don't you?'

'Yeah, I guess. This is probably a silly question but have you remembered to bring everything you need for this evening? All your magical stuff?'

'Duh! Of course. And you?'

'Eh, yeah. They were the first things I put in my bag.'

After a minute or so of silence, Archie added, 'I kept an eye out last night. Didn't notice any shady characters in the street, you'll be glad to know.'

'Yeah, same here. I checked a few times. Maybe it was your imagination after all.'

Archie still wasn't sure. 'I'll keep checking, day and night, just to be on the safe side.'

'Yeah, me too.'

The first half of the day went by slowly for Archie – mainly because he was clock-watching. It wasn't until dinnertime that something eventful happened. Unfortunately, that eventful something was another confrontation between Isabelle and Carly.

Archie was playing football with Ryan when they heard a commotion on the other side of the playground. Carly was right in Isabelle's face, squaring up for a fight, by the look of things. And of course Laura and Ruby were right behind their friend, sporting suitably mean expressions.

'You know, I often wonder if she'd be so brave if she didn't have her buddies backing her up,' Ryan said.

'Probably not,' Archie replied.

They couldn't hear what was being said, so they made their way toward the commotion.

Then Miss Burrows appeared from seemingly nowhere and got in-between Isabelle and Carly.

'Well, well, what a surprise,' the headmistress said. 'You pair are at loggerheads again.'

'She started it!' Isabelle said as she glared at Carly. 'She threw a stick at my head – *again!*'

'No I did not!' Carly said, trying to look as innocent as possible. 'Stop blaming everything on me, why don't you!'

'Yeah!' Laura chimed in, backing her up. 'Stop blaming everything on her.'

'She didn't throw anything,' Ruby said to Miss Burrows. 'Honest, she didn't. I can swear on my life.'

'That won't be necessary,' she responded, trying to calm the situation. 'I didn't see who started this – and quite frankly I don't care. This business between you pair is becoming tiresome now,' she said, looking at Carly and then Isabelle, 'and it needs to *stop*.'

Ruby opened her mouth to say something, but Miss Burrows silenced her with a raised finger.

Archie noticed his brother in the background, having a giggle with his mates at the situation. And they weren't the only ones watching. Others were gathering around as well, gawking.

'I don't want to hear another word from any of you,' the headmistress said to the girls. 'If I get even a whiff of trouble between you lot over the next few days, I'm putting you all in detention – for a week!' She waved them all away with quick flicks of her fingers, 'disperse, please! *Disperse!*'

The girls did as they were told: Carly and her friends going to one side of the playground and Isabelle going to the other.

Archie and Ryan joined her.

'That Carly has got a screw loose,' Ryan said, shaking his head whilst throwing dirty looks at her. 'And her mates aren't much better.'

'Are you okay?' Archie asked Isabelle. 'Did she hurt you?'

'No, the stick didn't hurt me,' she replied. 'I was surprised, that's all. And I'm getting sick of being harassed. I need to do something about her. Something that'll make her think twice about even looking at me the wrong way, otherwise she's just going to continue making my life hell.'

'Who's making your life hell?' a familiar voice said.

Archie turned to see Sally standing next to him.

'I take it I missed something while I was in the toilet,' she said.

Ryan explained what'd happened. 'They obviously watched you walk away and seized their chance,' he added.

'Oh,' Sally said, looking guilty. She apologized to Isabelle: 'I'm sorry I took so long; I should have realised that this could happen.'

'You've got nothing to apologize for,' Isabelle said. 'It's not your fault.'

They all looked toward Carly and her friends, who were

still glaring at them.

'So what have you got in mind?' Ryan asked Isabelle. 'What is that you think you can do that will stop the crazy one and her demented minions from harassing you?'

'I don't know yet,' Isabelle replied, narrowing her eyes as she glanced in Carly's direction. 'But something will come to me.'

Archie once again hoped he would be there to witness it.

The rest of the day went by without any further incidents of nastiness.

History was Archie's last lesson. After the bell rang he stayed seated for a minute, slowly putting away his things. Even though he was as eager as hell to get himself to classroom 56, he knew there was no point rushing because the lesson didn't begin until 3:45.

'Come on, slowpoke,' Ryan said, appearing at his side, 'it's the end of the day, let's get out of this place.'

'I'm doing an after-school activity,' Archie informed him, 'so you may as well get going.'

'Really? And what after-school school activity would that be?'

'Draughts.'

Ryan burst out laughing. 'What? Seriously?' he said, looking at Archie gone out. 'You are joking, right?'

'No. Miss Burrows holds an after-school class every Thursday.'

'I know she does. But ... since when have you liked draughts? Have you ever played the game?'

'Erm, no. I just thought it'd be something different to try.'

'Are you going on your own, or with someone else?'

'Isabelle's giving it a go with me.'

Ryan smiled. He raised his eyebrows to form a teasing expression.

'And don't give me that look. She's not my girlfriend; she's just a friend.'

The teasing expression slowly changed to more of a blank one as the smile disappeared from Ryan's face.

'Well, I suppose I should leave you to it then,' he said as he began backing away towards the door. 'I don't want to get in the way of anything you're doing with your new "friend".'

Archie opened his mouth to suggest that they could go kart racing at the weekend, but it was too late – Ryan had already gone. Archie pondered whether to go after him, but he decided against this. Better to let him cool down and try to catch him at a better moment, he figured.

'You're not usually one to dither and hang around,' the teacher said as he appeared at Archie's side. 'You're normally gone like a shot when the bell rings. Is there something I can help you with?'

'No, I'm fine, thanks,' he replied, snatching up his bag and exiting the room before the teacher could ask him any more questions.

Archie took a slow walk up the middle stairwell, resisting the constant urge to rush. As he walked along the top corridor, approaching room 56, he expected to see a group of students by the door, waiting to go inside – but there were only two boys and a girl. He recognised all of them, but it was the girl who caught his attention and he began to think that he must be in the wrong place. No way could *she* be a witch. No way! As Archie got closer, he double-checked the number on the door. Yep, he was in the correct place, all right. Miss Burrows had definitely told him that the magic class was held here. The blind on the other side of the glass had been pulled down, so he couldn't see inside the room.

'If you want to play draughts, you need to ask Miss Burrows first,' Laura said to him as she saw him approaching. 'You can't just turn up, I'm sorry to say.'

'I'm not here to play draughts,' Archie responded. 'I'm here for the magic class.'

'Don't say that,' one of the boys said. 'Voices echo in these corridors and you don't know who might be listening.'

Archie had seen him around before, plenty of times. He was in year six or seven, ridiculously tall for his age and hence not difficult to miss. Archie was sure he was called Brad, or was it Chad, or something like that?

The other boy was in the year above Archie. His name was James and he wore square, thick lens glasses which made his eyes look very large.

'No way are you a wizard,' Laura said to Archie. 'There must be a mistake.'

'That's exactly what I thought when I saw you,' he replied. 'Please don't tell me that Carly is a part of this. Please don't tell me that she's a witch. That *really* would be a depressing piece of news!'

'Keep your voice down!' Brad, or Chad, or whatever he was called, said. 'If Miss Burrows hears you, she won't be happy.'

'Yeah, she won't be happy at all!' Laura said, looking at Archie as if she wanted to make him disappear right there and then. 'And, no, Carly isn't a part of this, so you can wipe that worried look off your face.'

James checked his watch. 'It's gone a quarter to,' he said. 'Miss Burrows is normally here by now. I can't remember her ever being late before.'

Speaking of being late, Archie thought, *where the heck are you, Isabelle ...*

He heard footsteps behind him and turned to see her and the headmistress approaching down the corridor. And there was someone else with them who Archie hadn't expected to see ...

'Sally,' Archie said in a low voice. Surely she couldn't be a witch as well ... could she?

'Apologies for the delay in my arrival,' Miss Burrows said as she unlocked the door and opened it. 'I had some business to take care of.' She pulled her wand out of her bag and muttered some words as she moved it around the entrance. Then she stepped to the side and beckoned everyone to enter.

'Chop, chop – come on, let's get on with it, my little witches and wizards.'

Isabelle and Archie handed in their permission slips as they passed the headmistress.

Archie noticed some dirty looks being exchanged between the girls as everyone made their way into the room.

Laura went to the back, which is where Archie had expected her to go. Brad, or Chad, or whatever he was called, seated himself to the left, with James. Sally and Isabelle took seats together on the right, which just left Archie wondering where to plonk himself.

'There's plenty of seats available,' Miss Burrows said as she shut the door and made her way to her desk. 'Make yourself comfortable wherever you like, Archie.'

He seated himself in the centre of the room, at the front.

Miss Burrows unpacked some books and a few other things from her bag and then addressed the class: 'It's all change today as we have new starters. Please welcome Isabelle and Archie to the group,' she said, gesturing towards them, 'and please make sure that you help them wherever possible. This bit of a jump in numbers might have come as a shock to you all, but I'm sure we can all work together if we put our minds to it. We have one witch absent due to illness. Laura, you've raised your hand already. Why are you raising your hand?'

'Does this mean we're going to have to do some boring beginner spells this lesson?' Laura asked her.

'No, I'll find you something more challenging to do, so don't worry.'

'So what happens if someone wants to come here and play draughts?' Archie inquired. 'And what happens if someone walks in on us while we're doing magic? Shouldn't you at least lay some boards out on the desks with the pieces, so that it looks like we're playing?'

'Miss Burrows has been holding these classes for some time now,' Laura chirped in from behind him, 'so don't you think she'll have already considered all of that, eh?'

The headmistress explained: 'Before we entered, I cast a charm in the doorway that will let me know if anyone is approaching.' She brought everyone's attention to a small stack of draughts set boxes on a shelf to the left. 'I can have those unpacked and laid out in a matter of seconds. With regards to someone wanting to play draughts, I'm sorry to say that I have to dissuade them from practising the noble hobby at the school. A simple charm does the trick.'

'Well, that sucks for the draughts fans, if there are any,' Archie said. 'But do you really have to bother with some sort of alarm bell charm where the door is concerned? Wouldn't it be easier to just lock it?'

'Locking the door would look suspicious,' Miss Burrows answered. 'Anyone trying to enter would want to know why we were locking ourselves away to play a board game. Plus, there's the caretaker to consider. Mr Jones is a bit of a busybody, as you've undoubtedly noticed. The last thing I want to do is arouse suspicion with him. Memory wipes can be tricky to perform and so I'd rather avoid them, where possible.'

'Fair enough,' Archie said.

'Have you got any more questions?' Miss Burrows asked him. 'Or can we continue with the lesson now?'

Archie could feel that everyone was staring at him and he didn't like it. 'Eh, yeah, sure,' he said, happy to have the focus of attention deflected away from him.

'Okay,' Miss Burrows said, looking around the room at everyone with a keen expression, 'let's form two groups. Laura, you can pair up with Brad and James. Archie, you go with the girls.'

'Do I really have to?' Laura said, disgusted at the prospect.

'You don't have to do anything you don't want to,' Miss Burrows said impatiently. 'And you don't have to be here if you don't want to be either. The choice is yours, my dear.'

Begrudgingly gathering up her stuff, Laura dragged her feet as she moved to be with the boys.

Archie picked up his bag and seated himself across from the girls.

'You've been lumbered with me,' he said to them.

'I think we'll cope,' Isabelle said.

'Why didn't you tell me that Sally is a witch?' Archie asked her in a low voice.

'I'll explain after class,' Isabelle replied. 'For now, just be quiet – otherwise you'll get us shouted at.'

Miss Burrows appeared next to them. 'Are you okay to do some beginner spells with Archie?' she said to the girls. 'Sally, you've been attending for quite some time now, so I know these will be a little below you. Just look at it as a refresher. Isabelle, you're new like Archie, but I witnessed you proficiently perform a spell, so I dare say that you're already a more than competent witch.'

'I've been practising magic for years,' Isabelle informed her, 'but I don't mind doing some beginner spells with Archie to help him out.'

'Me neither,' Sally said.

'Excellent!' Miss Burrows said, smiling at all three of them. 'I do love to see teamwork amongst my students. Now, if you'd all like to turn to page 14 in your spell books, you can get shrinking and unshrinking things. And don't go shrinking each other. Yes, it's hilarious – but just don't do it. You're here to learn magic, not have a laughfest.' She left them to it and went to sort out the other group.

'I really wouldn't want someone to shrink me,' Archie said as he skimmed through his book to the correct page. 'Imagine if it went wrong and I got stuck at a micro size. Have you seen that movie *Honey I Shrunk the Kids*? It'd be like that. Ants and spiders would be huge compared to me. And they'd be trying to eat me, along with loads of other insects.' He shuddered at the thought. 'I *hate* spiders.'

'Me too,' Isabelle said, putting a reassuring hand on his

arm, 'so we'll make sure you stay normal size.'

'So what shall we shrink then?' Sally said, looking around for something to use.

'Not your brain,' Laura said from the other side of the room. 'I don't think it'd be possible to make it any smaller!'

'*Hey!*' Miss Burrows said, glaring at her. 'I'll have no nastiness in this lesson, little miss. You're not with your troublesome friends now, so there's no need to show off. You keep things civil or don't bother attending. Have you got that?'

'Sorry,' Laura said, 'but I just couldn't resist.' And she couldn't help but throw a mean look toward Archie's group.

'You just concentrate on summoning fireballs and then extinguishing them,' Miss Burrows said. 'You've been wanting to do it for weeks and now's your chance. It's a difficult spell and requires a *lot* of concentration. Are you sure you're up to it?'

'Yes, I'm up to it,' Laura assured her.

'Me too,' Brad said eagerly.

'And me,' James said, grinning at the prospect.

'Well, have at it then,' Miss Burrows said, stepping back and beckoning them to commence.

'Fireballs?' Archie said to the girls. 'They're going to be summoning fireballs? Is that wise?'

'Miss Burrows is keeping a close eye on them,' Sally said, 'so don't worry; they won't burn the place down.' She continued to look around for something they could shrink, but she couldn't see anything appropriate. 'Look, we'll just use my book. I know this spell by heart, so I don't need it anyway. Shall I go first?'

'Sure,' Isabelle said.

Archie nodded.

With a twinkle in her eyes, Sally produced her wand, pointed it at the book, then said the magical words: 'Remormodent Parvusio!'

Archie watched in amazement as the book shrunk to

about a fifth of its original size.

'You need to roll the Rs and say the O with some oomph, just like I did,' Sally said to him. 'It may not be the most interesting spell you'll ever perform, but it's definitely a handy one to know for hiding stuff and carrying things you wouldn't otherwise be able to carry.'

Archie thought of his cauldron, which was still tucked away in his bag.

'And once you've shrunk something,' Isabelle said, 'you'll then need to unshrink it at some point.' She did the reverse spell – 'Reformodent Crescoria!' – and the book popped back to its original size. 'Again, rolling your Rs, then sounding the S out in Crescoria, like a hissing snake.'

Isabelle had looked as if she were performing the most mundane of tasks, but to Archie what she had just done – what both the girls had done – was nothing short of awesome. He just hoped he could pronounce the words correctly and not make himself look like a fool.

'Go on then,' Isabelle said, encouraging him. 'Your go. Picture in your mind what size you want it to be.'

Pulling his wand out of his bag, Archie pointed it at the book and attempted to say the magical words: 'Remormodent Parvusio!'

And ... nothing happened. Archie's shoulders slumped in disappointment.

'You didn't say the O with enough oomph,' Laura said from the other side of the room. 'Oh, and you're gripping that wand too tightly. There's no need to be so tense. Just relax a little.'

'Er, excuse me,' Miss Burrows said, looming over her. 'You need to forget about them and concentrate on what's happening here.'

James had conjured a small fireball and was levitating it in the palm of his hand with a big grin on his face. 'And on only the second attempt, too,' he said proudly.

'Cool,' Archie said. 'I can't *wait* to do something like that.'

Isabelle said, 'Forget about even attempting something like that for now.'

'It can take a lot of practice to truly master such a spell,' Laura said. She nodded towards James. 'He was only able to do it on the second attempt because he's a square-head geek who studies and practises magic any chance he can get.'

'Or it could just be because I'm a powerful wizard,' James said indignantly. He was so busy glaring at Laura through his thick-lens glasses that he didn't notice the fireball beginning to grow larger and brighter above his palm.'

Miss Burrows had heard and seen enough. She clapped her hands together, getting everyone's attention. 'James, please keep an eye on what you are doing,' she said irritably. 'Laura, please stop interacting with the other group – otherwise I'm *really* going to lose my temper. Concentrate on what's happening in your group and you might be able to perform the spell when it's your turn.' Miss Burrows looked toward Archie and the girls. 'I know what's happening on this side of the room must seem a lot more interesting but please just focus on the task I've set you, otherwise we won't be able to cover everything I want to cover in this lesson.'

'Okay,' Isabelle said to Archie, 'give it another go. And remember to roll the R in Remormodent and give some oomph to the O in Parvusio. You can do this. I *know* you can.'

Steadying himself, Archie gave it another try ... and was pleasantly surprised when the book shrunk to the size that he'd imagined.

'Well done,' Sally said. 'You just performed your first spell.'

'Bravo!' Isabelle said, giving him a quiet round of applause. 'And now you've got to get it back to how it was before.'

Archie did this at the first attempt.

'Wow!' Sally said. 'I think we may have a natural here. It took me about six or seven attempts to do both spells when I first attempted it.'

'Yeah,' Isabelle said, 'it took me three or four , if I

remember rightly.'

Something occurred to Archie. 'Why didn't your parents shrink all your stuff when you were moving in?' he asked Isabelle. 'All the furniture and other bits? You wouldn't have needed a removal van, because you could have fit it all inside of a large holdall.'

'We wanted to appear to be as normal as possible,' she explained. 'Which meant moving in properly and not having everything just mysteriously appear out of nowhere. *That* could have raised some eyebrows. The last thing we want to do is attract attention to ourselves, for obvious reasons.'

'Ah, yes,' Archie said, 'I never thought of that. But your parents told my parents that you're from down south and then your parents – or whoever was driving the van – made the second journey in a ridiculously short time. And both vanloads were unloaded in a ridiculously short time too. Wouldn't *that* raise some eyebrows?'

Isabelle gave him a tired look. 'Well, it raised yours,' she said.

Sally puffed her cheeks out and twiddled her thumbs, which was enough to let Archie know that he should just shut up.

Laura let out a giggle on the other side of the room, but it wasn't directed towards them. Brad had just tried to manifest his fireball but had only managed to produce a cloud of thick, choking, black smoke.

'Now come on, you know that laughing at other students' attempts at magic is a big no-no. This is your last warning to behave yourself, Laura,' Miss Burrows said to her. 'One more incidence of silliness or dissent and you're out of here. And just remember that it's your go in a bit and that the last laugh could be on you.' She then cast a spell which sucked up the smoke with the tip of her wand.

Laura looked on sullenly, her bottom lip pooching slightly out.

Archie, on the other hand, was amazed at what he was

witnessing. 'Cool! She's using it like a hoover.' he said to the girls. 'I still can't believe that Laura is here. How can she be trusted to keep this a secret and not tell Carly, or anyone else for that matter?'

Sally said. 'If she was going to say something to anyone, I think she'd have done it by now. Our headmistress is a smart lady. Do you think she'd have let her take part if there was any danger that she might expose what we're doing here? I think not. And Laura isn't as bad as what you think she is. When she's not with Carly, she's okay – kind of. I think she's just been around her for that long that the meanness has just rubbed off on her and she feels the need to maintain this hard-girl image, even when Carly isn't around. I'd imagine the same is true of Carly's other sidekick: Ruby. Believe it or not, Laura helped me with a potion I was struggling with in the last lesson.'

This came as a surprise to Archie, who couldn't imagine Laura helping anyone with anything.

'*Yay!*' she blurted.

Archie turned to see that Brad had successfully managed to summon a fireball on his second attempt, much to his delight.

'Very well done,' Miss Burrows said, congratulating him.

'Nice one, mate,' James said, wiping hair away from his fringe.

'Right,' Archie said, turning his attention back to the girls, 'so what are we doing next?'

Isabelle tapped the book with her finger. 'We're shrinking and unshrinking this until we're told otherwise,' she said. 'You practise a spell until it becomes second nature – until you can do it without even giving it any thought.'

'Okay,' Archie said, readying himself again.

'Uh-uh,' Sally said, shaking her finger at him. 'It's my turn.'

'But you must be able to do this spell blindfolded,' Archie said.

'It doesn't matter,' Isabelle said. 'You can never do a spell too many times.'

'Okay,' Archie said, gesturing for Sally to go ahead. 'But will we be doing anything else in this lesson?'

A figure appeared at his side and he knew it was the headmistress without even looking.

'You want to shoot lightning from the end of your wand and make things disappear in a puff of smoke, yes?' she said, but she didn't wait for an answer. 'The worst thing you can do with magic is try to run before you can walk. This can result in disappointment and potentially dangerous outcomes. Concentrate on the tasks I set you and you'll soon get to the more interesting stuff. You did well with that first spell. Now keep up the good work.'

Laura had summoned her fireball and somehow made it larger than the ones the other two had managed. It glowed brightly above her palm as she smiled and looked around to see who was watching.

'It's a shame you can't show the same dedication to your school work as you do to your magic,' Miss Burrows said. 'You'd be quite the student.'

The fireball dimmed a little as the smile faded from Laura's face.

About halfway through the lesson, the headmistress called a halt to what the two groups were doing and congratulated everyone on their performances. 'Next, I'd like you to take turns immobilizing each other with the statue spell,' she said to Laura and the two boys. 'Again, this is not an easy one, by any means – but I'm confident you can all handle it with some practice.'

'I don't know whether to be excited or not,' Brad said with a torn expression. 'I'm looking forward to immobilizing you pair but I'm not looking forward to being immobilized.'

'Me neither,' said James.

'You're such a pair of wimps,' Laura said, sneering at them.

Archie remembered reading about the statue spell the day before and was excited at the prospect of seeing it cast (even if he wasn't the one doing the casting).

'Will they be able to breathe while they're immobilized?' he asked.

'Yes,' Sally answered.

Miss Burrows addressed their group: 'You can try levitating things. Anything you like, as long as it's not breakable. I'm going to get some paperwork done, but if any of you need anything or have any questions, don't hesitate to ask.' She went back to her desk.

'I guess we may as well use this again,' Sally said, giving her book a poke with her wand. She did not look enthusiastic.

'I'm sorry you're having to do boring stuff with me,' he said. 'Maybe next week they'll pair you with someone else and you can do something more interesting.'

'There's no boring stuff in magic,' Isabelle said. 'It's just that some spells are more exciting than others.'

'I'm not going to lie,' Sally said to Archie, 'I would really like to have done the statue spell, but I'm sure we'll get our chance to do it at some point, so no problems there.'

'You can do it next week,' Miss Burrows said, looking up from her paperwork. 'Don't worry, you won't miss out.'

Sally smiled at her and then said in a low voice: 'Damn, I forgot that our headmistress has superhuman hearing.'

Miss Burrows glanced at her with an expression which suggested that she could still hear her.

Sally rolled her eyes as if to suggest that she might never speak again. And then she did: 'Okey-dokey,' she said, raising her wand, 'I guess I may as well go first again.'

When it was Archie's turn – Motus Moblata! – he managed to make the book float on the third attempt, much to his delight. It felt good to finally do the spell that he'd witnessed Isabelle perform when he'd first laid eyes on her. She gave him an approving nod and smile.

On the other side of the room, it was Laura's turn to be

immobilized. James performed the spell and struck her motionless in an instant.

'Can we keep her like that?' Sally said.

'You do know she can hear you, right?' Brad said.

'Err, yeah, of course,' Sally replied, clearly lying. 'I was just joking.'

When James performed the reverse spell on Laura, the first thing she did was turn and glare at Sally with a look of thunder on her face.

'I really was joking,' Sally assured her.

Laura opened her mouth to say something, but the headmistress beat her to it. 'All right, it's nearly time to go,' she said as she rose from her seat and moved in front of her desk so she could address the class. 'Begin packing away your things, please. As usual, make sure you don't forget anything. We wouldn't want any of your magical items to fall into the wrong hands, now, would we?'

Archie began packing away his things.

'So, did you enjoy your first lesson?' Miss Burrows said as she came towards him.

'Oh yeah,' he replied, smiling. 'And I can't wait till I can immobilize people and make fireballs and mix potions and ride around on a broomstick. I'm *especially* looking forward to that last one.'

'Yes, everyone is always very eager to ride a broomstick,' Miss Burrows said.

'So where do you do that, then?' Archie inquired. 'Not in here, obviously.'

'Why, in the sports hall, of course,' Miss Burrows said. 'We'd love to do it outside, but we can't for reasons I'm sure I don't need to explain.'

'Cool!' Archie said. *Oh my God, magic is awesome!* he thought, twitching with excitement.

The other group said their goodbyes as they were leaving.

Archie noticed that Laura was glaring at Sally, who'd noticed too and was keen not to hold her gaze.

'Are we allowed to practice magic at home?' Archie asked the headmistress.

'You would even if I told you that you shouldn't,' she replied, giving him a knowing look. 'All I ask is that you exercise some common sense and only do spells and potions you've already done in class. Do not attempt anything liable to burn your house down, or cause physical harm to anyone, or draw unnecessary attention to you. Are we clear about this?'

'Crystal,' Archie replied.

'Right, I'm going to have to shoot off as I've got somewhere I need to be,' Miss Burrows said as she began putting her papers back in her bag.

'Me too,' Sally said, slinging her bag over her shoulder as she made for the door. 'See you tomorrow!'

After they'd gone, Archie once again asked Isabelle why she hadn't mentioned that Sally is a witch.

'I didn't tell you because I wanted it to be a surprise. When I first started here, I felt drawn to her – because, as you know, I'm a vampire. That's why I became friends with her. The mightier witches and wizards are easier to identify, due to the power they emanate. Ones like Sally, who aren't very powerful at all, are not so easy to identify. But I picked up enough from her to know what she was.'

'Sally isn't very powerful? But she shrunk that book with no problems. And she made it float.'

'They're easy spells. I'm not sure she would even be able to produce that fireball that the others did. We'll find out exactly what she can and can't do in the weeks and months to come.'

'And what about you? Are you a powerful witch?'

Isabelle gave him a curious look. 'I'd like to think that I'm not too shabby,' she said with a smile playing at the corners of her mouth. 'I've got some game, as the saying goes. Which brings us to the next question that you're going to ask. How powerful are *you*? Let's just say that I knew there was a witch or wizard around as soon I moved into our new home. Even though I was a good distance from you, I was still picking up those vibes, as I like to call them. I told my dad about you and he said that you could be "one to watch"'.

'You said that you weren't going to tell your parents about me because they'd worry about what we'd get up to together.'

Isabelle shrugged. 'I know I did,' she said, 'but I changed my mind. After I gave it some thought, I figured they'd be happy for me to be in your company, because I'll be safer around you. And that's exactly how they saw it.'

'Ah, right, okay. So I'm like your powerful guardian angel, or something, yeah? Is that how they'll view me now?'

'Not quite. But if it makes you feel better to think of yourself as one, then you go right ahead.'

'Yeah, yeah, I like that,' Archie said, grinning like a buffoon.

He couldn't believe what he'd just heard. Not only was he a wizard, he was a *powerful* one at that (and even a bit of a guardian angel to boot, by gab!).

'You made those spells you did look very easy,' Isabelle commented.

'Crikey, I didn't think I could be more buzzing than I was when I first found out I was a wizard but I'm *really* buzzing now. I can't *wait* to see what I can do!'

'I'm eager to see what you can do too. But it's going to have to wait because we need to get out of here before the caretaker comes sniffing around.'

They walked home together, talking mostly about magic. But as they rounded the corner onto Salt Road, Archie asked Isabelle if there'd been any news regarding Barrick and his efforts to find her and her family.

'Well, I've been looking over my shoulder everywhere I go and I haven't noticed anyone following me, so I guess that's a positive sign. Fingers crossed that it stays that way.'

'Maybe I did imagine that shadowy figure. Did you tell your parents?'

'No. And I'm not going to, either. As I said to you before, it'll just cause unnecessary panic. I'd need evidence of something a little more concrete than a shadowy figure which may or may not have been across from our house before I turn our lives upside down again.'

As they approached her house, Archie noticed the downstairs curtains open a little and a large, round face appear in the gap.

'Err, your dad is staring at us,' Archie said.

'I know. Just don't stare back, or you might encourage him. He's quite eager to talk to you.'

'Is he?' Archie said, slightly alarmed. 'Why?'

'He's intrigued by your power.'

'Ah,' Archie said, not sure how he felt about this. 'And what about your mum? Is she intrigued by my power? Does she want to have a powwow as well?'

'My mum is curious, yes. But only because my dad told her about you. She's not a witch. She's just a Normal: like the rest of your family.'

'Oh, right,' Archie said, enthralled by this new piece of information. 'Your parents do know that I'm a noob, right? They do know that I don't actually know any magic yet, yeah?'

'That's not true. You know how to levitate and shrink things and do a Force Push.'

'I do,' Archie said, puffing his chest out proudly. 'But I don't know how to defend myself as such. The last time I asked if you could teach me some magic you said no, but things have changed since then. So ... will you teach me some spells?'

'I can do – at the weekend. Some of them can be very tricky to master, but I'm sure you'll handle them.'

'Cool!' Archie said, imagining himself shooting lightning bolts from the tip of his wand.

'My dad is still staring at us,' Isabelle said, 'so I better go in before he comes out.'

Archie waved goodbye to her as she disappeared down the pathway and into the house. He looked towards the curtains and saw that the face was no longer there. He figured that Mr Lockhart was probably quizzing Isabelle in the hallway, asking her what they'd been talking about.

Not lingering for a second longer, Archie made for his own house and was of course greeted by Mrs Wiggins as soon as he entered through the front door.

'So, how did it go?' she inquired. 'Did you enjoy your draughts session?'

'Yes,' Archie replied, trying to look as enthusiastic as possible. 'It was very ... interesting and ... challenging ... and strategic.'

'Will you go again?'

'He will do if he wants to get a reputation for being a *dork*,' Oliver said as he passed him on the way to the kitchen.

'Ignore your brother,' Mrs Wiggins said. 'The most strategic and challenging thing he does in a day is getting out of bed.'

'That's not fair,' Oliver said, 'I play some very challenging and strategic games on my XBOX, I'll have you know!'

'That's not something I can be proud of you for, though, is it?' Mrs Wiggins said.

Mr Wiggins appeared behind her. 'Did you win any games?' he asked Archie. 'I do love draughts. We've got that set in the garage, if you're interested? I'm not much of a player, but I might be able to give you a run for your money, what with you being a novice and all.'

'Maybe tomorrow,' Archie said as he began edging towards the stairway.

He made it to the landing before he was halted by his mum's voice calling up to him: 'Your dinner is in the microwave! It's pepperoni pizza! Don't let it go to waste!'

As if I would, he thought.

In his bedroom, he got his magical items out of his bag, laid them on his bed, and marvelled at them. He'd enjoyed his first lesson every bit as much as he was sure he would. Now that he'd got a taste for doing magic, he wanted to do more – and he wanted to do it now! *Miss Burrows told me it was okay to practice at home*, he thought, reaching for his wand. He figured he could levitate something – but then he heard footsteps *thudding* up the stairs and abandoned the idea. The last thing he needed was Oliver catching him with all his new items, so he stashed them under his bed, out of sight. Archie decided that if he was going to practise then he needed to be sensible about when and where to do it. This clearly wasn't the time or place, what with his whole family being at home and liable to burst in on him at any moment.

With his tummy grumbling from hunger, Archie knew that the best thing he could do was scoff the pizza, so that's what he did.

Later that evening, when Archie retired to his bedroom, he checked the street for signs of anything unusual. There were no shadowy figures to be seen and nothing else untoward caught his eye. A quick scan of the moonlit sky did not reveal any night-flyers on broomsticks, ready to swoop down and exact retribution. And so Archie really was beginning to think that his imagination had got the better of him a few nights before. *The shadowy figure really must have been no more than a trick of the light*, he thought as he closed his curtains and got into bed. It didn't take him long to drift off to sleep.

In the early hours of the morning, Archie opened his eyes slightly and, after a moment of disorientation, he noted the time on his digital clock: 02:30. He yawned, wondering why on earth he was awake at such a ridiculous hour. A strange sense of something being not quite right was welling up inside of him.

Sliding from beneath his covers, he went to the window

and pushed the curtains back. He checked the street and saw nothing untoward. The sky was still dotted with stars and free from flying broomsticks. As far as he could see, there was no reason to feel alarmed. And yet he still did feel alarmed. So much so that he stood there for about ten minutes, checking left and right and scanning the sky.

It wasn't until he'd finally decided that he was wasting his time that he made the decision to go back to bed. As he went to close his curtains, he stopped and watched as two cone-shaped headlights appeared at the end of the road and began edging slowly closer. Pressing his face to the glass to get a better look, Archie watched as an unusual-looking, long, sleek, black car with a red lightning bolt down the side pulled up across from Isabelle's house. Archie couldn't see who was in the vehicle but sirens were sounding inside his head.

Snatching up his mobile phone, he fingered Isabelle's name and she picked up after the fourth ring, sounding groggy and disorientated.

'Erm, you need to look out of your front window,' Archie said in a low voice.

He heard her get out of bed, the sound of a curtain being hastily pushed to the side. And then Isabelle replied: 'Oh God, I need to wake my parents.' She didn't sound groggy and disorientated now. Not in the slightest.

Archie could now hear her moving through the house, opening doors.

'Should I call the police?' he asked her.

But she didn't reply because she was too busy explaining to her parents that they were about to be descended on by a bunch of gangsters.

Archie repeated the question, this time with a lot more urgency: 'Isabelle, should I call the police?'

'No!' she replied. 'Do not do that! Do *not* involve them!'

'Why?' Archie said, pacing back and forth in his bedroom. 'Why don't you want them involved? They'll be able to help.'

'No, they won't; you'll just be putting them in harm's

way.'

Archie heard Isabelle's father yelling in the background: 'Get off that phone and get dressed! Get dressed *NOW!*'

'I've got to go,' Isabelle said. And then there was silence.

'Hello! Hello!' Archie said, clutching the phone tightly to his ear. 'Isabelle, are you still there? D'you want me to come around? D'you want me to come and help? Hello! *Hello!* Are you still there?'

The continued silence of a terminated call told him that she wasn't.

Archie heard bedsprings pinging and the sound of his mother groaning.

Oh poop! he thought. The last thing he needed was for the rest of his family to get involved in this and put them in danger. He stayed still for a few seconds: long enough to be sure that she wasn't about to come investigating a disturbance – then he went back to the window to see what was happening across the street.

Five men, dressed in dark suits, were now outside of the vehicle, looking and pointing towards their target house. Archie remembered the description he'd been given of Barrick and how tall he was, so he was easy to pick out. He led his followers across the street and then held his hands out to either side of him, halting them.

'He knows the Bubble Barrier is there,' Archie whispered. 'He's sensed it.'

Isabelle had told Archie not to call the police, but he was of a mind to do it anyway. He thumbed the numbers into his phone and then paused for a second with his finger over the enter button. They won't be able to help. That's what she'd said to him.

Looks like it's down to me then, Archie thought as he reached under the bed to retrieve his wand. He quickly got dressed, tucked the wand down the front of his bottoms, then crept downstairs to put on his trainers. As he was edging through the hallway he heard bed springs pinging and his mother once again groaning, so he waited for a minute before he turned the key in the door and exited soundlessly onto the pathway at the front of the house.

Keeping low, he moved towards the fence which separated his house from Isabelle's. He could hear a fizzing noise as he got closer and wondered what could be happening. But it was all too obvious what the new arrivals would be doing and a peek over the fence confirmed that they were trying to break through the invisible barrier. Barrick was standing behind the four other men, who were blasting the barrier with lightning bolts from the tips of their wands. Resting his back against one of the panels, Archie listened as Barrick spoke: 'That's it, boys, keep your beams concentrated on the same area and we'll soon be through this.'

Archie wondered what was happening with Isabelle and her parents. Had they fled from the house through the back door? Were they on their broomsticks, flying high and away from danger?

What Barrick had to say next scuppered any thoughts of that. 'Ha-ha! Look at their scared little faces staring out at us. They've probably just realised that there's no getting away this time. They've realised that they're surrounded on all sides and that their time is up.'

Archie heard a whizzing sound and looked up to see another five people on broomsticks, silhouetted in the moonlight, looping overhead. Realising that he would be spotted by them, he relocated himself beneath a hydrangea tree which was at the end of the fence, close to the pavement. The small tree's lollipop head screened him well from the broomstick riders.

Barrick had said that the house was surrounded on all sides, which meant that the rear of the property was covered by his men too. Which meant that there really was no way out for Isabelle and her parents. With the odds stacked so heavily against him, Archie wondered what he could do to help.

He figured that he could try a distraction – but he wasn't sure which type of distraction he could create. He only knew two spells ... And then it came to him. Isabelle had told him that he was a powerful wizard, so now it was time to put that power to the test.

Peaking around the side of the fence, he pulled out his wand and pointed it at Barrick's car.

'Keep at it, boys,' the Barrick said, 'another minute or two and you'll be through it. Then we can have some fun – and a good dose of retribution.'

Not if I've got anything to do with it, you aren't, Archie thought as he continued to point his wand at the car. And then, in a low but forceful voice, he said the magical words for the spell he was attempting to cast: Motus Moblata!

He watched and ... nothing happened. The car did not move. It stayed exactly where it was, its wide tyres firmly grounded on the tarmac.

Archie gave it another go: saying the words a bit more forcefully this time (while still keeping his voice as low as possible). And ... nothing happened again.

Meanwhile, Barrick's men were very close to punching a hole through the barrier with their lightning strikes. Archie knew that if he was going to do something then he needed to do it *now* – before it was too late.

Focusing on a new target, something which should be somewhat less of a challenge, he levelled his wand at the nearest suit and once again said the magical words. Archie watched in amazement as the man began levitating above the ground with a look of terror on his rugged face.

Archie's distraction had the desired effect. All the suits broke off the attack to look around and see who was casting the spell.

'It'll be them in the house!' one of them declared.

'No,' Barrick said in a cool, calm voice, 'I'm shielding you from them.'

Realising he was about to get busted, Archie moved to

hide back behind the fence. But it was too late – Barrick's gaze was already upon him.

The suit that Archie had been levitating let out an '*Oomph!*' of pain as he dropped to the pavement in a crumpled heap. The other suits picked him up and steadied him so he wouldn't fall back down.

Archie wanted to run – but he didn't; he stood his ground and readied himself with his wand. He wasn't sure whether to try the levitation spell again, or have a crack at shrinking someone ...

'Well, well, well,' Barrick said, eyeing him curiously. 'Look at what we've got here. 'A little wizard – and a brave little one at that. And also perhaps a stupid one. You had a free shot at us. You could have used any spell and you chose to make one of us float above the ground.' He made a *tsking* sound and shook his head to show his disapproval.

Archie didn't like being called stupid, but he wasn't about to admit to being a noob just so this Barrick wouldn't think he was an idiot. 'I've called the police,' Archie said. 'It won't take them long to get here, so you and your thugs should just go now while you can.'

'Thugs?' one of the suits said, pretending to be offended. 'Who are you calling a thug, short stuff?'

Out of the corner of his eye, Archie could see Isabelle and her parents looking on from inside the house.

Above him, the suits on broomsticks circled like vultures, swooping in out of the darkness.

'As if I'm going to be worried about the police,' Barrick said, taking a step closer to Archie and raising his wand. 'I feel a great deal of power emanating from you. I'm sure that you would have gone on to become a fantastic wizard. But I don't have time to waste here, so it is with deep regret that I'm going to have to snuff out your flame before it becomes a raging fire.'

A surge of despair swept through Archie as he raised his wand in an attempt to at least try to defend himself.

'You leave that boy alone!'

Archie turned to see that Isabelle and her parents were now standing in the garden. Isabelle and her father had their wands at the ready and Mrs Lockhart, looking terrified, was clutching a rolling pin to her chest with a shaky hand.

'He's nothing to do with this,' Mr Lockhart said, 'so just let him be!'

'Ah, you're so brave over there behind your barrier,' Barrick said, turning his attention to the Lockhart family. 'But not safe. We're nearly through it, so you may as well step out on the pavement and get this over and done with. You have a debt to pay – and it's a heavy one.'

'There's no debt to pay,' Mr Lockhart said, his bald head glistening with sweat. 'Your brother was drunk and tried to assault me. All I did was push him away in self-defence. It's not my fault that he hit his head on a rock and it's not my fault that he died.'

'It's pointless trying to explain it to him,' Mrs Lockhart said, her eyes as wide as saucers as she looked frantically around, trying to account for everyone who'd come for vengeance. 'He's made up his mind and nothing we say is going to change anything.'

Barrick levelled a finger at Mr Lockhart. 'You are a wizard – and a good one at that!' he said. 'Are you seriously trying to tell me that you couldn't have prevented him from falling and hurting himself? And don't give me any wishy-washy excuse about not having your wand with you or not being able to pull it out in time; you could have stopped what was going to happen and we both know it.'

'Yes, I could have prevented him from falling,' Mr Lockhart admitted, 'but I didn't know he was going to hit his head on a rock. It was dark in that car park, so I couldn't see the ground very well.'

'It's dark where you're going,' Barrick said as he raised his wand and pointed it at Mr Lockhart. 'I think it's time to finally break through this barrier, don't you?' Barrick opened his mouth to say some magical words ...

But then, out of the sky, three dark hooded figures on broomsticks landed near Archie.

'Haven't you got enough of your people here already?' he said to Barrick. 'Do you really need any more?'

'Nothing to do with me,' he said with a slight look of concern on his face.

Archie distanced himself from the new arrivals. *Who the heck are these people?* Archie thought.

'Please leave this family alone and let them live their lives,' the figure in the middle said.

Archie recognised the voice ...

Miss Burrows!

She took a step forwards and pulled back her hood. And then the other two stepped forwards as well, pulling back their hoods to reveal Mr Gibb, the PE teacher and Mrs Hickinbottom, the owner of the Enchanted Cove.

'Who in the blue hell are you lot?' Barrick said.

'Who we are is of no concern to you,' Miss Burrows replied. From inside of her robes, she produced her wand. 'You just need to leave this place and not return.'

Barrick gestured towards the suits on the ground and in the air. 'You are heavily outnumbered and have no chance of winning here. And so I'll give you a bit of advice. Get your bums back on those broomsticks and fly away, back to wherever you came from. If you're as smart as I think you are, then that's exactly what you'll do. And then I'll forget I ever laid eyes on you. Or you can just stay ... and die. The choice is yours.'

Miss Burrows signalled towards a house on the right: number 34. 'We seem to have attracted an audience,' she said. 'That woman who's in the upstairs window with the phone cupped to her ear? Who do you suppose she's calling? Her mother? Her brother? Or could it be the police? I know which one my money's on.'

'Well now that's easily sorted,' Barrick said, pointing his

wand in the woman's direction.

'And what about those people over there?' Mr Gibb said loudly as he pointed towards a house a few doors down on the left. 'Are you going to "sort" them as well? Looks like there's a whole family in that window beneath the eaves, watching this circus unfold.'

'I'll do whatever it takes to get revenge,' Barrick said.

'Not with us around, you won't,' Mrs Hickinbottom assured him.

'We'll see about *that*,' Barrick said, gripping his wand tightly as the suits lined up behind him, ready to fight. The ones on broomsticks landed and fanned out behind the others, also readying themselves to fight.

Archie did a headcount: ten baddies vs seven goodies. He didn't like the odds. And Barrick had mentioned that the rear of Isabelle's house was covered, which meant that there were other baddies around as well. No, Archie did not like these odds. He did *not* like them at all.

But he stepped out in the open anyway. If he could disable one of the suits with either of the spells he knew, then that would at least be something. He would be of some help to Isabelle and her posse, rather than a bystander who would need saving or just be in the way. He was *determined* to take at least one of the suits down.

And so was Isabelle, judging by the fiery look she was sporting. She looked at Archie and nodded. He nodded at her with a fiery look of his own.

'Your chance has passed,' Mr Gibb said to Barrick. 'You should flee while you still can.'

'And that's exactly what you'll do,' Miss Burrows said, mimicking what Barrick had said a short while before, 'if you're as smart as I think you are.'

A look of total rage spread across Barrick's face, a momentary crack in his otherwise cool facade. And then he regained his composure and issued a warning. 'This is not over by a long chalk, missus. I'm going to find out who you are – who *all* of you are,' he said, taking in the three wizards before him and marking them each with a sinister glare, 'and you will pay dearly for your interference here today. You have no idea who you're messing with.'

'Actually, we do,' Mrs Hickinbottom informed him. 'We know full well who you are – and you don't scare us.'

Archie noticed a lump forming in her throat as she spoke, which suggested that she was scared but putting on a brave face. Archie hoped that neither Barrick nor any of his cronies had seen this.

'People are filming us on their phones, now, look,' Miss Burrows said, nodding towards Archie's house.

With some alarm, Archie turned to see Oliver in the spare bedroom window with one hand pressed against the glass and his iPhone in the other. He mouthed some words – something like: 'What are you doing?' And Archie's mouth dropped open in shock.

Oh crikey, he thought, *that's it – I'm for it now!* He looked towards the window again and noticed that Oliver wasn't there anymore. Archie figured that he'd gone to wake their parents. *Yep, I'm definitely for it – BIG time!*

'Like I care if anyone is filming me,' Barrick said to Miss Burrows. 'That's a mess I'll leave you to clear up.' He turned his attention to the Lockhart family and levelled his wand at Mr Lockhart. 'You've just made things worse for yourself and your family. I know where to find you. And if you move again, I'll find you *again*. Revenge is inevitable – and I'm going to savour *every* second of it.'

Barrick glared at Mr Lockhart as he began backing away towards his car with his men. But the most intense glare was reserved for Miss Burrows and her helpers. Especially the headmistress. Barrick did not blink as he got in the driver's side and gunned the engine. The suits who'd arrived on broomsticks took to the air and began whizzing about overhead.

Miss Burrows and the other two moved onto the pavement so that they wouldn't get mowed down by Barrick as he pulled off. As he passed, he locked eyes with Archie and didn't blink. The suits in the back gave him a more sinister look and then the ones on broomsticks whizzed away into the night, disappearing in the blink of an eye.

Archie wondered how long it would be before the police arrived. He figured they couldn't be much more than a quarter of a mile away at the most. This was assuming that the woman from number 34 had actually called the police, of course. Archie didn't know her name, but he did know her well enough to know that she was the sort of busy body to do just that.

'Thank you for coming so quickly,' Isabelle said to Miss Burrows and the other two.

'Thanks for coming at all,' Mr Lockhart said. 'If it weren't for you, we'd have been done for – and that's for sure.'

The Lockhart family stepped across the lawn and out from the protection of their magical bubble. Skittering forwards in her high heels and bursting into tears, Mrs Lockhart embraced the headmistress and began thanking the other two over and over.

'It's okay, you're safe now,' Mrs Hickinbottom assured her. 'You and your family are safe.'

'The magical community comes together to protect their own,' Mr Gibb said proudly. 'That's how it's always been – and rightly so.'

Archie felt himself shrink a little as Mr Lockhart's gaze fell upon him.

'And thank you, young sir, for standing up for us,' Isabelle's father said. 'What you did was brave and you performed that levitation spell very well for someone who's only just been introduced to magic.'

Archie could feel his cheeks flushing red as all eyes fell upon him. Isabelle smiled at him and he smiled back.

And that's when Mrs Wiggins burst out through the front door and blustered onto the pavement. She looked very concerned as she secured her dressing gown around her waist and took in everyone before her.

'What is going on here?' she said to Archie. 'Why are you out here with all these people?' Her eyes widened as she recognised the headmistress and the PE teacher. 'Miss Burrows and Mr Gibb, why are you standing in the street with my son and our next door neighbours in the small hours of the morning? And Oliver mentioned some sinister-looking individuals in suits, who did not look to be of a friendly persuasion?'

Mr Wiggins and Oliver, both dressed in their pyjamas, came up behind her, eyeing everyone suspiciously. Mr Wiggins looked especially blurry-eyed and confused.

Miss Burrows held up her hands in a calming gesture. 'Now I know that this must all look a bit strange, but if you'll just allow me to explain everything ...'

She was cut off, mid-sentence, by the arrival of the police. Two cars rounded the corner at the end of the round and drove quickly towards them with their blue lights flashing.

Miss Burrows gave Archie a tired look and said, 'Now this is a mess that's going to take me some time to sort out.'

And that's when another dark figure descended out of the night sky on a broomstick and landed next to Isabelle.

Sally! Archie thought.

'What's happening?' she said, looking around at everyone. 'Are you all okay? Sorry I'm late; I had a nightmare trying to get out of the house without my parents noticing me. Where's Barrick? Has he fled?'

'Who in the heck is Barrick?' Mrs Wiggins blurted. She gestured towards Sally. 'And did my eyes just deceive me or did this girl just land on a broomstick?'

'Yep, she definitely landed on a broomstick,' Oliver confirmed.

'I'm still in bed and dreaming,' Mr Wiggins said, shaking his head whilst looking flummoxed. 'I must be.'

Miss Burrows rolled her eyes at Archie. 'Yes, this is *definitely* going to take some time to sort out,' she said, holding up her wand as she turned to face the police officers who were advancing toward her.

The following day, Archie woke to the sound of his mother's voice yelling up the stairs, telling him to get his backside out of bed. 'You're not going to have any time for breakfast if you don't get down here now,' she said. There was a pause and then she added, '*Helllllo!* Can you hear me?'

Poking his head out from under the covers, he let out a croaky reply: 'Yes! I 'm getting up!'

He'd only got three hours' sleep. How he'd managed to get any at all, given everything that'd happened the night before, was a source of amazement to him. He stayed motionless for a minute or two, thinking about Barrick and his attempt to get to Isabelle and her family. He thought about Miss Burrows and the other two who'd come with her to help. And of Sally. It'd been a shock to see her as well, floating in at the last second with her better late than never appearance. But what'd surprised Archie the most was how he'd stood up to Barrick and the suits. He would never have believed that he could be so brave and so scared at the same time. And the thank you from Mr Lockhart had been the cream on the cake, making him feel the proudest he'd ever felt in his life.

'ARCHIE!'

Springing out of bed, Archie got himself dressed and rushed downstairs. He was greeted in the kitchen by Mrs Wiggins, who looked far from impressed.

'You went to bed early enough last night,' she said as she finished off a slice of toast, 'so why have you got up so late? Not playing on your phone until the early hours, I hope?'

'Of course not,' Archie replied, grabbing an apple off the side and heading back into the hallway.

'Is that all you're having to eat?' Mrs Wiggins said as she followed after him. 'That's not much of a breakfast. You'll be starving come dinnertime.'

'You're always telling me to eat more fruit,' Archie said, taking a bite of the apple. 'So here I am, eating fruit. I'll have a banana as well, if it'll make you feel better.'

'It would,' Mrs Wiggins said, retrieving one from the kitchen and handing it to her son.

By the front door, Archie slipped on his shoes and slung his bag over his shoulder.

Then Oliver came down the stairs and pushed his way past, en route to the living room. 'Oh look, it's the dork of the house,' he said.

'Well, I have to look on the bright side,' Archie said. 'Things could be worse – I could be you.'

'Dork!' Oliver said from the living room.

'Idiot!' Archie replied.

'Bonehead!'

'Berk!'

'Tool!'

'Moron!'

'Shut up!' Mrs Wiggins said, giving Archie a steely look because he was the one in front of her. 'Just give it a rest, the both of you! It's too early in the morning for fallouts!'

Mr Wiggins appeared at the bottom of the stairs, adjusting his tie. 'An argument is not the best way to start the day,' he said, wetting his fingers and running them across his eyebrows. 'Not that there's ever a good time of day to argue, of course.'

'He started it,' Archie said. 'Like he *always* does.'

'That's a scandalous accusation!' Oliver protested.

'It's the truth,' Archie said.

'Yeah, well, if you weren't such a dork ...' Oliver said. He was still in the living room.

'Just shut up, you fool!' Archie retorted.

'Twit!'

'Chump!'

'Clown!'

'Nincompoop!'

'Ha-ha! Is that the best you can do, bruv?'

'*QUIET!*' Mr Wiggins yelled, his nostrils flaring.

Everyone fell silent and stared at him, surprised by this rare, momentary outburst of anger.

And then Mrs Wiggins grabbed Archie by his shoulder and bundled him outside. 'Don't worry, I'll deal with your brother,' she said. 'He's just being off because he's got a dental appointment and you know how much he hates the dentist.' She closed the door with a bang, the sound of which was still reverberating in his ears by the time he reached the end of the driveway.

Why do I have to live in a house full of nutters? he thought. *Why can't I be part of a normal family?*

Archie stood on the spot where he'd faced off against Barrick and his suits the night before. It felt as if it'd been nothing more than a dream or the result of an overactive imagination. But he knew full well that a gangster vampire wizard and his followers really had been outside of Isabelle's house, trying to get to her and her parents so they could exact revenge. The thought of how close they came to getting that revenge made Archie feel weak with worry. And it wasn't just his next door neighbours he was worried about. There was Miss Burrows and the two others to consider. Barrick had promised to make all of them pay (Sally was the only one not in the firing line at the moment, but that was only because she'd turned up late). And, of course, Archie needed to consider himself and his family. By getting involved, he'd put them in danger as well. The realisation of this was beginning to hit home as he stayed rooted to the spot, staring down the street in a daze.

'Hey!'

Archie looked towards Isabelle's house and saw her approaching up the driveway. She was dressed all in black, with her hair tied up in a ponytail.

'I take it this means you're not going to school,' Archie said.

'My dad doesn't want me going anywhere today. He says it's too dangerous and Miss Burrows understands. My dad was a bit funny about me coming out here to see you, but I managed to convince him that I'll be okay with you to protect me. You'll probably see the curtains twitch in a minute because he isn't going to let me out of his sight for long.'

'After everything that's happened, I don't blame him for being concerned. I'd be the same if I was in his position. But he can't keep you locked up in your house forever. He'll have to let you out at some point.'

'Well, they've had me "locked up" for about an hour, since I got out of bed. My parents just want some time to think about what we're going to do next. My mum wants us to move again, but my dad says that there's no point. He says that Barrick will find us no matter where we go.'

'So you're just going to wait for him to come back. Next time he's going to be well prepared. He obviously didn't anticipate that there would be people brave enough to help you.'

'That's because there probably aren't that many people brave enough to stand up to him. But, yeah, you're right; he'll be well prepared next time. And so will we.'

'When you say we? Who do you mean, exactly? You and your parents, obviously – but what about Miss Burrows and the other two? Have you got them on speed dial, ready to leap into action if anything goes down? How did they even know that you were in trouble? How did they find out that Barrick was after you and your parents? And what about Sally? How did she find out?'

'Crikey,' Isabelle said, signalling for a time-out with her hands, 'ease off with the questions, yeah? Or at least hit me with just one at a time.'

'Sorry,' Archie said, 'but if my family's in danger then I need to know every detail of what's happened so that I can be ready for what's coming.'

'I didn't ask you to get involved in this. It was your choice.'

'Yes, it was my choice. I'll admit that part of me regrets getting involved because of the danger to my family. How dumb was I not to think that my parents and brother could get dragged into things! But ... a part of me doesn't regret helping you one bit. And if I had to make the choice again, knowing what I know now, I'd still help you.'

This made Isabelle smile. 'Thank you,' she said, gushing a little. 'You're quickly becoming my best friend. As far as Miss Burrows goes, it was Mrs Hickinbottom who put her onto me. When I went into the shop and bought the ingredients for the Bubble Barrier potion, Mrs Hickinbottom was very concerned and knew there could be something wrong. People only put them up when they need protection from someone or something, so she was sure that I was most likely in danger. Unbeknown to me, Mrs Hickinbottom and our headmistress don't just know each other; they happen to be very good friends. So Mrs Hickinbottom told Miss Burrows about me and she knew exactly who I was straight away.'

'You're lucky that they're friends. If Miss Burrows and the other two hadn't shown up, we wouldn't be having this conversation now, because we'd most likely be dead.'

'I didn't feel lucky when she summoned me to her office and began interrogating me. At first, I just told her that I was practising magic and had always wanted to put up a barrier because I thought it'd be something cool to do. But Miss

Burrows was having none of it. She told me that she could smell the lies coming off me and that I should just tell her the truth and be done with it.'

'How do you smell lies?'

'I don't know and I didn't ask. But it felt good to tell her about everything that'd happened. And I felt such relief when she told me that she would help me. And, of course, she got Mr Gibb and Mrs Hickinbottom involved too. Safety in numbers and all that. As far as Sally goes, she could tell that something was bothering me at school (something far more troubling than Carly and her friends). I kept telling her that I was okay and that nothing was wrong, but she's a bit like Miss Burrows in that she can detect lies. I told her that I didn't want her involved but she was insistent. She told me that I'd stood up for her where Carly was concerned so she wanted to be a proper friend and return the favour.'

'There's a difference between standing up to the school bully and taking on a gangster vampire wizard who's hell-bent on revenge. Are you sure she knows what she's getting herself into here?'

'She knows exactly what she's getting herself into. I told her everything about him and about everything that's happened.'

Archie was impressed. 'Okay, well, she sounds like a proper friend, especially considering you haven't known her for long.'

'A bit like you,' Isabelle said, smiling at him again. 'You are both *proper* friends.'

Unable to hold her gaze, Archie looked up and down the street at the different houses. 'Miss Burrows did a great job of making our neighbours forget about everything they saw last night. Although, I do have to wonder what will happen if she missed someone. She told me that she erased all the video footage that was recorded – including Oliver's – but what if she didn't do it right? What if someone uploads something to Youtube? How would Miss Burrows clean up a mess of *that* magnitude? She isn't going to hunt down everyone who views it and wipe their memories, I'm pretty sure.'

'She wouldn't need to. Youtube is full of videos of people doing fake magic, so that's what people would think it was:

just another fake video. And, besides, Mr Gibb was keeping a close eye on all the houses while it was all kicking off and he was adamant that he knew which ones we'd been watched from. Plus, I can't see our headmistress not doing a proper job of erasing footage from mobiles. She's *way* too thorough to make that sort of mistake.'

'Yeah, you're probably right,' Archie had to admit. 'My parents don't remember anything that happened and neither does my brother.'

'The spell Miss Burrows used on the police to persuade them that they weren't needed was pretty cool as well, don't you think? That's advanced magic and takes a *lot* of practice to master.'

'Miss Burrows has to be the coolest head of school ever.'

'Definitely.'

Archie was surprised by how unfazed Isabelle seemed to be by everything that'd happened. 'Aren't you worried at all? he asked her. 'If I was in your position, I'd be snatching glances everywhere, thinking that someone was going to jump out on me at any second.' He looked up and down the street again, snatching glances here and there himself. 'I'm worried – and I'm not even one of Barrick's direct targets.'

'The situation is what it is,' Isabelle said, looking as composed as ever. 'Of course I'm worried, but turning into a blubbering mess about it isn't going to help with things. My dad told me that one of the most important things is to stay calm and collected, so that's what I'm determined to do. I just wish my mum would take that advice. She's a blubbering mess at the moment.'

'I think my dad would be the same if he knew the trouble I'm meddling in. He's the blubberer in our family. I'd love to take the day off so I could be close to you, just in case Barrick comes back, but that would mean I'd have to pull a sickie and my mum knows when I'm faking it.'

'I'll be fine. He won't come back yet. He'll put a plan in place and then try to surprise us. We just need to be ready for him.' Isabelle checked the time on her phone. 'Erm, I think you might want to get a move on, otherwise you're going to be late.'

Archie checked his phone. 'Oh, yeah, crap, I'm going to have to jog,' he said as he took off down the road with his bag bobbing about on his back. 'We'll practice some spells when I get in from school, yeah? After I've had my dinner?'

'Yeah, of course,' Isabelle said, giving him a warm smile as he waved goodbye and then turned and began jogging.

Archie just managed to make it to school in time. The bell sounded as he neared the main entrance.

In his first class, Carly was being as irritating as ever, backed up as always by her two friends: Laura and Ruby (although Archie did notice that the former wasn't approaching the task with her usual level of enthusiasm, which could only be a good thing). Then Carly began throwing stuff at other students before focusing all her attention on Sally, who was doing her best to ignore her, but it wasn't easy when bits of balled-up paper were pinging off the back of her head.

The teacher was late arriving, so there was no one of authority around to intervene.

'Where's your weird friend?' Carly asked Sally. 'Has she stayed at home because of me? Is she too scared to come into school?'

Laura let out a kind of half-giggle. Ruby laughed out loud. And so did a few of the other students.

Sally, on the other hand, just sat rigid as a statue, staring dead ahead.

'Why don't you just leave her alone?' Archie said to Carly. 'And Isabelle isn't here today because she's ill. She isn't afraid of you. She isn't afraid of *any* of you. You just all need to shut your mouths and get a life.'

Ruby sucked in air dramatically as her eyes widened in surprise. Carly looked ready to powerslam Archie. Laura, on the other hand, didn't appear to be so sure of herself this time. She seemed torn between whether to support her friend or not (or at least that's how it looked to Archie). And the rest of the class watched with eager eyes, waiting to see what would happen next. The only person who looked worried was Sally – and Archie had a feeling that it was his wellbeing she was concerned about, not hers.

'Oh, you must like pain,' Carly said, seething.

Her seat scraped across the floor as she stood up. She went to advance on Archie ...

But then Laura grabbed her by the arm and said, 'Just leave it – he isn't worth it.'

Carly looked at her as if she'd been spoken to in a language she didn't understand – but then she said, 'Leave it? Are you kidding me? Have you gone soft or something?'

'Apologies for being late!'

Everyone turned to see that the teacher had arrived and was closing the door behind her. 'Take your seats, please, everyone – so we can get you all learning as quickly as possible.'

As Carly seated herself, she marked both Archie and Sally with dirty stares.

I guess Sally was right about Laura, Archie thought. *Maybe she is okay after all*.

At break time, Sally caught up with Archie in the playground and told him that she wanted to talk to him about something. They found a quiet spot around the side of the building so that they were away from the screams and shouts of other kids.

'It's about last night, isn't it?' he said, squinting in the sunlight. 'It's about the trouble with the Barrick and his suits, yeah?'

'It is,' she confirmed, 'but there's something else I want to discuss. Isabelle has enough on her mind without having to deal with Carly when she's here, so I think we should do something about that situation.'

'Really?' Archie said, liking the sound of this. 'What have you got in mind? Something magical, I hope.'

'Of course,' she said, grinning mischievously. 'When she was talking to her friends earlier, I overheard her saying that she was staying behind after school to do some overdue homework in the computer room, so I figured this could be our chance. With all the trouble she's been in recently, I guess she doesn't want any more black marks against her name.'

She told Archie about her plan and he didn't know whether to grin mischievously or look concerned.

'Are you sure this is something you want to attempt?' he asked her. 'Surely there must be another way? There has to be something else we can do that isn't so ... scary.'

'I'm all ears,' Sally said, waiting for Archie to put forward some suggestions.

He couldn't think of any. Not one. 'I get the feeling that's not going to be an easy spell to perform. Are you sure you'll be able to do it?'

Realising what he'd just said, Archie snapped his mouth shut and then sported a suitably guilty expression.

'Isabelle's obviously told you that I'm not very powerful,' Sally said, looking a little embarrassed. 'But that's fine; I don't mind that you know. I mean, it's not like you're not going to notice when we're in magic class, is it? There'll be things the others will be doing that I can't do, so I'd rather you found out now than later. And I *can* do the spell ... with your help. As long as you're holding the wand with me when I say the magical words, I can leach some of your power and that should work. That's assuming you're okay with that?'

'I've got no problem with that. You can vampire as much power away from me as you need.'

Archie was still concerned about what Sally had planned, but he was willing to go along with it. Powerful or not, Sally was clever and had been doing magic for a while so Archie trusted her judgement. He just wished he could get rid of the feeling of apprehension which was welling up inside of him.

'I can't wait to see the look on Carly's face!' he said, trying to sound positive.

'Me too! It's going to be hilarious! After that, it'll be one less idiot to worry about.'

'If only we could sort out Barrick so easily.'

'Hmm, yeah,' Sally said. 'It'll take something quite spectacular to get rid of him. I'm assuming Isabelle has told you all about him and what we're up against, yeah?'

'Yep, she's told me,' Archie replied, trying not to look concerned himself. 'But we'll be ready for him and his suits when he shows up again. I'll know more magic by then, so I should be able to do more than just levitate someone in the air to create a distraction.'

'Is that what you did?' Sally said, smiling.

Archie nodded. 'I tried to make his car float, but I couldn't do it – it was too heavy.'

'I wouldn't be able to do that and I've been doing magic for some time now.'

All of a sudden, at the far end of the building, a football rolled into view and Ryan appeared. He looked at Archie, who looked back at him. And then Ryan scowled, scooped up his ball, and disappeared as quickly as he'd appeared.

'Would I be right in thinking that you need to go and talk to him?' Sally said.

'Yeah, you would,' Archie confirmed. 'I'm meeting up with Isabelle later so we can practice some spells at her house,' he said as he began making his way back towards the playground. 'You should come. I'm sure she wouldn't mind. We need to get in as much practice as possible and you might learn something new.'

'Sure, that's something to look forward to. I'll drop her a text and let her know.'

Archie told her what time to be there and then added, 'I might even ask Miss Burrows if she can give us more than one lesson a week. I'm sure Isabelle will be a good teacher, but our headmistress is the one who'll be able to prepare us best for what's coming.'

'Yeah, *definitely* ask her about that. And meet me on the second floor after school. I'll be waiting in the library.'

'I'll be there,' Archie assured her.

On the playground, he found Ryan playing a triangular game of pass with two other boys from their year. Standing as close as he could without getting in the way, Archie tried to attract Ryan's attention – but he was having none of it; he just carried on side-footing the ball when it was his turn and refusing to even glance in Archie's direction.

Archie tried to be patient, but break time would soon be called to an end, so he decided to try something more direct to get his friend to talk to him. Intercepting the ball, Archie picked it up and gave it to one of the boys.

'Hey! Whaddaya think you're doing?' Ryan said.

Ignoring him, Archie asked the boys if they could play by themselves for a minute and they told him that that was fine.

'Err, that's not fine by me,' Ryan said, giving his friend a dirty look. 'If I wanted to talk to you, I'd have done so when I saw you a minute ago.'

'There's no need to be like that. I know I've been ignoring you a bit lately, but that's only because I've had some important stuff to deal with. We're still friends as far as I'm concerned. But I get why you're being off with me. I'd probably be the same if I was in your position.'

'So what's this "important stuff" you've been dealing with?' Ryan said, folding his arms across his chest and eyeing Archie with a raised eyebrow. 'It's something to do with that new girl, isn't it? It's something to do with Isabelle?'

Archie nodded as he was happy to give away that much information.

The bell sounded to end break time.

'So come on then, what's this "important stuff" that you're doing with her?' Ryan asked him. 'If she's your girlfriend now then that's no big deal. There's no reason to be cagey about it. And there's no reason to dump me. You *can* have a girlfriend and a best friend too, ya know. I get that you'll want to spend a lot of time with her, but –'

Archie waved his arms around, cutting him off. 'I told you before; she's not my girlfriend. She just ... needs my help with something, that's all.'

'And what does she need your help with?'

Archie didn't want to tell his best friend lies, but he didn't want to tell him the truth either, because he knew that by doing so he would put him in danger. Archie had already put his family in the firing line; he didn't need to do that with Ryan as well. He wanted to keep him well and truly away from Barrick and his suits.

'Oh, well, I guess that's the end of this conversation,' Ryan said.

'I'm sorry but I can't tell you about it, mate,' Archie said. 'I just *can't*. Can we still be friends, though?'

'You've got a new best friend, so it looks like I'm surplus to requirements.'

'Don't be like that.'

One of the teachers called across the playground to them: 'Come on, you pair, get a move on, will you! You'll be late to class!'

Archie didn't like the idea of being late. He knew that all eyes would be on him as he entered the classroom, so he set off across the playground with Ryan at his side. Not a word was exchanged as they entered the building, Archie going one way and Ryan the other.

Archie's second to last class was with Miss Burrows, which Archie found to be quite a surreal hour for him. It felt strange being there with her after everything that'd happened the night before. Archie found it hard to concentrate on his work (and not because Carly and Laura were there – not surprisingly, they were always well behaved in Miss Burrows' class). Archie kept glancing at the headmistress, trying to catch her attention. But apart from the occasional acknowledgement of his existence, she carried on with her teaching in the same strict, professional way that she always had.

After the lesson had ended, Archie was purposely slow to pack away his things and was the last pupil to make his way towards the door. Just as he was about to leave, Miss Burrows called him back, just like he knew she would.

'I may have to stand down as the headmistress of this school,' she said as she tidied some papers on her desk.

'Why?' Archie said. This was not what he'd expected her to say. But then he figured it out for himself. 'It's because of the danger to the students, isn't it? It's because you're worried that Barrick might find out where you work, yeah?'

Miss Burrows confirmed this with a slow and measured nod of her head. 'I was foolish not to have fully considered the ramifications of helping out Isabelle in her struggle with Barrick,' she said. 'But that's not to say that I wouldn't have helped her, even after giving the situation the proper due consideration that it'd deserved. I would perhaps have done it in a, shall we say, less direct way. One that didn't put the students in the firing line.'

'What will you do?'

Miss Burrows offered a slight shrug of her shoulders. 'I'm only seven years away from retirement and I've squirrelled enough money away for that to be an option,' she said, 'so that's the best way to go, I think.'

'Oh,' Archie said, disappointed at the prospect of this. He'd recently found out that Miss Burrows was the coolest headmistress ever and now she was about to call it a day. Damn! He wondered what would happen with the magic lessons.

As if reading his mind, Miss Burrows said, 'I'm sure we can make arrangements to continue your magical studies one way or another. I need to make sure that you, Isabelle and Sally are as ready as can be for what's coming, so somewhat of a crash course could be in order.'

'Ah, yes, I was going to ask you about extra magic lessons. I like the sound of a crash course. Hey, what about Mr Gibb? Will he be standing down, too?'

'I haven't discussed it with him yet, but my guess is that he'll be leaving as well.'

Double damn!

Archie couldn't remember ever being as disappointed as he was now.

'You should stay well away from Barrick,' Miss Burrows advised, 'because you will be of particular interest to him. You know what type of wizard he is, don't you? You know that he's a vampire, yes?'

'I know *exactly* what he is. Staying away from him is going to be difficult, seeing as I live next door to Isabelle. And I'm not going to not help her out just because of any danger to myself. Wizards and witches come together to help each other out. That's what Mr Gibb told me – or something like that – and it sounds like a good motto to live by.'

'It most certainly is. And not being late to classes would also be a good motto, don't you think?'

Archie got the message. Miss Burrows wanted to be on her own so she could ponder and plan things. So Archie gave her a kind of half-smile and went to leave.

'There's a battle coming, you know that, don't you?' Miss Burrows said to him just as he was about to disappear through the doorway. 'We all need to make sure that we're ready.'

'I'll be ready when I know some magic.'

This time it was the headmistress who got the message. 'I'll make sure you get the tuition you need,' she said. 'And we'll focus on attack and defence. I've already seen enough from you to know that you'll be a quick learner.'

Archie couldn't hide his delight at the prospect. He couldn't *wait* to start learning.

'Now get yourself down that corridor, me laddo. Go on – skedaddle!'

Archie skedaddled. And he was indeed late for his last class. Archie tried to enter through the door and make his way across the room as soundlessly as possible, but all eyes were on him anyway, including the teacher's.

'Well, at least you're making an effort not to try and disturb the class,' he said, regarding him with an irritated expression from behind his desk, 'so I suppose that's at least something.'

Focusing on the floor, Archie walked to his desk on legs which felt like jelly. He usually sat next to Ryan, but his former best friend had decided to plonk himself next to someone else on the other side of the room. This left Archie feeling very alone.

A few sniggers erupted from the back and Archie didn't need to look up to know which culprits were laughing at him. After what'd happened in the first class – with Archie jumping to Sally's defence – he was sure that he would be the brunt of Carly's rage for the next fifty-five or so minutes. And that's exactly how things played out.

Every time she made a joke about him, he felt like turning around and hurling abuse at her and Ruby. Every time a piece of balled-up paper pinged off the side of his head, he felt an overwhelming urge to throw it back at them. The teacher kept repeatedly chastising Carly, but she took no notice of him. Like Mr Callum, his lack of authority made him a doormat with the children in general, never mind the school bully.

And so Archie gritted his teeth and rode out the storm, knowing that, if all went well, he would have the last laugh soon enough. *Oh, I can't wait to see the look on your face when Sally and I do what we've got to do*, Archie thought.

When the final bell rang, Archie stayed seated while everyone else filed out of the room. He tried to catch Ryan's eye with a slight wave of his hand, but Ryan couldn't even bring himself to look at him, so it was a wasted effort.

Archie had noted that Carly and Ruby had gone left out of the doorway, so he went right and made his way quickly up to the second floor.

In the library, Sally was in the history section, thumbing through a book about medieval England.

'That's my favourite era,' Archie said. 'Although I wouldn't have wanted to be a wizard or a witch back then. If you were caught doing magic ...' he ran a finger across his throat, 'you met a grisly end.'

'Good job we're living now, then, isn't it?' Sally said as she snapped the book shut and slotted it back on the shelf.

'What are we going to do if there's other people in there and she isn't alone?' Archie said. 'What will we do if her friends are with her?'

'Let's take a look and see what's what. Then we'll decide whether to go ahead or not.'

'Okay,' Archie said, eager to get on with it, 'lead the way, my magical friend.'

'How did things go with Ryan?' Sally asked as they made their way along the corridor. 'Are you back to being besties again now then?'

The look that Archie gave her was answer enough to that question.

'Oh, right – well, I'm sure you'll make up with him at some point.

Archie hoped she was right.

When they got close to the computer room, Sally told him to stay put while she strolled past and glanced through the glass at the top of the door to see who was inside. From the look on her face, it was not good news.

'There's someone else in there, isn't there?' Archie said to her as she returned.

'Yep,' she confirmed. 'That's the bad news. The even worse news is that it's Laura.'

Archie managed one word in response: 'Oh.'

'Well, I guess that's that,' Sally said as she began to walk away. 'We'll just have to wait for another opportunity.'

'Hang on a minute,' Archie said, staying where he was. 'Are we just going to call it a day at that? We can think of a way around this, can't we? If we can just get Laura out of that room, then it's game on.'

'And how are we going to do that?'

The door to the computer room opened and Archie's breath caught in his throat as he waited to see who would appear.

'I'll be five minutes, tops,' he heard Laura say. And then there she was, right in front of him with a curious look on her face, which changed to a glare as she closed the door. 'I hope you're not planning on going in there,' she said, hooking a thumb towards the computer room, 'because Carly's got work to do and she isn't going to share air with you pair.'

'Oh, well, that's okay,' Sally said, 'we'll leave her to it then.' She turned to leave, but her accomplice stayed put. 'Err, time to go, Archie. I'm sure there'll be another opportunity for us to do what we need to do.'

'So why are you here?' Laura asked them. 'You do know you need to book time in the computer room in advance, right? You do know that, don't you?'

'Yes, of course,' Sally answered. 'We booked our time.'

'Really?' Laura said in a challenging tone. 'Did you now? It's just that when the teacher logged me and Carly down earlier I didn't notice your names listed.'

'We did it late,' Sally said.

'What time?' Laura asked.

'Err ... it was just before dinner break,' Sally said, bumbling her words out.

'Oh, right,' Laura said. 'Do you know what, you need to improve your lying skills, 'cause they're not up to scratch. I booked mine and Carly's slot just *after* dinner break – and guess what! Your names weren't listed. So why are you really here? What are you pair up to?'

'Sally lied about booking us in,' Archie admitted. 'We thought we could get away with not bothering. Just our luck that you happened to be here, eh.'

Laura stared at him, weighing him up. 'I can believe that you would do something like that, but *you*,' she said to Sally, 'no way would you turn up here without booking yourself in first. Not a goody two shoes like you. No way!'

'I'm not a goody two shoes!' Sally protested.

'Yes you are,' Laura insisted. 'And if you don't tell me why you're really here, I'm going to get Carly and we'll see what she makes of this.' She folded her arms across her chest and waited for a reply.

'I ... erm, we ...' Sally said, stumbling her words out again with clearly no idea what to say.

'We've come here to teach Carly a lesson,' Archie said, deciding that honesty was the best approach. 'We want to make sure that she doesn't bother us or Isabelle ever again.'

'Archie!' Sally said, aghast at his outburst. 'Please tell me that I just imagined that you said that?'

'Nope, you didn't imagine it,' Laura said with a sly grin spreading across her face. 'Hmm, wonder what Carly will make of this bit of news.'

'You're magical, like us,' Archie said. 'Doesn't that mean anything to you? Where's your loyalty?'

'What about the loyalty to my friend?' Laura countered. 'Should I just forget that?'

'Your friend is a nasty piece of work,' Sally said, 'so, yes, maybe you should.'

'Oooh! Maybe I should tell her that too,' Laura said, sporting a stern look, which then melted away into a toothy smile. 'So ... what's the plan? How are you going to teach Carly a lesson? How exactly are you going to make sure she doesn't bother any of you again? Which spell were you about to cast?'

'It doesn't matter what we were going to do,' Sally said. 'We've been busted. Our opportunity has gone. And we probably won't get another one because you're going to be looking out for her all the time now. Come on, Archie, we may as well go. She's going to tell Carly no matter what we say, so there's no point hanging around.'

Sally began walking away, so Archie followed her.

'Hey! Hold up!' Laura said. 'I want to know which spell we're going to cast. I can't help you if I don't know what the plan is.'

Both Archie and Sally stopped dead, as if they'd been frozen by a spell that Laura had just cast. Archie looked at Sally and she looked at him, asking a question without saying a word. Something along the lines of: did she just say what I thought she thought she said?

'I told her that I wouldn't be gone long,' Laura said, 'so she's probably beginning to wonder where I've got to right now.'

Sally regarded her through narrowed eyes. 'You're either joking or trying to lead us into some sort of trap?' she said. 'Which one is it?'

'Neither,' Laura replied. 'I know she's my friend, but I'm sick of being bossed around by her. And I suspect that Ruby is too (even though it doesn't look that way). I think that Carly needs pulling down a peg or two – and then maybe she'll be all right. So I'll ask you again – what's the plan?'

Archie and Sally exchanged another look: one which suggested there was a smell of poop in the air.

'I think we should just leave,' Archie said to Sally.

'Yep, I'm with you on that one,' she replied.

And that's exactly what they were about to do ...

'Crikey – I'm offering to help you and you're just going to walk away,' Laura said, throwing her hands up in frustration. 'Fine. I'll just deal with her myself then. Although I don't know how I'm going to do it. I'll have to look through my spell books when I get home to give me some ideas.'

Archie and Sally stopped dead again and looked at each other.

'Erm, I think she's being serious,' Archie said.

'Yeah,' Sally said, looking as surprised as he felt, 'I think you might be right.'

Laura gestured for some hustle. 'That door could open at any second,' she said, 'and then we're going to have some explaining to do.'

'Fine, fine,' Sally said, 'I guess we'll have to trust you. Magical folk sticking together and all that.' She giggled nervously, then edged closer to Laura and explained what needed to be done. 'I know what you're going to say: that I'm not powerful enough to do it. But I was going to have Archie hold the wand with me, so I can channel his power.'

Archie tried to gauge Laura's reaction to their suggestion, which he figured was a mixture of shock and surprise.

'Well, you're right about you not being powerful enough to pull it off on your own,' she said to Sally. 'Even I might struggle with *that* one. And you do realise that what you want to do is dangerous, right? Not to mention the fact that it'll be as scary as hell. Are you sure you want to attempt this?'

'It's only dangerous if it isn't cast properly,' Sally stated. She stuck her chest out proudly and added: 'We're not scared. And I'm very confident that I can "pull it off", as you say ... with Archie's help, of course.'

'I'm doing it,' Laura said. 'Not you.'

'With my help?' Archie asked.

'Hell no!' Laura replied, clearly offended by the notion that she would need help from a noob (albeit a powerful one). 'I take it you've got a book with you that's got the spell in it? Because that's not one you're going to know off by heart, now, is it? It's not one you'll have practised in class with Miss Burrows.'

Sally produced the book from her bag and handed it over. 'It's on page 246,' she said. 'You've got your wand with you, yes?'

'Of course I have. I never go anywhere without it (I don't care what Miss Burrows says).' Laura regarded the book inquisitively. '*Advanced Magic: an A to Z guide* by Graham Goodbody. Are you sure you want me to do this particular spell?' she said.

'Yes,' Sally said after only a little hesitation.

'We're sure,' Archie said, committing himself.

'I have to immobilize her first,' Laura stated. 'It'll keep her where I want her for at least five minutes, which should be more than enough time to do the second part of the procedure.'

The sound of a chair scraping across the floor in the computer room made all three of them look towards the door in alarm.

'That'll be Carly,' Laura said, 'coming to see where I've got to. You pair should go and just leave me to it.'

'No way,' Archie protested in a low voice. 'I'm not missing this for anything.'

'Me neither,' Sally said, grabbing his arm and leading him into a classroom on the other side of the corridor.

After closing the door behind them, they positioned themselves on either side of it, out of view, and listened ...

'Where have you been?' they heard Carly say. 'You told me that you were going to the toilet and that you'd only be five minutes at the most!'

'Yeah, sorry I took so long,' Laura replied, 'but I got talking to someone on the second floor and,' she rolled her eyes as if to say, well, you know how it is, 'I just couldn't get away from her 'cause she wouldn't stop yapping.'

'I bet it was *you* who wouldn't stop yapping,' Carly said. 'Come on, I want to get this work done so I can get out of this place. I've got far more interesting things to do than being here. And so have you.'

After hearing the door to the computer room shut, Archie gave Sally a nod and they both went back into the corridor.

'This could still be a trap, you know,' Sally said in a low voice. 'She could be telling her about us right now.'

'She isn't,' Archie replied as he peered in through the glass in the top half of the door.

Carly was sitting on the left side of the room at one of the terminals, which were all lined up against the wall. She was studiously analysing the screen in front of her, while Laura, seated to her right and slightly back had the magic book open and was perusing the relevant page.

'What's happening?' Sally asked Archie.

'Laura just gave me a thumbs up,' he whispered back. 'And now she's pulling out her wand. Crikey, she's actually going to do it. I hope she doesn't muck this up.'

'I want to see!' Sally said, a little too loud for Archie's liking.

'Keep your voice down,' he said, moving aside to make room for her.

They peered in and looked on eagerly as Laura pointed her wand at Carly, then began chanting the magical words to immobilize her. A few seconds later she was as stiff as a statue, with both hands splayed above the keyboard and a look of severe concentration etched into her brow. Archie had to resist the temptation to burst into the room, spin her around and do Take the L right in front of her.

Sally giggled. 'Oh, you have no idea how much I've been waiting for this moment,' she said.

'I can imagine,' Archie commented.

In the classroom, Laura now had the book resting on her lap and was running her finger across the pages.

'I hope she can do this on her own,' Sally said.

'What will happen if she can't?'

Sally shrugged. 'She'll probably ask for you or me to help her, assuming she can bring herself to do that,' she said. 'Okay, she's ready.'

Laura had risen from her seat and backed away from Carly so that she was closer to the door.

'She's positioning herself so she can get out of there quickly,' Sally noted.

'I'd be standing even closer to the door if it was me,' Archie stated.

He checked down the corridor in both directions. He half expected to see a teacher or a student or – God forbid! – the caretaker ambling into view, which would have put the sliders on the whole operation. But there was no one else to be seen. And yet Archie had an overwhelming feeling of being watched, so much so that it made his skin prickle with gooseflesh.

'I'm nervous,' Archie said. 'My stomach feels like it's been tied in knots.'

'That's how I feel,' Sally said. She raised her hand to show how much she was shaking.

In the computer room, Laura had begun saying the magical words, repeating the same phrases over and over with her wand pointed at Carly: 'Canbasa Illati Tempura! Elita Canbasa Dervena! Terbaco dede Ellsuc eta ... Canbasa Illati Tempura! Elita Canbasa Dervena! Terbaco dede Ellsuc eta ...'

After a minute or so had passed and nothing appeared to be happening, Archie said, 'I don't think it's working. Should one of us go in and help, d'you think? Should I go in?'

'No. Give it longer. And if she wants help, she'll ask for it. Interrupting her mid-spell could be dangerous, for all we know.'

What Sally had said made sense, so they continued to watch the strange spectacle taking place in front of them. *I'd have thought that someone was mad if they'd suggested to me a few weeks ago that I'd be watching an immobilized Carly having a spell cast on her by one of her best friends*, Archie thought. He was amazed at how his life had been turned upside down in such a short space of time. His life had become a lot more exciting. And dangerous.

'Okay, I think something's happening,' Sally said, beginning to shiver.

Archie shivered too as they both peered in through the glass and watched as some sort of spectral mist began to form by Laura.

'It's a good job I'm not in there,' Archie said in a low voice, 'because I'm not sure I would be able to resist the temptation to run away.'

'Me neither,' Sally said, also keeping her voice hushed. 'Say what you want about Laura, but she's one heck of a brave girl and one heck of a witch.'

Although, to Archie, she looked anything but brave at the moment. Her eyes were wide and the hand holding her wand was visibly shaking, probably from a mixture of fear plus a sudden temperature drop which had no doubt taken place inside the room. Archie could see her watching them out of the corner of her eye as she continued to say the same magical words over and over, with her breath now frosting in front of her: 'Canbasa Illati Tempura! Elita Canbasa Dervena! Terbaco dede Ellsuc eta ...'

It was about another minute before the next stage of manifestation took place. Out of the mist, the slender figure of a woman began to form, waxing and waning in and out of existence. Archie couldn't make out any discernable features, but he knew all too well who she was: the Lady of the Stairs. Long bony fingers, translucent, there and yet not there, reached out towards Carly, caressing her cheek ...

And that's when Laura got up, tucked the book under her arm, and tip-toed quickly towards the door.

Opening it as soundlessly as he could, Archie let her out and then closed it behind her.

The three of them then peered in through the glass. They watched as the Lady of the Stairs leaned in close to Carly and began whispering in her ear.

'What did you tell her to say?' Sally asked Laura as quietly as possible.

'Exactly what you t-told me t-to,' she replied, her teeth chattering. 'That she should s-stop bullying other students and be n-nice to people ... or else.'

'Or else what?' Archie said.

Laura shrugged. 'I dunno ... I f-figured an open-ended w-warning would carry more malice than a more specific th-threat. Look, can we get out o-of here? Being near that g-ghost has really unnerved me.'

Archie had felt unnerved and he hadn't even been in the room, so he could only imagine how terrified Laura must have felt with a ghost – an actual *real* ghost – forming right next to her.

'I'm with Laura,' Sally said, edging away from the others, 'we should just leave them to it.'

'But what if someone tries to get in the computer room after we've gone,' Archie said, making a valid point. 'They're going to have a nasty shock when they see what's going on in there. It's the caretaker I'm more worried about than anything.'

'At least one of us should stay behind to head off anyone venturing near here,' Sally suggested.

'And how e-exactly do you plan on h-heading them off?' Laura inquired.

'I'd use a persuasion spell,' Sally replied. 'I'd convince them that they need to get home straight away.'

Laura nodded. 'Yeah, yeah, that'll w-work,' she said. 'And it's not too difficult to do, so you should be able to p-pull it off.'

Cocking her head slightly to one side, Sally regarded her with an inquisitive look. 'I take it you want *me* to stay behind,' she said. 'Is that what you're hinting at?'

Laura gave her what appeared to be a half-mocking, half-pleading smile. 'Well, I'm g-going to catch my death if I stay here much l-longer,' she said, hugging herself in an attempt to keep herself warm. 'Plus I was the one who h-had to cosy up with a ghost to do the s-spell, so I think I've earned the right to sk-skedaddle, don't you?'

That was a fair point, Archie thought. 'Look, me and Sally will stay behind,' he said. 'You get yourself out of here.'

Laura didn't need prompting twice. She gave the book to Sally and then began backing away down the corridor.

'Well, this after-school t-time has turned out to be a damn sight more i-interesting than I thought it would b-be,' she said. 'See you later, losers. Tomorrow is g-going to be a verrry interesting day.'

Sally and Archie watched her as she disappeared down the corridor.

'Who's she calling a loser,' Sally said. 'If anyone's a loser around here, it's her. Her and her even bigger idiot of a friend, who's getting a good dose of Karma right now, I'm happy to say.'

'I don't think they're friends now. Part of me wants to look in through the glass and part of me doesn't. How long did you say that the statue spell lasts? How much longer do we have to wait, do you think?'

Sally checked the time on her phone. 'It should be wearing off any time around now.'

They couldn't hear any noise coming from inside the classroom.

'So what happens after Carly legs it out of here?' Archie inquired. 'Will the ghost just disappear? What's to stop the Lady of the Stairs from looking for another victim?'

Hugging herself because of the cold, Sally said, 'She'll just go back to what she was: a tormented spirit who roams the stairwell and corridors, giving people chills and the occasional spooky sighting.'

'Are you *sure* that's what'll happen?'

Sally replied yes, but she didn't look one hundred per cent certain, as far as Archie could see.

The sound of a scream and a chair scraping across the floor in the computer room signalled that the statue spell had finally worn off. A few seconds later, Carly flung the door open and burst into the corridor with a look of terror on her face. She ran past Archie and Sally as though they were invisible and then disappeared down the north stairwell, the sound of her screams gradually fading away.

'I'd say that had the desired effect,' Sally said coolly. 'Wouldn't you?'

'Definitely,' Archie agreed. 'And I can't wait to see what she's like at school next week. That's assuming she turns up. Judging by how scared she was, I'd say we might never see her again.'

'Let's hope that that's the case.'

They both looked towards the open door to the computer room.

'Should we ...?' Archie began to say.

'I'm quite happy to just leave,' Sally said as she began backing away down the corridor.

'I think we should check to see if the ghost has gone,' Archie suggested.

Sally motioned for him to do just that. 'By all means do,' she said, still backing away.

'You're just going to leave me to it?' he said, aghast at the idea of being abandoned.

Ceasing her retreat, Sally said, 'Okay, I'll wait here. But I'll be ready to scarper out of this school at the first sign of anything scary. Just so you know.'

'It's good to know that someone's got my back,' Archie said sarcastically as he began edging towards the door.

'It's still *really* cold in here,' Sally said, shivering, 'so that doesn't bode well.'

There were no noises coming from inside the classroom. Archie took this as a positive sign, despite Sally's warning about the temperature.

Pausing just before he reached the doorway, Archie glanced back to check that Sally was still there, which she was.

'Go on then,' she said in a low voice. 'If you're so insistent on doing this, then just do it. I don't want to stay here any longer than I have to.'

Steeling himself, Archie stood in the doorway, looked into the classroom and ... saw nothing.

Exhaling a deep, frosted breath of relief, he turned his head to happily report his discovery back to Sally.

'It's okay,' he said, 'she's gone.'

But then a voice iced with malice whispered in his ear: 'Oh no I haven't.'

Archie didn't waste a second. He bolted down the corridor with Sally at his side.

They did not look back.

'Probably a good idea not to tell anyone about this,' Sally said as they exited the school and darted across the playground.

When Archie got home, he had to fabricate a story about why he was so late getting in from school. The best he could come up with, after being put on the spot by Mrs Wiggins, was that he'd been playing football on the field with Ryan and lost track of time. She seemed suspicious of his explanation, but she accepted it nonetheless (even though she noted that being late seemed to be becoming an unwelcome habit for him in recent times).

He'd arranged to meet Sally outside of Isabelle's house at 6.30 pm and she turned up on the dot. This was the first time he'd seen her wearing something other than a school uniform: faded blue jeans, a white, flowery top, and a pair of black Kickers shoes.

'Why are you looking me up and down like that?' she inquired, giving him a funny look.

Archie shrugged. 'I Dunno,' he said. 'I just thought you'd be dressed in something a bit more ... dorky.'

'Dorky?' Sally said, scowling at him. 'Who are you calling a dork?'

Realising his mistake, Archie began backtracking straight away. 'I'm sorry,' he said. 'I wasn't calling you a dork; it's just that at school you're quite square and so I figured you'd dress square in your spare time.'

'Wow! Now you're calling me square as well. Are you fixing for a punch in the eye or something? Just because I study at school doesn't make me a square – or a *dork!*' She looked Archie up and down with an expression that suggested she wasn't impressed by what she was seeing. And she was about to tell him just that when a voice spoke up ...

'Are you pair going to linger there all day, or are you coming inside?'

They both turned to see Isabelle standing in the doorway giving them a curious look.

Archie took off towards her, eager to distance himself from Sally.

A minute or two later they were out in the garden, standing in the spot where Archie had first met Isabelle and witnessed her doing magic. On the way through the house, Isabelle had picked up a book titled: *Defence and Attack spells for the Magical Mind*. Archie couldn't wait to start performing some of the spells that it contained.

'The trees and overgrown bushes hide us from view here,' Isabelle explained, 'so this is the best place to practise.'

Archie noted what she was wearing: a black t-shirt, leggings, and trainers. 'Do you always dress in black when you're not at school?' he asked her.

'I like dark colours,' she explained. 'They match my dark mood.'

'Oh, so you're having a pop at her about how she's dressed as well, are you?' Sally said, giving Archie a hard stare. 'What is it with you and judging people by what clothes they're wearing?' She looked him up and down again. 'What's with that cheap, white t-shirt? It looks like it came out of a three for ten pounds pack. And what brand of trainers are you wearing?' She moved closer so she could examine them. 'Falcon? Never heard of that. Hardly Nike or Adidas, is it?' She focused on his jeans. 'And they look cheap, too. I'm going to guess that they're not Levis or Wrangler.'

'Whoa! *Whoa!*' Isabelle said. 'What's with all the insults?'

'He started it,' Sally explained. 'He called me a square – and a *dork!*'

'I did not call you a dork,' Archie commented. 'I just said that I thought you'd be dressed more like a dork because you're such a square at school.'

'There, you see,' Sally said, growing more and more agitated by the second. 'Who do you know that wouldn't be triggered by a comment like that?'

Isabelle gave Archie a searching look. 'Perhaps you should engage your brain before you open your mouth,' she said.

'And an apology could go a long way to resolving this situation, you know.'

'I've already apologized,' Archie said, beginning to wish that he hadn't gotten out of bed that morning. 'But, okay, I'll apologize again. I'm sorry, Sally, I didn't mean to offend you; it's just that ... sometimes I say stuff that other people would keep to themselves (or, at least, that's what my mum reckons, anyway). And for what it's worth, I think you're pretty cool. The way you handled things at the school this evening was very admirable. If Laura hadn't turned up, I'm sure you'd have summoned the Lady of the Stairs with no help from anyone else. I'm sure you'd have been just as brave as her and not got up and ran away when the ghost was breathing down your neck (not that ghosts can breathe, I'm sure, but you know what I'm saying). Although you did want to leg it at the end, after Laura had gone. And, on reflection, that was *exactly* what we both should have done ...'

'Oh my God, just shut up, will you!' Sally blurted. 'You started so well and then you had to spear off in the direction of stupidity again. We agreed that we weren't going to tell anyone about it, *remember*?' She put her head in her hands and groaned.

'Err, what's all this talk about a ghost?' Isabelle said. 'And what have you pair been up to?'

Archie looked at Sally and she looked at him.

'I suppose I better explain,' she said, 'otherwise you'll only end up putting your foot in your mouth again, won't you?' She didn't wait for a reply. 'You've been having a lot of problems with Carly,' she explained to Isabelle, 'and I – or *we*, should I say – thought that it was a bucket-load of stress that you really could do without, given everything else you're having to contend with at the moment. So we decided something needed to be done about it. Although I will hold my hands up and say that this was my idea to begin with,' Sally held her hands up to emphasize this point, 'and so I accept responsibility for anything which might have gone wrong.' She paused before resuming. 'Okay, as I'm sure you know, the school is haunted by a woman known as the Lady of the Stairs.'

Isabelle said, 'I'm new so I don't know anything about a ghost. Although I must confess that there has been a few times where I've felt like I'm being watched. And sometimes it can get really cold in some classrooms and corridors and especially around the stairwell on the north end of the school. I'm guessing that that's where the ghost mostly hangs out, what with her name being "the Lady of the Stairs" and all.'

'You guess correctly,' Sally confirmed. She told her about the teacher and how she'd been killed by one of the students who'd pushed her down the stairs, fifty or something years before.

Archie joined in with the explanation: 'Mrs Smallwood has been haunting this school ever since, wanting vengeance – and to punish any kids who are misbehaving. Or, at least, that's what I've been told. I'm sure some of the teachers here have spread that rumour just so they can get kids to behave. Although that certainly hasn't worked with Carly.'

'I'm loving this history lesson about the spooky goings on at the school,' Isabelle said, 'but what has this got to do with the school bully?'

Sally looked down at the ground as she spoke. 'I, erm, thought it would be a good idea if Carly were to get a real nasty scare.' And then she explained what'd happened and how Laura had become involved. 'I think we've done the right thing. You should have seen Carly's face when she ran past us in the corridor; I've never seen anyone look so scared before. It was *awesome*. The coolest thing ever.'

Isabelle could not suppress a smile. 'I wish I could have been there to see it,' she said. 'I get why you've done what you've done and I don't blame you for doing it – but did Laura do everything correctly? Because if she didn't ...' She shook her head, indicating that the consequences of botching the spell would *not* be good.

'Yes, as far as I know, she did it all correctly,' Sally reported. 'Although ...'

'Although what?' Isabelle said, giving her a searching look.

Archie explained about what'd happened just before they'd left: about how he'd reported to Sally that the ghost had gone, only to then have it whisper in his ear: oh no I haven't!

Isabelle's searching look changed to one of deepest worry. 'Ah, that's not good,' she said. 'That is not good at all. In fact, it's bad. *Very* bad.'

Archie and Sally exchanged worried looks.

'When you say bad,' Archie said, 'how bad are we talking? On a scale of one to ten?'

'I don't know exactly how bad,' she replied, 'I just know that things are going to get hair-raising at school if that spell wasn't cast correctly, which it sounds like it wasn't. You may have solved one problem and created another – bigger! – one. You'll have to tell Miss Burrows – you know that, don't you?'

Archie stayed silent. He was almost as afraid of the headmistress as he was of the ghost.

'It was my idea,' Sally said, raising her chin as a show of bravery, 'so I'll do it. I'll tell her on Monday. She knows what Carly's like, so I'm sure she'll understand – kind of. And I'm sure she'll know what to do.'

'You don't seem surprised that Laura helped us,' Archie said to Isabelle.

'No, I'm not surprised,' she replied. 'Carly treats everyone terribly, so I can't imagine she treats her friends much better. Although that might be about to change, thanks to you pair and your new buddy.'

'Err, I think calling her our buddy is a bit of a stretch,' Sally said. 'I think it's more a case of the enemy of your enemy is your ally kind of thing.'

'Yeah, I'd say that's closer to the truth,' Archie agreed. 'Where are your parents?' he asked Isabelle in an attempt to veer the subject in a new direction. 'Your dad's Mercedes was missing from the driveway when we arrived.'

'He's out shopping and my mum's upstairs in her bedroom,' she replied. 'She'd normally go with him, but there's no way she's leaving me on my own – not after what happened.'

'I'm surprised that he's left you pair alone,' Archie said, 'given that there's a vampire wizard and his gangster posse out to get you. They could rock up at any moment and I have a feeling that your bubble charm isn't going to hold them off for very long.'

'Well, we need food to survive, so we've got to do the shopping and other things,' Isabelle explained. 'And the only reason he agreed to go out was because I told him that you pair were coming round. He won't be long. And as far as the Bubble Barrier is concerned, my dad has repaired it and Mrs Hickinbottom is going to give us some rare ingredient that'll make it much stronger.'

'Barrick and his suits will still be able to get through it though,' Archie said. 'All you're doing by strengthening it is delaying the inevitable. Am I right?'

'That's a defeatist way to think,' Sally said. 'I'm sure that Isabelle and her parents have already considered this and put a plan in place to deal with the situation. And you don't have to help out if you don't want to, Archie. No one's forcing you to be here.'

'I wouldn't be here if I didn't want to help,' he responded. He got the feeling that she was still being off with him because of his nerd and dork comments. 'Look, it's beginning to get dark, so I think we should start practising. I'm *very* eager to learn.'

'Archie is right,' Isabelle said, 'we should start. But as far as a plan goes,' she produced a small vial of purple liquid from her pocket and held it up in the palm of her hand, 'this is the best we've come up with so far.' She smiled. 'Barrick can't attack what he can't see, right?'

'Invisibility potion?' Sally said in awe.

'Key-rect,' Isabelle confirmed. 'It's not much but it's enough to get the three of us away safely if the worst comes to the worst, which it most certainly will at some point. Mrs Hickinbottom went above and beyond to get us the rare ingredients needed for this potion.'

'Awesome!' Archie said, wondering how strange it would be to be invisible. 'But that's not going to stop Barrick from pursuing you. Like with the Bubble Barrier, you're only delaying him from getting to you. All the time he's alive, you and your family won't be able to get on with your lives.'

'So what do you suggest?' Sally said. 'That we kill him?'

'It may be the only way,' Archie said.

'He is right,' Isabelle had to admit. 'It may be the only way.'

A short silence followed as all three of them digested the gravity of what was being suggested.

It was Archie who broke it. 'Do your parents have any friends that are willing to help you out?' he inquired. 'Anyone from down south, where you came from? Surely there must be some wizards or witches that you can call on.'

'Most of my parent's friends are too scared to help,' Isabelle explained as she pocketed the vial. 'And my parents don't trust anyone anymore. We told nobody about us moving and yet Barrick *still* found us. We have no idea how. And don't ask me if there's a spell or potion for that, because the answer's no.'

'What about family?' Archie said. 'Have you got any relatives who've got your back? Surely there's someone other than us pair, the teachers from the school and Mrs Hickinbottom from the – '

Isabelle halted him mid-sentence with a raised hand. 'No, no, and no,' she said, 'and I don't want to discuss it any further. Let's just say that it's a subject best avoided and that we should get on with practising our magic, yes?'

Archie was curious as to why it was a subject to be avoided, but he was smart enough not to press the issue. 'Fine,' he said. 'Well, whatever we decide to do we're going to need magic to do it, so...' he pulled his wand out from beneath his t-shirt and held it up, 'let's get ourselves ready.'

Sally held hers up to show that she was ready. 'Those gangsters aren't going to know what's hit them,' she said with a determined look on her face.

Isabelle, the girl in black, opened her book and turned to the relevant page. 'We'll start with something simple,' she said, her big brown eyes glinting with eagerness. 'And then we'll quickly progress to the more interesting stuff. I'd be quite excited about this, if I wasn't so terrified.'

'I'm terrified and excited, too,' Sally said.

'And me,' Archie said.

The branches on the nearby trees rustled as a cool strong breeze whipped up around them.

And then Isabelle began to read from the book as the other two listened ...

Dear readers, as you've probably guessed, this is not the end of the story. This is the first instalment of what will be a very long tale. Please follow me on Twitter for news and updates: https://twitter.com/CjLoughty

Follow CJ Loughty on Facebook for news and updates:
https://tinyurl.com/wudx96za

Also by CJ Loughty:

If you like Harry Potter and you like horror, you'll love INTO THE DARK ...
A new home. A new town. And a (terrifying) new start.

Ella Tickles is certain that the new house she and her family are about to move into is haunted. Her parents and brother try to convince her that she's being silly. But when the black mould on the walls and ceilings begins to move like it's alive, Ella knows something has to be done. She learns from a neighbour that the house has been cursed by the previous owner, Maud Bellingham, who was a witch. No matter what anyone does to get rid of the mould, it keeps coming back – with vengeance. Whilst visiting a magic shop, Ella learns of a way to lift the curse. And she also learns something else: that she is a witch, too ...

Printed in Great Britain
by Amazon